Desert
of
Solitude

By

Steven Richard
Harris

First Edition: July 2024
ISBN: 978-84-09-62321-1

In memory of Las Abejas de Acteal

I can´t breathe.

I´m suffocating in the thick stench of death, swimming in the murky waters that have me trapped. Dead arms drag me deeper into the abyss below as I try to fight my way free from the tangle of bodies that´s pressing down on me, sucking on my life, draining away the last vestiges of energy that remain inside my muscles. I swim against a tide of flesh that blocks my way, pushing me back the few centimetres that I´d liberated around me. I reach inside myself – to my other self – and from somewhere deep within I gather the strength to squirm and twist free from my closest captors. Enough space to turn my head a little, searching now for a route out of my watery grave. Up there, somewhere high above, a shaft of light beckons in the darkness. A beacon that guides my clumsy movements, glaring at me, screaming and daring me to haul myself nearer to its promise of escape.

I´ve been here before. Everyone has. But this time it´s different. I´m floating. Not in the nutrient-rich amniotic fluids of our mothers that prepare us for this world, but in a dense tar of limbs of *campesinos* and *rebeldes* that has me bound to another. Tzotzils, Tzeltals, Ch´ols, Tojolabals and other Mayan indigenous groups now one indistinguishable mass, united in their fateful cause. The smell of drying blood and faeces tries to throw my senses off course as I search for the light. My hope. My shining salvation.

It´s there again, above me. I climb towards its allure, using the limbs of my fallen comrades to ascend; supported in death as much as I was in life by my adoptive family. The odour in my nostrils and the approaching beam wake parts of my body that before had stubbornly refused to acknowledge the horrors of the present.

Tingling in my extremities, crawling over me like the insects that had been my recent companions – my spies – mutates into sharp, then blinding pain in my right thigh before creeping its way up to my ribs.

I´m on fire, pierced with a red-hot blade of agony that renders my renaissance near impossible.

But I have to breach the surface. To cry out to show I´m alive, to feel and breathe an air not rancid with murder, loss and regret. The light – *my* light – disappears. But mercifully it´s soon back again. Someone´s out there. I reach for the gap between the upper layer of discarded corpses. It´s impossible, it´s too small and I´m too weak. I´m stillborn. The air I crave is within my grasp but heaving myself through this deathly quicksand has defeated my punctured body. I´ve lost too much blood. Blood that´s flowed into the red clay ground and mixed with the fluids of the day-old dead that lie with me here. My blood brothers and sisters. This is my destiny then, is it? I will stay in this rotting womb forever, fetid, becoming part of this humid land that was never mine to defend. I have finally found my place.

No. Not now. Not yet. I´m not ready. Let me stay here until I disappear, absorbed by the earth. I float upwards, pulled by the arm I´d left outstretched above me. Towed along the river of resurrection. A piercing pain in my head as the sunlight that floods my final resting place – my birthplace – slams into my closed eyelids and burns a dark red stain into my consciousness. My other arm is released from its slumber by my side and I slither out into the daylight, groaning as I´m thrown down on my shattered right side. Senses begin to stir and I hear the nostalgic buzzing of insects. The damp smell of the jungle quickly replaces the suffocating blanket of air I´d been inhaling in my tomb at the bottom of the muddy ditch. Keep your eyes closed. I don´t want to see what´s around me. Not yet. I´m not ready. I roll onto my front and lie face down on a torso that used to belong to someone I´d shared the bus with in another life. Who could it be? Miguel Ángel? Guadalupe? I push my shaking arms into the soft mounds which now support me. I find myself on my hands and knees. OK, I´m ready now. I can cope with the scene I´ve already blindly recreated in my mind. I´m ready to see their smashed faces and broken bodies again.

A heavy blow in the centre of my back sends me crashing down again onto Miguel Ángel or Guadalupe, or whoever that used to be. Back into the embraces I´d freed myself from moments before. A familiar metallic click, the cold barrel of what can only be a gun in the nape of my neck. I open my eyes; my vision blurs and I squint against the alien brightness in an attempt to see my saviour. I make out the outline of the thick undergrowth by the side of the road that leads into the impenetrable twisting vines and trunks of the jungle. Are the rest of them out there? Are they safe? People are here, standing nearby. But it´s not them. I can see muddy boots, smell cigarettes as they admire their catch. Nobody speaks. The insects roar their disapproval.

This scene doesn´t last long. A flash of pain breaks my reverie and I return into the arms of the underworld, the butt of the rifle inviting my blood, once more, to run into the soil I´d naively tried to protect with my life.

The automatic doors of the arrivals hall opened just long enough to catch a glimpse of Dan, who was already waiting for me to clear customs. I fidgeted impatiently while the young official checked every pocket and seam of my backpack, but his silent diligence captivated me as he unrolled my carefully-packed clothes, studying them inch by inch, which somehow calmed my frayed nerves. Finally satisfied that my collection of old t-shirts, baggy shorts and unfashionable underwear posed no serious national security threat, he left them – along with the rest of the contents of my baggage – strewn along the long table behind which he probably spent more than half his waking hours.

I smiled and waved at my soon-to-be travel companion, the constant stream of arriving passengers forcing the doors to Mexico uninterruptedly open so we had no difficulty exchanging a mix of finger-pointing, shrugs and other gestures as we tried to convey what was going through our minds. With a nod of the head, the customs officer abruptly left me alone with my scattered possessions and automatically moved on to his next victim, who was observing me with unashamed curiosity as I gesticulated to the waiting Dan.

Under other circumstances, the tiredness after such a long flight and this unexpected delay to the start of my trip would´ve left me irritated and grumbling, but I was excited about finally arriving in South America and I went about packing up my things as quickly and efficiently as I could.

*

Dan had been given six to twelve months to live. That was ten months ago. As I stuffed the last remaining items into my backpack, I observed him from the customs area. He´d lost weight and was twitching and moving from side to side, giving him a bird-like appearance that looked out of place among the steady flow of people on the other side of the automatic doors. He´d kept his hair short after the operation and the large scar on the side of his head where surgeons had removed the majority of the lymphoma was evident, even from the distance that separated us. But here he was. A dramatic last-minute decision having been made, he was eager to come along for the ride – at least on the initial part of my Latin American adventure – and after having arrived a couple of nights before me in order to explore the museums and galleries of Mexico City, he was now waiting nervously for me to join him in the busy arrivals hall.

A graduate in Anthropology, Dan was an interesting person to talk to, although we weren´t exactly close enough to be called real friends. I mean, on the few occasions that we´d actually spent any time together we´d got on reasonably well, though our conversations were mostly limited to commenting on topics that dominated our mutual friends´ interests; namely sport, alcohol and the opposite sex. I was keen to get to know him better and now I had the chance. But at present he was undoubtedly still firmly classified – to me at least anyway – as Michael´s brother.

Circumstances had brought us together after Mike had been offered a job too good to turn down and Dan had, in a way, stepped in to take his place. But I was nervous. He was going to travel with me for three months of the twelve I´d planned to be away. What was going to happen after two months? His official expiry date would be up. He was a ticking clock and I selfishly didn´t want anything to disrupt my well-laid travel plans.

I did my best to push these thoughts to the back of my mind as I approached him, happy to be sharing the first leg of my journey with someone who I could, in theory, talk to easily about more than just the mundane that I was used to. I held out my hand. He gave me an enormous hug.

We stepped out into the warm air and grey concrete surroundings of the airport and stood watching the torrent of green and white Volkswagen Beetle taxis fight aggressively for space on the roads that flowed past the terminal. We joined the melee, and after paying too much to be stuck for too long in a tailback that seemed to stretch virtually the whole way from the airport to the city centre, we found ourselves in the relative quiet of the La Condesa neighbourhood.

Dan had excelled himself before my arrival and found a private apartment for rent for the week that we´d be staying in Mexico City. We stopped outside an imposing angular building and while Dan looked for the keys to the outside gate that protected the property, I surveyed the giant block of flats painted in different tones of green, its sleek linear appearance hinting that it was probably built sometime in the nineteen-twenties or thirties. Dan´s futile search in every one of his pockets prompted the child-like security guard to jump up from his plastic chair on the other side of the gate and let us in with a key attached to an extendable wire tethered to his belt.

"*Buenas tardes, señor.*" He greeted me warmly, familiarly, as if he already knew me. I smiled and nodded back to him politely.

As we climbed the worn and slippery stone stairs to the second-floor apartment I heard a clinking sound in the pocket of my trousers. I pulled out the keys to the flat and handed them to Dan, who amazingly didn´t even give it a second thought that they´d somehow found their way into my possession on the way from the airport. He must´ve dropped them. I must´ve picked them up without thinking. That´s all. I´m jetlagged, no big deal.

High ceilings, large lead-framed windows and wooden flooring met us as we entered and I stood for a few moments admiring the simple beauty of the place before becoming aware of a weight that was forcing my shoulders to sag. I felt weak after the journey and so slung my recently disorganised backpack into a corner near the front door. Dan disappeared into another room as I continued to study the architecture around me in the living area, losing myself in thoughts of gangsters and speakeasys. I looked out through the large sash window, which framed an identical apartment just metres across the private road that ran through the heart of the block, splitting it into two identical sections, one reflecting the other. Bougainvillea and snaking cacti scaled the outside of the building, gripping it tightly and doing their best to claim the structure and sacrifice it in honour of Mother Earth, to render it no more than a verdant mountain punctuating a once vibrant modern civilization.

Creaking floorboards behind me. Dan had returned and I crashed back down to Earth. He was holding a small, chipped shot glass in one hand and a bottle of Don Julio tequila in the other.

"Welcome to Mexico", he proclaimed and filled the glass dangerously up to the top. We downed two in quick succession, sharing the solitary vessel with me making sure that I drank from my side of the glass without Dan noticing too much my reticence to our saliva mixing. An uncomfortable silence then fell between us. Blood rushed into my cheeks with embarrassment at finding nothing appropriate to say. We avoided eye-contact, suddenly nervous about being alone together without the support of our more vocal mutual friends´ banter, both trying not to start the journey off on the wrong foot by saying something out of place or giving away too much about who we really are outside of our normal habitat and comfort zone. Dan picked up the bottle again and instead of pouring another, squinted over the top of his glasses at the label.

"Apparently, the difference between tequila and mezcal is that tequila has to be made from the blue agave plant, while mezcal can be made from any type of agave. At least that´s what I´ve read anyway." He frowned, unsure how to continue, taking refuge in his fixation with the bottle in his hand. "Well, whatever way you look at it, I suppose it doesn´t really make much difference what colour the plant is once you´ve had a few." He poured us another shot, which vanished immediately.

I felt obliged to make some kind of effort and so smiled idiotically at his offerings before the burning in my stomach and fierce guttural growl reminded me that I´d only picked at the tiny, tasteless meal given to me on the plane and had hardly eaten anything over the course of the last twenty-four hours.

We headed out onto the cracked streets of La Condesa, the concrete slabs under our feet pushed upwards by the roots of the huge ficus trees that provided welcome shade from the harsh sun of the Central Altiplano. Shards of pavement jutted out aggressively, bringing the crash of tectonic plates I´d studied at school into mind, reminding me of the devasting earthquakes that can strike the city at any moment.

In the fading afternoon light, we wandered past a mix of Spanish colonial and Art Deco buildings, dodging low-hanging electrical wires as we searched for somewhere suitable for my first meal on Mexican soil. Seeing the familiar sight of what looked like an oversized doner kebab, we sat down at the entrance of a *taquería* – little more than a garage with a counter, hotplate and a random selection of different coloured stools and tables. Dotted around the dim eatery were a blend of different people: businessmen, young Mexicans, and European or American travellers, reflecting the area´s diverse mix of trendy locals and globetrotting visitors. We ordered several *tacos de pastor* and watched as chunks of flesh were sliced off the compact lump of meat that had attracted us here, quickly fried and then stuffed into tacos.

Soon we were diving in, red lines of spicy juice running down our wrists in rivulets of molten lava, which we tried desperately to mop up with transparent paper napkins. We washed the food down with an unpleasantly warm *Dos Equis* beer, which somehow had done the trick of extinguishing the fire that had been burning in my stomach earlier courtesy of Señor Don Julio and his blue agave beverage.

"So, what have you been up to here then?" I asked, picking out a chunk of fatty meat that had got lodged between my front teeth.

Dan began to fill me in on his time alone in the city, his passion for history and culture shining through as he enthusiastically explained about how he´d spent the entire previous day exploring the vast National Anthropology Museum, located on the edge of the sprawling green space of the Bosque de Chapultepec, not far from where we were now sitting on our brightly-painted squat furniture.

"It's unbelievable. It's got the most amazing collection of Mesoamerican artifacts you're ever likely to see anywhere. It's mind-blowing. Really. There are pieces from the Toltecs, Zapotecans, Mayans and incredible giant stone heads carved by the Olmecs around a thousand years before Christ. You've got to see them, really. The detail's incredible and the expressions on their faces so lifelike. They're kind of African in appearance, or like the Easter Island heads. You know, there must be a connection between all these ancient peoples and their cultures, they're so similar in so many ways. I don't know. They're just captivating. Really."

I was keen to listen to Dan's experiences; happy not to have to talk about anything myself. I lifted my empty bottle of beer into the air and signalled for two more to be brought our way. The waiter raised a thick eyebrow in surprise, presumedly at the speed with which we'd polished off the first two bottles.

"But I guess the most amazing thing in the whole place has to be the *Piedra del Sol,* the Aztec Sun Stone. I guess you've probably seen it. It's a huge, round stone circle carved with symbols representing the five suns and their gods."

I nodded, masking my ignorance as the waiter exchanged our empty bottles for full ones, staring and frowning at me as he did so. Why did he look at me that way? Why do they *all* look at me that way? What do I do to deserve their scorn wherever I go?

Dan didn't notice the glances and continued eagerly. "By the way, we're in the era of the fifth sun right now, but that's another story altogether. Anyway, most people think it's some kind of calendar but others refer to it as maybe a place of sacrifice or even a surface where gladiatorial battles took place. Something along those lines. Whatever way you look at it, it's probably one of the most important artifacts ever found in Mexico and, above all, it's very, very cool."

As I listened to Dan, I was filled with envy. He was here, seeing and living things he´d read about and studied, absorbed in a passion he felt something for. He had a purpose for his trip. A reason to be here on this journey through the ancient civilizations of Mesoamerica. But me? What was I doing here listening to this educated acquaintance of mine in my bubble of ignorance? Who exactly am I anyway? I have no idea who I am, no idea of how I work, no idea of how to feel good with myself, in peace, happy. Happy with myself and who I am without others wanting me to be something I´m not, evaluating my every move like the taco-wielding owner of this place. I know my own beliefs are not mine. My way of thinking is not my own. I´m denying myself, who I really am.

How has this come to be? I guess it´s because I´d never learnt how to develop myself, my thoughts. I´ve just been a passenger in this body, unable to resolve my own emotional and internal conflicts. Really, all I want to be is the person who I am; to be worth the person I am. To be set free. But how can I? I don´t have any criteria of my own. The important things I´ve learnt come from outside the body that carries my soul. Parents, teachers, bosses, peers and now Dan, who was sitting in front of me droning on about Mexican archaeology. The behaviours we have, we adopt, and I´d come to realise that I´d never made a decision by my own intuition or from my heart.

But how could I if I don´t know who I am? Or *what* I am. I don´t even know where I come from. Or where I´m going. And I have absolutely no idea how I got here. Why I´m now sitting in a little taco bar listening to Dan. It must´ve been my idea to be here, right now in the middle of Mexico, but I can´t remember when or where I made it. Am I having an existential crisis, something like that, whatever that really is? What I think I am is what others say I am. Is that it? The perception of myself is not real. Is that it? All that I feel exists inside me is an internal conflict I don´t know how to resolve. A pain, an emptiness.

The only thing that I do know for sure is that I didn´t want to be back in what was referred to as *home*. I wanted to be anywhere else but there right now. I wanted to travel; I think. Or was that what other people wanted me to do? I knew somewhere deep down beneath the pain and emptiness I wanted to see the World, but I didn´t really know what it was I wanted to see exactly. What world. I didn´t want to "find myself" and have some life-changing enlightenment about my path in this existence, no. I wasn´t escaping from something either as for me there can be no real escape.

Apathy. That must be the word. That´s what all of this translates to on the surface. That´s what all the people see. That´s how it all seems. So that´s the word I´ll use for the pain and emptiness. I was apathetic with my life. With the world around me. With the people around me. With everything.

I did have a life once, sometime before I landed here. I had parents and they´d given me a good, solid upbringing I suppose. From what I can remember, I was clearly in the bracket of middle-class judging by the holidays we´d had and the fact that there were lots of books on the shelves at home. There were books about travel, crime, politics and authors like Salmon Rushdie, Jack London and Jeffery Archer stood out on many of the spines. I´d often flicked through the travel books imaging myself in far flung places away from the grasp of my surroundings; the others I left untouched.

I´d scraped through a degree in something to do with business management and then worked as an admin temp during the week and in a record shop at the weekends to fund my trip. Did I? Did that really happen? Was that really me? I can see myself doing these things but the memories feel false, imposed, staged. The film I´m replaying in my mind has me as the central character with no career plans, no goals, no ambitions. A me who wanted to apparently see the World, it´s true, but it was really a way also for me to delay my destiny. Or at least delay thinking about it.

Whoever or whatever I am, was, or will be, listening to Dan now spewing out his passion only served to highlight my own misgivings, inadequacies and fears that I´d failed to leave back at a place once called home.

*

Over the following days in Mexico City, I indulged Dan´s desire for culture and history, returning again to the vast brutalist anthropology museum, its grey stone angles a harmonious counterpoint to the exhibits it housed. I listened as Dan dragged me around telling me about ancient civilizations, myths and legends and the creation and destruction of the five suns at the hands of Quetzalcoatl and Tezcatlipoca, almighty creator-god brothers once worshipped throughout this part of the World, destined to destroy each other. And of course, ample time was dedicated to the fascinating Olmec colossal heads on display and Dan´s effusive running commentary on their appearance, probable meaning and significance in the field of archaeology.

We visited many other museums, galleries and countless churches and other places of worship too, their spires leaning drunkenly as their foundations succumbed to the unstable ground on which they were built. I thought of the dreaming spires of Oxford, leaning spires, crashing down, being pushed up by the crust of the Earth in an impossible nightmarish Escher´s reality, sharp edges of stairs piercing the sanctity of inverted crypts.

We walked for miles around the metropolis, unrealistically trying to cram as much as we could into our short time there, attempting to get a feel of the vibrant city and how its twenty million inhabitants lived their fragile lives. Shining, glass-fronted buildings were springing up in many places, in particular along the Paseo de la Reforma, stealing the skyline away from the colonial landmarks. Passively watching this transformation stood the Torre Latinoamericana, towering over the city centre as it had done for the past forty years, its LED clock reminding everyone not to be late. Through grimy windows it stared out over the vast expanse of the city, passing no judgement, just observing, waiting for the next seismic shift that would rattle the area to its fragile core.

But in some neighbourhoods there was still a feel of how life hadn´t changed over the previous decades. This is what attracted me the most. Vendors on bicycles piled high with crates of fruits, vegetables and live songbirds, wove their way through the lanes of heavy traffic. Between the throng of pedestrians, shoe-shiners plied their trade on the pavements, their clients looking down on their penitent servants from atop their thrones. I gazed at my old battered trainers, wishing that I could somehow be part of the spectacle.

We wandered through markets, sensorial hubs where rural life temporarily invades and takes over urban areas for a change, rather than the other way round. Stalls of limes, avocados, dried chilies, spices, and sheets of fried pork *chicharrones* were punctuated by groups of women preparing corn tacos, rolling the dough into small balls and pressing them automatically into circular discs. There was absence in their eyes, slaves to the hundreds of thousands of repetitions throughout their lifetime on the same square-metre patch on which they´d grown up. We ate at the markets, trying whatever our stomachs could manage. Fried stuffed *gorditas,* spicy *enchiladas, pozole* soup and whatever salsas were on the low tables covered with brightly-coloured plastic tablecloths.

The hours of the days were devoured too, passing quickly, merging together. We headed to the north of the city, the busy crammed streets where tourists were normally hard to spot, fighting our way for space on the pavements, mouths watering at the plates of food that only the bravest visitor should dare to try.

We explored the popular southern district of Coyocan as well, making the obligatory stop at Frida Kahlo´s Casa Azul, joining the busy lines of people intruding on a life – like many – cut far too short in this country. Most visitors were engrossed in the artist's studio, paintings and personal artifacts on display for all to see. Dan's attention, however, was stolen away by the numerous pieces of ancient art collected by her husband, Diego, that were scattered around the patio and garden. A frown was hewn deep into Dan's forehead as he observed the looted sculptures; an expression that only receded once in the peaceful gardens of Leon Trotsky's nearby house as we imaged the great thinker – and Frida's one time lover – tending to his hens and rabbits, his brilliant mind a constant hive of activity, theory and counter-theory.

We travelled further south of the city to Xochimilco with its canals, garishly decorated flotilla of gondolas and floating Mariachi bands. And, thanks to Dan's insistence that it just couldn't be left out of our itinerary, we spent a day marvelling at the giant pyramids of Teotihuacán.

*

Seeing Dan in situ, among his beloved ancient ruins, was a thing to behold. He dragged me around the vast site, stopping at the base of nearly every pyramid and thumbing through a guidebook he'd produced from the small backpack that held everything that a serious day-tripper would need. He read aloud as much information as he could find about the temples' former use, their ornate carvings and the mighty gods they were built in honour of. The sun crashed down on us as we walked up and down the length of the dusty, shadeless Avenue of the Dead but Dan was relentless, talking away endlessly to himself as much as to me.

"The layout of the site's supposed to be in alignment with the three stars of Orion's belt. I mean, that could've been just a coincidence, but it's *exactly* like the main pyramids at Giza, which also have the same configuration." He looked at me excitedly as if he'd just made the discovery himself. I tried to look impressed at this link between Mexico and Egypt but I was more concerned, and increasingly embarrassed,

14

about the small group of people who´d sidled up to us and were now eavesdropping amusedly on Dan´s passionate explanations.

"This could explain the ancient super-race theory that claims that they somehow found a way to impart knowledge of astrology and geometry around the World. Remember the African-looking Olmec stone heads? That must be more than a coincidence, surely." Dan was staring down the straight line of the Avenue of the Dead, deep in thought, the hot wind and dust blowing in our faces.

"Well, we do all come from Africa originally, don´t we?" I dared to add, hoping that the people around us would disappear and Dan would read to himself rather than out loud. But he wasn´t listening. He looked down at his watch over the top of his glasses and rushed off in the direction of the on-site museum. I gratefully followed in his shadow as I´d become used to doing, not so much in search of yet more stone artifacts, but looking forward to a welcome respite from the scorching sun and the chance to escape from the prying eyes that hunted us.

*

Despite our aim to explore every far-flung corner of the city we could, and despite our urge for a wide variety of unique experiences, we often found ourselves repeatedly traversing the huge expanse of the Zócalo, the central square surrounded by snaking rivers of motor vehicles in the heart of the capital. This is where the reality of life for many of the city and country´s residents started to become apparent to me. This is where indigenous people from all parts of the nation were represented in all their colourful and pitiful glory. This is where elderly men and women, their skin dark and leathery from years of scraping a living in the harshest of conditions, came to sell what little they could produce or salvage. These people didn´t have the luxury of a lifetime on a market stall. They sat on the ground, lined up along the railings outside the cathedral or scattered around the vast public space with its enormous flag of red white and green. They sat in the burning sunshine, many with their backs to the opulent presidential palace, risking another day selling nothing or being brutally evicted by heavy-handed police with orders to clean up the city. Spread at the feet of many were undersized cobs of maize and small plastic bags of limp vegetables. Some sold wicker baskets or other handicrafts, trying to tempt a sympathetic tourist into parting with a few pesos. They were ancient people with ancient traditions and knowledge that one day would die with them. Their ancestors had created immense, modern cities before any European arrived to impose a new way of life and beliefs on them, but now they were reduced to little more than beggars. And, guiltily observing these outcasts, something inside me moved. Like two land masses fighting each other for space along a fault line, something moved inside me; nothing more than a tremor, a release of pressure, but for the first time in as long as I could remember, I could feel my inherent apathy begin to slowly disappear.

Dan´s Spanish was far better than mine and he could manage to hold down – albeit with some difficulty – a conversation with most of the people we came across. The subjects were invariably limited to directions, food and drink and tourist-related activities, but his secondary-school level Spanish was coming in more than handy and undoubtedly improving daily. I, on the other hand, despite having studied diligently a wide range of vocabulary in the weeks before our trip, was left to occasionally prompt Dan with translations of the names of some of the more unusual fruits and vegetables when visiting markets or restaurants. This lexis somehow had stuck with me, to the detriment of other more useful expressions, which for the life of me I just couldn´t remember.

In spite of our combined linguistic handicap and increasing lack of energy due to the self-inflicted ill effects of some dishes that we really shouldn´t have tried, we´d managed to fulfil Dan´s desire to see the remnants of the most important ancient Mesoamerican cultures in and around the capital, while also ticking various boxes of not-so-important things that I´d added to the wish-list too.

So, feeling that our work in the capital was done, we left the sedate safe-haven of our apartment in La Condesa behind and made our way south-east to the city of Puebla.

*

Located halfway between Mexico City and Veracruz – the coastal gateway between the New and Old World where most of the supplies and reinforcements for the Spanish conquest had arrived – the gloriously named settlement of Heroica Puebla de Zaragoza was a place we were definitely both looking forward to visiting.

We delved enthusiastically into the city´s murky colonial past, wandering streets dominated by religious buildings of one type or another, their imposing facades made even more intimidating by the dark-grey Cantera stone of the architraves surrounding their enormous doorways. We lapped up the seemingly endless history of a city that was built by the Spanish, occupied by the Americans and laid siege to by the French. I pretended to be interested in the mix of renaissance and Mexican baroque architecture as Dan flicked through his guidebook for an anecdote that I might find interesting and inspire me to keep plodding along the dark pavements obligingly like Sancho Panza by his side.

The ecclesiastical gloom of the centre was punctuated by brightly-coloured buildings, tiled frontages and neighbourhoods full of small shops and stalls selling white onyx and marble handicrafts, ornate rugs and textiles – a throwback to a once thriving fabric industry in the city. Dan had dug deep and found a suitable anecdote for me from somewhere in the back of his mind, or his guidebook.

"You know, the red dye that´s used to colour the cloth actually comes from an insect." He waited to continue until he had my full attention. I reluctantly gave in. "You know the flat cactus leaves that we´ve seen people selling to eat? The *nopales*? Well, little bugs attach themselves to the surface and form a kind of white sticky cotton-like infestation. Traditionally the native indians – but I guess anyone who´s cultivating them today – scrape off the bugs, dry them and then they can be crushed into a bright red power. It´s also used in lipstick and food colourings and is quite common in things like sweets too."

"So, like, we´ve been eating insects for years without even knowing it?" I feigned surprise, doing my best to play along.

I looked at the deep crimson of the intricate rugs around us, imagining an old woman in traditional clothes harvesting the insects in the heat and dust of the dry lands where little more than cacti are able to take a foothold. In my mind´s eye she was old but with jet black hair. Her cracked feet supported by nothing more than thinly-soled shoes made of dried grass. She was painfully thin.

From what we discovered, today there were very few indigenous Nahuas, Totonacs or Otomies still here in the artistic quarter, the very people who shouldered the heavy grey stones used to construct the

New-World edifices now forced out into scratching a survival in substandard living conditions on the outskirts due of the growing city. Most of the handicrafts we saw on sale were now probably made in huge sweatshops where the workers were paid peanuts in return for producing something that would adorn the walls of some middle-class living room in Europe or North America. An anger was forming a knot inside me, tightening my nerves.

It was dawning on me that I was just going through the motions with Dan. I enjoyed his company and we´d already seen some amazing things but I was finding our days stretching out in front of me like an eternity. Too full of activity; too devoid of real meaning. I tried to take my mind off the dualities I was observing and distracted myself instead in search of food, in particular the thick spicy *mole* sauce typical of the region; the mix of chilli and chocolate somehow invigorating me – temporarily at least.

By now, however, we´d grown tired of street food and the risks involved for our delicate constitutions and so stretched our budget by experimenting with other dishes we hadn´t seen or tried before. The patriotic *chiles en nogada* caught our eye with its creamy sauce, pomegranate seeds and parsley representing the three colours of the national flag that we´d seen fluttering unashamedly above the capital´s poverty-stricken main square.

We satiated Dan´s anthropological thirst for ancient civilizations again too with a side-trip to the church-heavy city of Cholula, both of us keen to see what was claimed to be the largest pyramid in the World. Dan was excited; I, simply along for the ride as usual.

*

Built by mythical giants, the temple of Tlachihualtépetl could house the two great pyramids of Teotihuacán – the Pyramid of the Sun and the Pyramid of the Moon – inside its volume and still have room to spare. So, we were extremely disappointed, to say the least, to find little more than an enormous grassy mound with a depressing concrete

19

basketball court at its base. Sat atop the once dominant landmark was a pale yellow colonial church, stark against the overcast sky – a reminder for all to see for miles around of the crushing defeat and massacre of the Cholutecas at the hands of a Hernan Cortés led army.

But there is always something to see, something to learn, the World an open-air museum, an immersive art gallery full of life, history and anthropological delights. The seemingly ugly and underwhelming places offering more clues to the real life of the people and their home than carbon copy city centres overrun with similar coffee shops and fast food chains. At least from Dan´s perspective it was anyway, and he went about energetically exploring the rest of the archaeological site with glee. I decided that it would be best to pull myself away from him. I needed a rest. I needed to escape his dominance. His presence.

"Take your time mate, please. I´ll just be over there." I pointed to a kiosk with some tables fanning out from it not far from where some teenagers were trying to throw a deflated ball through a netless hoop on the basketball court in the shadow of the once mighty Tlachihualtépetl.

"OK. I won´t be long." Dan danced away and disappeared down a grassy slope, which no doubt hid another architectural gem of a bygone dynasty just waiting for him to discover.

I used the time to write a postcard I´d bought of the Zócalo back in Mexico City, its giant flag unfurled by the breeze to show, in full glory, an eagle devouring a rattlesnake. The scene of hunter and prey was perched for eternity above the now infamous prickly pear cactus, the pads of the plant a staple throughout the country, present as much in the national symbol as on the streets, where weather-beaten old men and women sit and scrape off the spines in preparation to sell *nopales* for a pittance. There were no indigenous hawkers on the square in my postcard. My parents would like this.

As I finished writing empty words that were not my own, I felt something lightly touch my elbow. I brushed it off without looking, not giving it much thought. Some kind of insect maybe. I flapped my hand aimlessly to try to make it go away. Harder this time, I now felt the strike of something solid on my upper arm, repeating again and again and starting to get more and more painful. I looked down, shocked and angered at the intrusion. I stared into the piercing eyes of a huge serpent, its body snaking away endlessly into the distance, covered in emerald feathers and shining scales. The creature prodded me hard again with its beak-like jaws, huge fangs protruding from its gaping mouth, more colourful bunches of feathers formed a ruff around its neck. Its animal appearance had a human-like air to it and I was captivated by its expression; unimaginable knowledge burning brightly behind its eyes. It struck me again hard and a stream of blood began to flow down my arm. It wanted my bones. My bones would bring harmony and balance to its world, I could read that in its eyes, its mind. Fear washed over me, I couldn´t move and the beast´s fangs were sinking more deeply into my flesh, the blood now surging out of my wounds, cascading down onto the ground below and disappearing between the cracks in the slabs of stone that supported myself and the animal. I pulled away from its grip and I suddenly opened another set of eyelids I didn´t know I possessed. I blinked at the bright light that had me blinded.

Through blurred vision I could make out a shadow close by, which slowly converted into someone in a dark-blue uniform. An annoyed-looking policeman was standing over me and the bench I was lying on, the truncheon he´d been poking me with now lowered and in the process of being sheathed back into its belt – but worryingly on hand should I make any sudden movements. I looked around and saw the kiosk café on the other side of the small square with a fountain in the middle. I noticed that I was holding Dan´s guidebook, my completed postcard tucked inside it.

The police officer was saying something to me loudly and his body language told me that I could easily wind up in a quite a bit of trouble if I wasn´t careful. But then Dan was suddenly there, reeling off something impressive in Spanish and showing the officer his passport, which seemed to calm and satisfy the policeman, who thankfully soon wandered off without looking back in my direction.

There was nothing else to see or do here. We knew we had to leave Cholula now even without Dan and I discussing the option together. We jumped into a taxi and headed straight back to Puebla; the World´s largest pyramid disappearing slowly from view behind us and the heavy clouds above drawing away to reveal the volcanic cone of Popocatépetl bellowing his smoking rage at our backs.

*

We punctuated the rest of our time back in the city of Puebla by dropping into dark bars in the historic centre to down shots of home-made liquors, tequilas and mezcals. I was getting too good at this. The burning in my stomach I´d experienced upon arrival in the country was fast disappearing and I was beginning to favour hanging out in *mezcalerías* rather than climbing the steep steps of ancient pyramids. I needed to drink; I really did. Drink to forget those serpentine eyes that had fixed me with their poisonous stare. When I closed my own, they were there and all I could do to eliminate them was to try to lose consciousness. Mexico – and Puebla as it turns out – was turning into a very good place to do this.

After several drunken days, the city´s initial charm started to fade. The balloon sellers, hidden by a cloud of colour and defying the laws of gravity, which had amused us at first, went ignored. The historic streets we´d explored now all seemed to be dug up in order to improve transport, build new infrastructure, introduce ecological projects and sanitize public services. We wouldn´t see the results, maybe nobody would, but for us right now it simply made strolling around the old town quite hazardous and selfishly less enjoyable. So, we unanimously decided it was time to retrace the footsteps of the *Conquistadores* and set off towards the port city of Veracruz on the Gulf coast.

We were glad to finally head down from the Central Altiplano, the unrelenting sun having left our skin burnt and taut and the altitude stealing the breath from our lungs as we climbed near-vertical hillsides and scrambled up and down pyramids. Although being on the coast afforded us a more beneficial level of oxygen, the air was dense and humid and we both started to quickly develop dark stains of sweat on our t-shirts. In search of a sea breeze – and something cheap to eat – we made for the run-down port area that dominated the city.

The skeletal bodies of stevedore cranes raised themselves over the docks and piles of containers blocked out the horizon. Inland, the landscape was backed by austere port authority buildings that separated us from the old town. It wasn´t exactly the Caribbean getaway that we´d imagined. Looking for something to fill our stomachs, we were approached by a teenage boy who was walking towards us in the opposite direction, his clothes dirty and torn. He must´ve been somewhere around sixteen years old by my reckoning, although his tough dark skin and slight frame made it difficult to tell exactly how old he was. He looked directly at me and I prepared myself as I´d done so often over the past two weeks. *Lo siento*, I would apologise, deeming him neither desperate nor indigenous-looking enough to warrant my charity, despite his shabby appearance. As he drew closer, I could see that his eyes were red and watery. I could sense Dan, who´d been walking at my side until now, move just a shade behind me. Coward.

The three of us stopped and faced off on the street for a few tense seconds. The boy didn´t ask for money though; instead, stretching up as far as he could on his toes to my eye-level, he screamed into my face a long shrill sound that left Dan and I reeling backwards. I could smell stale alcohol on the boy´s breath and as we turned on our heels and scurried away as quickly as we could from this strange encounter, we could hear him laughing hysterically and shouting at us in an accent, or dialect, impossible to understand.

Dan and I didn't need to speak. We knew what each other was thinking. Dan would be shaken, imagining that we could've been killed with a knife; I, beating myself up about how I could've done things differently to avoid contact in the first place.

I'd had my fair share of close shaves throughout my life in the U.K. as I walked home after pub closing time. I'd been beaten up badly once too as I foolishly took a late-night shortcut through what I thought was an empty park. But this was different. Two worlds had collided here by the port, whereas back home I'd been attacked by my own kind. The thought of this left me decidedly unsettled.

We left the deserted dockside and started to walk along the seafront *malecón*, lines of palm trees and nineteen-seventies apartment blocks and hotels giving us something of a safer feel. We started to relax as we strolled along the promenade of the *Ciudad de Tablas*, our footsteps covering the area where slaves and low-paid workers salvaged the wooden boards from unseaworthy ships, a fact – according to Dan's trusty guidebook – that lent the city its once popular pseudonym of the City of Boards.

I didn't dislike Veracruz as such. It had its charm with its pretty Plaza de Armas central square that once housed the National Government of Mexico and the city also boasted a visit-worthy collection of cream-coloured churches and buildings. And so, we continued in tourist mode by visiting as many sites as possible over the course of the next couple of days. It had a gritty character being a port town and the mix of a more tropical climate and the growing tourist infrastructure made it an interesting and varied place to spend some time. But, in comparison to the metropolis of Mexico City and the colonial might of Puebla, we were left slightly underwhelmed.

We were also on edge. It wasn't our brief encounter with our first local from Veracruz that did it, but something else that was in the air. Something that made us look over our shoulders more than once. The growing knot in my stomach? The sense that all of my memories had been placed into me artificially and every day I was forgetting who I was? The dread of realising the truth? I don't know. This strange feeling was accentuated further still with a visit to the Fortaleza de San Juan de Ulúa.

The fort, which in previous incarnations had been used as a dock, warehouse, garrison, prison and even the headquarters of the *Santa Inquisición* was an impressive structure, its angular walls jutting out aggressively into the sea. Outside, bright sunlight reflected off its exterior walls, highlighting the light-coloured petrified coral incrusted into the stone blocks that made up a large part of the construction. Inside, it was a different story. It was dark. We were surrounded by an unearthly mix of life and death. The walls were alive with dark mould, the ceilings dripping with slimy stalactites. But it was death that was ever more present here, stalking our every move as we walked through grimy tunnels and past dungeons and cells with names like *Purgatory*, *Limbo* and *Hell*; rusty hoops still visible on the walls where prisoners or opponents of the Catholic faith were strung up, crucified.

Liquid dominated this dank place. Outside, the sea lapped at the feet of the sloping defences; inside, the cells flooded waist high, the putrid water once mixing with the tears and blood of the condemned. We passed through dimly-lit arches, half expecting to be set upon at any moment and beaten to death, Dan hiding behind me as he'd done as we'd looked in vain for something to eat in the port.

*

Back in the old town, the night before we were due to hug the coast towards Campeche, we decided to have one last wander around the pretty Plaza de Armas and stroll under the more inviting arches of the buildings that flanked its sides. Not far from the square, up a small side street, Dan stopped at an open door through which well-trodden steps, sagging in the middle from years of footfall, led up to the first floor. He was staring at the sign above the entrance. *Pulquería*, it read. Before I could ask him what it meant, he was already well on his way inside.

"Come on," he encouraged from halfway up the worn stairs.

We entered the bar area and studied our surroundings quickly, doing our best to not seem out of place but failing miserably, in no small part due to our clothes, despite our rapidly darkening skin colour. On one side of the room was the bar, its shelves filled with an array of bottles of spirits, CDs, ceramic figures and an assortment of candles, many of which with Jesus and his shining sacred heart glowing out from the middle of his chest. In the centre of the upper of the two shelves sat a picture of the Virgin Mary, framed with false flowers and fairy lights. The bar itself was full of plastic tubs in which sat huge bottles filled with thick liquids of varying colours.

"*Pulque*," Dan said, "I've been meaning to try it."

The barroom was close to full so we grabbed one of the only tables that didn't have groups of locals huddled around it. Traditional *Son Jarocho* music from the area was blaring out of the speaker above our heads, probably thanks to the older, local clientele that made up the majority of the people there. I recognised the melody as something familiar and was trying to figure out where I knew it from when Dan, shouting above the music, broke my train of thought.

"It's made from the agave plant," he yelled in my ear. "Like tequila and mezcal but I think it comes from the sap in the middle of the trunk, or something like that."

I shrugged my shoulders in reply. "OK. Great," I mouthed and gave an enthusiastic thumbs up.

The bartender meandered over slowly to our table, a look of indifference on his face as we ordered. He shuffled even more slowly back to the bar, took a ceramic jug from a shelf above, filled it with a white viscous liquid from one of the larger plastic tubs and sauntered over to us with it spilling over the brim onto the already sticky floor. We took turns to sip at the slimy fermentation, grimacing as the unfamiliar bitterness invaded our taste buds. However, before too long we grew accustomed to the pre-Hispanic brew of the gods and worked our way through another brown jug. Our bodies relaxed and our tongues loosened.

"So," I shouted over the music, which had now changed to Mexican pop in response to a younger crowd that had started to gradually take over the place. "Are you going to be alright? I mean ..." I pointed at the side of my head, emboldened by *pulque* unlike any other drink before, poaching the elephant in the room at last.

"I don´t know, we´ll see. It wasn´t great at first but things are going better than they said they would. Anyway, I´m OK at the moment, well more or less." He smiled and held up the decorated jug as if making a toast. "They cut out the bad stuff and zapped the rest. I mean, anything can happen from now on. I might end up being epileptic for the rest of my life or something but I´ve got the all clear for the time being, so, umm let´s see what happens."

I held out my jug this time in order to properly smack them together and say cheers but my hand was empty. I looked at it and it started to flicker, like a malfunctioning hologram. I looked at Dan. He was the only one with a drink. He began to flicker too. Fuck. The *pulque* must be stronger than I thought.

"But I could drop down dead at any moment too," Dan said suddenly, solemnly.

I spat the contents of my mouth into my jug, which had appeared again in front of me, finding his comment darkly hilarious. Luckily, Dan found this contagious and we were both laughing out loud together for the first time since arriving in Mexico, the thought of his possible demise strangely bringing us together. The bartender, like the group of young people at the next table, was giving us the evil eye from across the room.

I hadn´t noticed the people arrive but now the bar was full, which created a lively atmosphere that we were both enjoying. Animated by our drinks we talked about all kinds of subjects that had been overlooked until now. Family, relationships with friends, love and plans for the future – taboo topics among our football-mad group of amigos back in Essex – were all given a good going over. We were putting the World to rights, gesticulating effusively as we did so. I was sure that as Dan waved his arms wildly I could see vapour trails in the air around him, or his aura, or something like that if they really exist. We´d just started a character assassination of the current British government when our pearls of wisdom were cut short by a group of three who asked politely if they could sit down at the unused stools that were tucked under our table.

Our new table-mates were an odd-looking bunch to say the least. Two men and one woman, whose combined appearance to me in my current condition was nothing less than comical. One of the men was incredibly short and thin and had a large head with a thick matt of black hair that sat atop his child-like body. He had a huge mouth and an expressionless face. A Pez dispenser, I thought and smiled to myself. The other man was possibly the largest guy I´d seen in Mexico so far; a fact accentuated by the wide-brimmed cowboy style hat he wore. After so many *pulques* I wasn´t even sure if he was just a figment of my imagination I´d just made up. He seriously could´ve been a bad guy in a film, a *bandido*, or something like that. His shirt matched the western style of his hat and was unbuttoned to reveal a forest of hair in which a gold crucifix was partially engulfed and the scar on his pock-marked face added to the drama further still. But he smiled at us warmly, which of course allowed us to see a shining gold tooth. His girlfriend – I assume this due to their close proximity and intertwined fingers – was unusually attractive amid this scene, her deep brown eyes framed with dark eye-liner, her ebony hair long and flowing. She spoke to us in a simple English.

"Where are you from?"

Dan wanted to practise his Spanish so I sat back and left him to it. "*Soy de Inglaterra. Cerca de* London. *Me llamo* Dan."

She grinned, and I noticed that Pez dispenser and Bandido were both now smiling too. "Nice to meet you," she said, as she stretched out her hand, taking Dan´s softly in her own. Her companions didn´t offer theirs.

We spent the next hour or so exchanging comments in English and Spanish, Dan much more forward than I was, glad to get the chance to push himself out of his linguistic comfort zone. Raquel, as she´d introduced herself, translated for her two friends, who stared at me with a strange drunken mix of amusement and hatred.

It was my turn to get another round in and as the room was now far too packed for table service, I swayed my way over to the grumpy bartender, who was angrily watching me approach his territory. Before I could get my words out, he thumped his right fist into the palm of his left hand. I didn´t understand what he was doing and stared blankly at him like the idiot gringo I was. Was it some kind of sign language? He made the same gesture again, more violently this time. I started to get nervous and looked over my shoulder to Dan, who´d been deep in conversation with Raquel when I´d left the table, his eyes showing too much affection towards her than was advisable. He wasn´t there.

"Warning," the bartender said in English and again smacked his fist into his palm. "Warning," he repeated again and nodded with his head towards our table.

I finally got the message. Shit. Fuck, fuck, fuck. The bartender rubbed his fingers together making the international sign for money before punching his left hand again, which didn´t really help my growing state of anxiety.

"Warning," he repeated.

"Thank you, *gracias. Muchas gracias,*" I slurred, my mind racing much faster than my mouth. I threw a lot more pesos on the bar than our drinks cost and walked back to our group, dodging other drunken customers with great difficulty. Dan was back at the table talking gibberish again.

"We have to go now, we´ve … we´ve got an early bus tomorrow,

OK? *Muchas gracias por tu compañia*, thanks. Nice meeting you. Come on," I tugged at Dan´s shirt.

"Umm, OK," he answered reluctantly at first until he realised my state of mind. Even through the *pulque* haze he could see that something was definitely wrong.

"Wait," Raquel shouted. My blood froze. She scribbled a number down on the back of a business card of a taxi company she´d pulled out of a small embroidered bag she had with her. "My number. You call me tomorrow and we take you to the bus station, OK?"

Dan took the card and started to smile again.

"*Hasta luego.*" I guided Dan away from the table, through the crowd and to the top of the stairs.

"They´re gonna rob us. We need to leave. Now," I told him.

Dan looked back at the three of them through the mass of people in the barroom. None of them was smiling anymore and Bandido was now on his feet looking taller and more menacing than he´d done before, if possible. We flew down the stairs as quickly as our rubber legs could take us and pushed the door. It didn´t move. We pulled and pushed at it as hard as we could but it just didn´t budge. A barrier of solid wood sealing us in forever. We were trapped at the bottom of the stairs, the dim light not helping our state of panic. Behind us, heavy footsteps on the ancient wooden boards made us spin around; the loud music had prevented us from hearing anyone approach until they were just a metre or two away. They´d have a knife. What the screaming teenager at the port hadn´t done to us would be done now. For fuck´s sake make it quick. Dan closed his eyes.

The bartender pushed us aside roughly and reached for the latch on the door, opening it effortlessly with the hand that had mercifully warned us of our fate.

"*Pinche pendejo,*" he swore at our backs, as we lurched out into the safety of the warm night air.

The *maguey*. On the face of it, an inconspicuous spikey plant that can survive in the harshest of conditions. A simple agave, that like its close cousin the blue *agave tequilana* and other *agavoideae*, sacrifices its torso to be roasted, ground and distilled into tequila and mezcal and drunk in places around the World from dark *tinacals* full of locals in the province of Hidalgo, to sky bars in Manhattan.

But the *maguey* is so much more than this. It's a one-stop-shop that's provided people since pre-Hispanic times with fibre for clothes, rugs, ropes and paper. Its membranes are dried and used for wrapping food in preparation for roasting, and its thick green leaves utilised to seal in the heat and juices of meat as it's slowly cooked over many hours underground. It's flowers are eaten, its sugary sap a delicacy and the larvae that burrow between its roots fried and consumed. Nothing is wasted. It's sharp barbs have been used as sewing needles for centuries and any by-product left over from the production of its many gifts is given to animals to feed on. And then there's its heart; a virgin-white starchy root-like substance harvested when the plant has reached a decade old. Ripped from deep inside, this highly-prized commodity leaves behind a gaping wound, bleeding a sap that will almost immediately begin to ferment into the alcohol that very nearly got us mugged – or worse – the previous evening.

But today, as I woke up cursing the gods of *pulque,* I didn't care that the *maguey* plant had been revered by ancient people and depicted in Aztec scriptures. Nor the important role it's played in the life of people here for hundreds or even thousands of years. I instead simply fought the blinding headache that anchored me to the bed and turned to look at Dan, who wasn't exactly in a better condition than I was.

He'd made the gargantuan effort, at least, to be sitting up on the edge of a bed that looked like it hadn't been slept in, his feet planted on the floor. He was fully dressed in the same clothes he was wearing the night before, including his shoes, his glasses askew. He sighed heavily and shook his head.

"I´m never drinking again," he promised himself weakly.

I squinted at my watch. The bus that was going to take us westwards along the Gulf coast was due to leave in little over an hour´s time.

"Coffee," I mumbled.

We somehow dragged our sorry carcasses simultaneously away from our beds and I dressed myself by retracing the trail of crumpled, inside-out breadcrumbs I´d left scattered on the floor as I´d undressed on my way to my fitful sleep. Fifteen minutes later, we were sipping on steaming, watery coffee and trying to work our way through a large messy plate of *chilaquiles*. The soggy *tortilla* chips bathed in a spicy green sauce, eggs, onions and other accoutrements now not seeming quite so appetizing as they had when we´d ordered them and definitely not a good idea with a long bus journey ahead of us.

Soon after breakfast, with our stomachs more or less full but complaining noisily, we boarded a bus to Coatzacoalcos, half a day´s drive down the coast, where we´d spend the night. The following morning, we would – in theory anyway – get up at the crack of dawn to see another archaeological site Dan had earmarked and promised would be more than worth the effort to get there. I have to say that I wasn´t exactly looking forward to our plans for the immediate future, but right now where Dan went, I would follow.

*

After an uncomfortably endless journey followed by a sleepless night full of twitching muscles that did their best to jerk me away from any kind of rest, we were again wearily waiting for a bus that would take us to another unknown stop on our spiralling voyage.

The city of Coatzacoalcos was an uninspiring, low-rise, low-key place far off the foreign tourist radar. The meandering river of the same name divided the city in half, spewing its contents into the Gulf of Mexico in one direction and swallowing the rust-speckled container ships that came to load and unload their hidden goods in the other. Soon, we were on our way on the two-hour journey by bus, mini-van and the power of our own weary feet that would lead us to the original sanctuary of culture and art in the whole of Mesoamerica; San Lorenzo Tenochtitlán.

The lack of sleep and the effects of the alcohol we´d consumed in Veracruz enveloped me in an irreal world of blurred images and false memories, a dream in which the heat of the evolving day sapped the energy from deep within my body, feeding on the nutrients in my bone marrow and rendering me useless. I let Dan take over. Let him revel in the excitement of finally seeing the giant stone heads he´d told me about with such eagerness on our first night together in La Condesa. He thankfully had energy reserves enough for the both of us.

We waited for what seemed like an eternity in the mirage of the rising heat on the side of the main road where the bus had left us. Thirst clawed at our throats as we waited for the *colectivo* that was going to take us to what was once the biggest and most important city in Central America. Eventually, a mini-van pulled up beside us in a plume of dust, already near to capacity, stuffed with villagers with bags and boxes of various sizes perched on laps and clutched in arms. All eyes were firmly planted on us as we levered ourselves into the front seat next to the driver in a space barely enough for one small person to squeeze into. Our fellow passengers looked at us with tired curiosity, the deep dark pools of the eyes of the children fixing us in their vacant stare. There were few smiles.

*

After a long, bumpy ride dodging potholes on a dirt road we arrived at the village – little more than a collection of ramshackle buildings thrown together where the road appeared to widen. Dan asked the driver where the site could be found and he gestured in the direction of a sloping track that climbed a hill behind the village.

Sweating out the last of the *pulque*, Dan dragged us both up the mound, his enthusiasm and adrenalin the only reason why we were still moving at all. If this is supposed to be one of the most important sites in the whole of the country, then why aren´t there any signs around here telling us about it? Or people? Teotihuacán with its giant astral pyramids was packed, why not here? Dan consulted his guidebook, a frown on his face at the sparse information that was available to him.

We came to a sagging chain that blocked off the path to motor vehicles. If any ever came up here. Dan skipped over it and I reluctantly followed, starting to suspect that we were not about to discover an ancient city full of pyramids, formic lines of tourists colonising their steep sides. We reached the summit, grateful for the light breeze that was blowing in from the direction of the coast. From our elevated position we got our breath back and took in the surrounding landscape with its rolling hills, serpentine river and flood plain. It somehow reminded me of the English countryside with its sloping pastures, the brown cattle dotted here and there adding to the unlikely analogy.

I knew exactly what Dan was thinking. Where are the heads? The helmet-clad governor-warriors staring blindly across the lands they once ruled. We walked towards the only structure that we could see; an unfinished, doorless, square construction, its low breeze-block walls barely reaching chest height. It was covered with a blue, plastic tarpaulin that provided little protection from the heavy rains that the area was prone to. We peered inside, careful not to enter without permission, worried we might not be welcome if discovered here unannounced. Inside, in the dim blue light, were various stone fragments and artifacts unearthed from somewhere among the grassy hills, trees and intermittent cows.

"*Les puedo ayudar?*"

We span around to see where the nervous offer of assistance had come from and saw that it had been asked by a young man, not much older than ourselves. He looked worried about what we were doing here up on this lonely hilltop.

"Hi, umm ... sorry to bother you, but we´re looking for the stone heads," Dan explained to our questioner in impressive Spanish, smiling innocently in order to try to convince him we weren´t some kind of neo-colonial tomb raiders.

The young man, in grubby cotton trousers and t-shirt, was definitely not like any of the many security guards we´d seen so far in Mexico. He had an academic air to him, a glint in his eyes that made us feel at ease, despite being caught red-handed where perhaps we shouldn´t be.

"Ah, OK. Please wait here for a moment, OK?" he said, gesturing with the palms of his hands for us to remain where we were. He rushed off down the side of the hill in the direction of another blue, plastic tarpaulin that we hadn´t noticed before. A few minutes later he was back, accompanied by a blonde-haired woman somewhere in her mid to late thirties dressed in a dark-blue shirt with sleeves rolled up to the elbows, and trousers – identical to her younger companion´s but even dirtier – tucked into ankle-high boots. To top off her stereotypical look of an old-fashioned explorer, on her head she wore a rattan pith helmet. As they approached, I could see that her complexion, hair colour and general adventurer´s appearance gave away the fact she obviously wasn´t from around these parts.

"Hello there. What brings you all the way out here then gentlemen?" she asked warmly in our mother tongue, surprise etched upon her face and a little out of breath from the climb up the slope. Her American accent confirmed my previous hypothesis.

"I´m, umm, here to see the giant Olmec heads if possible. I studied anthropology and I´m really interested in Mesoamerica. And, umm, wanted to see the heads in person if I can. I saw two of them in Mexico City and, umm ... they´re fascinating." The words stumbled out of Dan´s mouth and he couldn´t help but look around at his surroundings as he spoke, as if suddenly he´d catch sight of one of the sculptures he was searching for.

"Firstly, welcome to San Lorenzo Tenochtitlán." The woman smiled kindly at him. "Secondly, I´m afraid they´re no longer here." There was a little sadness in her voice. "They were all taken away, you know. Most of them are at MAX now and it doesn´t look like we´ll get them back anytime soon."

"I´m sorry, what´s MAX?" Dan asked.

"Oh, yes, forgive me. The Museum of Anthropology in Xalapa." She addressed Dan, I disappeared into the background and the depths of my self-consciousness. "The regional government took them away, or at least was offered them by some local hotheads in the community who used the *cabezas* as a bargaining tool in exchange for services for the village. You know, electricity, a school, better roads, things like that." The sadness quickly gave way to an anger she did little to try to disguise. "Services that the government would have, and *should* have, given them in the first place, of course."

Dan looked crestfallen. "I´m sorry to hear that," he muttered.

The woman smiled in resignation this time. "Sadly, the negotiation of archaeological resources has become quite a common occurrence among the communities in the south of Veracruz. And here," she scanned the hills and surrounding countryside with narrow eyes, "in what is the heart of Mesoamerican civilization, it saddens me to know that this place is still unprotected. People can just turn up and take what they want; the government, local entrepreneurs, looters."

I immediately thought of the artifacts that adorned the Casa Azul in Coyocan and the private collection of Frida and Diego.

"You know, I hope things change. That new generations learn the value of what they have and protect their cultural heritage, I really do. But right now, to be honest, it´s an uphill struggle."

Dan was lost for words. I stepped in reluctantly. "Well, if there´s anything that you think that we can do, you know, spread the word, something like that. Dan´s got lots of friends and fellow graduates in this field so it might, kind of, be useful. I don´t know."

"Thank you." She spoke directly to me for the first time, smiling warmly, although she was slightly puzzled at my appearance in the conversation. "I appreciate it."

"Ann!" a voice drifted up from the dig site down the hill from which she'd emerged. "*Ven aquí, por favor.*"

"Please excuse me, I should get back," she said apologetically, heeding the pleas of the voice that had asked her to return to the blue tarpaulin on the lower part of the site. "Please feel free to have a nose around, if you like. There's not a great deal to see right now but hopefully if you come back in a few months' time, things will be very different." She smiled knowingly, shaking my hand firmly and then, accompanied by her young colleague, headed back down the hill and disappeared under the plastic sheet in search of the great discovery that would perhaps change the fate of this undervalued and forgotten archaeological site.

*

As we made our long and dusty journey back to Coatzacoalcos I couldn't help but think about our brief meeting with the American archaeologist. Her determination to continue when seemingly all others around were fighting against her and her team. The passion she showed in adversity to protect a cultural dynasty that was not her own. The risks she herself personally faced.

Once again, the growing injustices I'd begun to see and understand in this beautiful, complicated country were weighing heavily upon me. At my side, Dan was also deep in silent contemplation and remained so as the bus pulled away from Coatzacoalcos and began its long journey to our next destination: Campeche.

The colourful, walled city of San Francisco de Campeche was the perfect antidote to the aggressive atmosphere of the port of Veracruz and the disappointment we´d felt at San Lorenzo Tenochtitlán. It provided us also with a welcome timeout from the crowded, colonial-rooted cities of the Altiplano with their countless religious monuments constantly reminding us of suppression and slaughter.

Here, at the entrance to the Yucatan peninsula in Campeche, among the spectrum of the flaking paint of the low, uniform buildings and the azure background of the Caribbean, we felt relaxed. We really needed it too. The constant sightseeing, the distances covered in such a short space of time, and the unchecked experimentation with alcohol that our bodies had yet to evolve to handle had taken its toll on our collective body and soul.

We rested, began to read the books that had weighed our backpacks down, caught up on much-needed sleep and wandered the pleasant streets occasionally visiting a church or museum or two without overdoing it too much. We walked the ramparts of the impenetrable walls that had protected the city from French and English corsairs and filibusters carried here by the alisios trade winds. Like us, they had been attracted to this place, not in search of rest and relaxation, but by the vulnerable New World wealth that passed through the fortified city on its way to fund an empire on the other side of the World.

We strolled along the *malecón*, the soft breeze and the sound of the gentle waves lulling us into a sense of security we hadn´t felt for some weeks now. We were not in a hurry. We sat and observed frigate birds skimming across the surface of the sea, their wings unmoving as they glided their perfect silhouettes against the rising sun. Pelicans rose and crashed clumsily into impossibly shallow water all around.

We got our first taste too of the ancient Mayan civilization at the compact site of Edzná, not far from the city, and were pleasantly surprised to see that we had the place to ourselves with not another single tourist in sight. I enjoyed the peace and quiet and the fact that we weren´t fighting for space on the steps of the main pyramids as we´d done at other larger, more popular sites.

We sat at the base of one of the smaller structures and Dan, once again, took up the mantle of tour guide.

"You know, there are quite a lot of differences between the Mayan cities and the other places we´ve seen so far. I mean, I guess the biggest one is that the Mayan kingdom wasn´t actually one state like many of the other civilisations as it was made up of different smaller kingdoms. So, that´s why many of the different sites in this region aren´t exactly that similar to each other, architecturally speaking."

He stroked his right ear lobe gently as he often did when trying to remember some interesting fact or another; an involuntary movement that had gradually developed into something of a habit on this trip. I listened with interest, imagining Dan in a lecture theatre somewhere giving his spiel to hundreds of undergraduates. The male students wanting to be like him; the female ones wanting to be with him. All of a sudden, I felt resentment towards him, his relative good looks, photographic memory and charismatic smile; none of which had been diminished noticeably by his brush with brain cancer. I buried these thoughts, guilty about feeling this way about someone living on borrowed time.

"If you look at the temples, with the Aztec or Mixtec ones, they used to have like a double temple on the top. So, that´s probably why on the other pyramids we´ve seen there are such large, flat areas." He flicked through the guidebook showing me some examples to refresh my memory. "The Mayan ones, however, are much steeper and more pointed at the top, if you like. Markets too were a feature of the Aztecs, who built their cities around grand central public spaces. I guess maybe the orography in Mayan areas prevented them from designing their cities like this."

Despite my previous wave of resentful feelings, as I listened to what Dan had to say I realised that this was part of what I could´ve been missing for so long. Someone to listen to, to talk to, and for the first time since I´d arrived I felt that I was finally enjoying the trip. An air of calm had entered us both and the stress of our close shave in the *pulquería* faded away and was starting to be replaced with something more of I guess what could be called – I hated to admit it – a holiday vibe. Was this feeling happiness? I don´t know. If happiness is the absence of suffering, then I guess just at this moment in time, I was.

But when was the last time I felt that I was truly happy? Was it when I was a boy when I didn´t understand what suffering was? An innocent child with an absence of beliefs, uncontaminated, virgin, unspoilt, a blank slate rich in natural resources. I desperately wanted to meet that boy, connect with him, learn from him. What was he seeing and doing to be so wise that everything he saw was new, engaging, fun? Or what *wasn´t* he seeing? And more importantly, when was it exactly that I passed from innocence to ignorance? Pity overtook me. I wanted to hold that young child, comfort him, shield him from what was to come. From what I would do to him.

Although sitting here in Dan´s company learning like a disciple from the great man as he orated the history of the rocks on which we sat, I could have pretended I was happy, there was something still missing, something that no holiday nor Mayan architecture could cover up. A handbrake was on, holding me back. Hooks were lodged into my flesh. If I pulled them out, the barbs would take part of me with them, leaving large gaping wounds that wouldn´t heal. And on my own I was too scared to do that. What *was* missing? What would make me confront what I was scared of looking at?

I was lacking something that would help it all make sense, and as we sipped margaritas in the sun, stuffed ourselves on *pan de cazón*, or took photos of the picturesque streets, these frivolous activities just seemed to heighten the impending fear that was creeping up on me that my life – and the lives of all of us – are completely wasted and we, us humans – the only living beings that think they own this planet –

are all doomed. Our fate left to unfold depending on circumstance; the unfortunate people in the global south doomed to poverty, famine, starvation, violence and persecution; us lucky ones in the North, doomed to a life of failure to live up to expectations, living under a sword of Damocles of regret, missed opportunities, guilt, fear and anxieties that shape us into who we are and who we will always be.

Having jointly decided that Campeche had served its intended purpose, and after pushing as far into the pit of my stomach my growing sense of desperation, we prized ourselves away from our temporary safe haven and took the monarchically named *Camino Real* towards the Yucatán capital Mérida. The names of the small towns and villages on our way there a reflection of their populations by becoming more and more Mayan along the route.

We stopped at Pomuch, where Dan wanted to see for himself the cemetery where in the days leading up to the *Día de los Muertos* relatives exhume loved ones in order to clean their bones, paint the funeral box in which they´re contained and clean or change the carefully embroidered cloth in which the remains of their deceased relatives are wrapped. There were still nearly three weeks until the celebrations but already an old indigenous couple were hunched over a small niche close to the entrance of the cemetery. We stood at a respectful distance and watched in silence as the woman carefully passed each bone to her partner, who in turn, using a small paint brush, meticulously cleaned each piece. The bones were small. A child´s bones. The man removed the dirt accumulated over the last year and as if placing a baby bird down on the ground, left them to one side on the clean handkerchief that was spread out nearby. Next to the couple a tin of paint was waiting for them to finish their first task before they would move on to the next. We didn´t make a sound; we took no photos.

*

Our path stretched northwards, past small towns, villages and hamlets. Hecelchakán, Dzitbalché, Tepakán. Places we´d never heard of. Places we´d never remember. Places that hid secrets we would never know, people we would never speak to. The empty streets lined with simple facades; masks that would never revel to us what lay behind.

As we breached the industrial outskirts of Mérida, the feeling of our futile existence on this planet I´d had so strongly before we left

Campeche crept back upon me. I turned to face Dan, who was sleeping, his head pressed against the window. I looked at the jagged scar on the side of his head. The hair was struggling to grow back there. Wispy bushes grappling for a foothold above the treeline. I leaned over more closely to study the tissue that had healed, wanting to run my finger over it. I closed my eyes and imaged what it would be like to lie on an operating table with my skull open. I saw myself wake up, the anaesthetic suddenly wearing off and feeling what had been done to my brain. I touched Dan´s head, gently at first and then I ran my fingers hard over his scar. The flesh was soft and gave way instantly, my index and middle fingers black glass knives that slipped inside, touching the soft tissue within. I could feel his thoughts, find out who he really was and why and where he was leading me, riding with me on the great caiman and down its crocodilian back into the swamps below. Two interlocked twins on our journey into the underworld, children of the one and only creator God. He opened his eyes wide and screamed. I screamed too.

The other passengers on the bus stared at us with varying levels of surprise, amusement and worry. As we woke from our dream, I knew our time was running out fast.

Mérida itself wasn´t the problem. It had a blend of colonial history from the time of the Spanish occupation, while at the same time sharing the Caribbean charm that we´d come to appreciate so much on our short sabbatical in Campeche. The city also boasted a grand array of restaurants: *taquerias*, *cantinas*, barbeque stalls and street food vendors that rivalled anything we´d come across so far in larger cities. And, predictably, like many places in this blood-stained corner of the World, it too held its own shameful history.

La Ciudad Blanca; the White City. Named so, according to what we´d read, due to the buildings of white stone that were constructed directly on top of the Mayan temples that once stood here. Many of the invasive new structures using the very same white limestone the Mayans had employed to build their places of worship and sacrifice. That was one theory. Or was the city´s nickname more racist yet?

Built on the back of the flourishing industry in the area – in particular the cultivation and exploitation of the fibrous agave plant that thrives in the climate and soil of the area and made into rope, rugs, sacks and roofing material among other things – Mérida became home to a host of rich landowners and entrepreneurs; the majority obviously white. We observed with disdain the mansions and palaces that testified to Mérida´s status as one of the wealthiest cities in the New World shortly after the Europeans arrived.

Whatever the origin of the city´s name – the pale stones used to construct churches and cathedrals; or the exile of indigenous people from the affluent city centre leaving only the rich pale-skinned to enjoy their splendid urban isolation – we found Mérida quite an interesting and pleasant stopover nonetheless.

However, after leaving the fleeting respite of *La Ciudad Blanca* behind and heading eastwards, the lingering unrest that I´d been bottling up inside began to intensify as we started to come across more and more tourists, day-trippers on package holidays, and transcendental backpackers.

I of course know and agree that everyone´s got the right to travel, to experience other places and see other cultures in the World. *We* were, for heaven´s sake. But there was a growing anger. Maybe I´d become xenophobic against my own race. Modern-day conquistadores exploiting the local population, travelling to far-away lands in search of a photo opportunity and a sun tan, darkening their skin to a shade similar to that of the local people they look scornfully down their noses at due to their natural pigmentation. Money is spent on over-priced excursions and inflated tips encourage a double economy where we´re seen as nothing more than a walking dollar bill. But why am I complaining about this? Tourists bring money to an area, improvements in infrastructure, don´t they? Am I being a selfish hypocrite to expect an economy not to grow? For people seen as lesser than us to not to try to achieve something in their lives? Can I expect to see people living as they´ve done for centuries and then go and gawk at them as if they were a living museum for me to stroll around with my inflated ego thinking I´m having an alternative experience and therefore better than those who want to just lie on a beach for two weeks? Am I? Can I?

I harboured a witch´s broth boiling inside me of resentment, rancour, victimism, indifference, guilt, and something else; another side of me I didn´t understand. And in my present state of mind, if I don´t understand, I attack, eliminate it and then crawl back under my rock again.

I was bitter towards the modern world and my bitterness was only accentuated further still upon seeing the lines of overweight, sunburnt day-trippers from Cancún crawling over the ancient pyramids at Chichén Itzá.

*

Until the colossal Olmec heads thrust their way into Dan´s consciousness, he´d always been fascinated with the Mayans more than any other ancient civilization. Their architecture, myths and rituals had

captivated him from an early age and to finally see one of the most –
if not *the* most – important Mayan cities in the World was something
he´d dreamt about for some time.

The site, fighting a constant battle against being swallowed up by
the lush vegetation that´s constantly stalking its structures, was
impressive, I have to admit. I followed Dan around faithfully, listening
to his explanations and watching the reconstruction work that was
being carried out at various temples. Labourers climbed wooden
ladders strung together with the fibres that had made Mérida rich,
groups of men tugged at pully ropes attached to large rocks, heaving
their bulk impossibly into positions they hadn´t enjoyed for hundreds
of years. We stopped and observed a worker place the stone head on
a reclining *chac mool* statue, the warrior complete once more and ready
to hold the sacrificial offerings that would appease the gods.

Despite the interest that the highly-motivated Dan was stimulating
inside me, something else was eating at me again, gnawing away at my
consciousness.

The tourists. Slithering themselves around the place like long lines
of albino slugs, a trail of rubbish and disrespect being left in their wake.
And so, what should´ve been a highlight for Dan and his
anthropological adventure was spoilt by my childish tantrums and
constant complaining. His patience having been worn thin, he turned
on me angrily.

"We´ve come all the way here to see something that I´ve dreamt
about seeing for Christ knows how long and you keep on acting like
this. Why don´t you just shut up for once?"

"*Me*, shut up?" I was incredulous at his outburst but not surprised,
as I´d seen him twitching and blinking with nerves as he´d tried to hold
himself back. "Why don´t *you* shut the fuck up? Banging on about
temples and shit all the time, making me look stupid in front of
everyone. What?" I screamed confrontationally, "You think I´m like
all the rest of these pricks, don´t you?" I pushed him hard squarely in

the chest and he was forced backwards several paces.

"Oh my gosh. Will you just look at him! Is he drunk?"

I span around at where the voice had come from and stared at the large woman in the Green Bay Packers cap who´d uttered those words. She´d slunk behind her even larger husband who was now trying his best to usher them both away and avoid the impending conflict they feared. These people feared everything. I turned back around and saw Dan walking quicky away from the scene. I followed him, keeping my distance, an urge to continue shouting abuse was stifled by my self-consciousness with all the startled onlookers around me. Eventually I drew level with him. We stood next to each other, both breathing heavily in unison.

"I´m sorry," I said at length, breaking the silence.

"I know," Dan replied without looking at me. He consulted the guidebook he held in his hand, flicked through a few pages and then, as if nothing had even happened between us, walked off energetically in the direction of the towering Temple of Kukulkán.

*

And so, if you can´t beat them, join them. That´s what I´d convinced Dan anyway after making our peace. I couldn´t quite talk him into staying in Cancún with its blocks of concrete, high-rise hotels, party-going tourists and noisy water sports, so we opted to spend a couple of nights in Playa del Carmen instead, around seventy kilometres further south on the Mayan Riviera. We´d watched with thinly-veiled horror as the skyline of the holiday hell of Cancún got nearer and nearer and then suddenly we were transported into another world as we weaved through streets lined with franchises from the U.S., Tex-Mex restaurants and neon-clad twenty-four-hour discotheques.

The bus dumped off its load of tourists who´d been in Mérida or Chichén Itzá and I was sure that as they squeezed themselves down the aisle, despite attempting to hide their faces, Mrs Green Bay Packers cap and hubby waddled off. To be fair, it was hard to tell the difference between most of the couples that we´d had the pleasure of sharing the journey with. Mercifully, we weren´t staying among these people and the bus began to chug its way southwards.

*

As we arrived in Playa del Carmen, we could see that it had a much more laid-back feel to it, in spite of the existence of the five-story hotels and apartments that spilled out rudely onto the once virgin beach. It was touristy, no doubt, with lines of bars and restaurants in its compact centre and along the seafront trying to tempt punters in with offers written in English, but the thatched roofs of the *palapas* here and there gave it an exotic feel. Hens pecked at the dusty earth beside the road as we explored our new surroundings and walked further from the heart of the resort part of town and its strolling holiday-makers, and with every step the place became more rural.

It was a false dawn. Nearly every empty plot of land had a billboard advertising new accommodation or tourist facilities and those that didn´t, had signs with the image of a grinning, white-toothed estate agent advertising its availability for purchase. Cranes rose above the foundations that had taken over the nearby countryside and wooden scaffolding hugged half-finished constructions that were ushering in an epoch of vast expansion and land grabs. A flood of buildings of biblical proportions wrought by a thoughtless race of people. The end of a world playing out slowly before our very eyes.

But for now, this was our little slice of low-key tourist heaven, where we´d forget about the "real" Mexico for a long weekend of beach-life, cocktails and sport on the large screens that occupied the walls of many of the bars. For Dan it was a useful distraction from temples and churches; for me, a punishment, a way of sabotaging myself by pitting my wits against the very beings that I´d grown to resent with a passion. A way for me, behind the pints of beer and tequila shots, to secretly pour scorn on their every move, their clothes, the way they walked, and the manner in which they called the waiter over to them. The way they breathed even. I was feeding the beast inside, and it was hungry.

Gone were the dark *cantinas* with their pictures and effigies of virgins nestled amongst the bottles of harsh liquors, replaced now with themed bars full of loud Americans, Brits and Dutch cheering on their chosen sports team. A flashback to a former life, when if I didn´t go to some dingy pub to see West Ham versus Spurs, then I´d be a friendless outcast and forced to drink on my own.

Dan and his damn intelligence however, was beginning to become suspicious of me and our reasons to be here. I had to change my tactics, to hide my intentions. There would be other quarry; another time. So, after a couple of days soaking up some rays and quite a lot of tequila in Playa del Carmen, we left the blocks of hotels with their package-holiday sun-seekers behind and mutually agreed to entrench ourselves for an indefinite amount of time in a complex of *cabañas* to the south of Tulum. The objective we convinced ourselves to believe: to both physically and mentally prepare ourselves before we would continue our journey onwards to Belize and Guatemala.

The main building of the complex was a small, plain, two-storied structure which served as reception, restaurant, bar and home to the young couple from Mexico City who ran the place. The palm-thatched huts were even more uncomplicated, with a sand floor, thin mattress on a fixed concrete base and a basic bathroom with a cold-water shower that provided a weak stream of slightly salty water. It was perfect. Just a short walk down to the white-sand beach and the clear blue waters. A world away from other places we'd laid our heads. It was also where Dan met Maggie.

Maggie was a nursing graduate from Seattle and travelling on her own, like many of the other guests we met at the *cabañas*. She had long, light-brown hair, a loping stride and a mischievous smile; and Dan fell for her almost immediately.

They spent their days talking about anything and everything, seemingly moving from one topic to another with complete ease, each conversation more interesting than the last. Although Dan and I had grown closer before our little spat at Chichén Itzá, the newly-enamoured couple's relationship was on another planet from the static dialogues and long uncomfortable silences my travel companion and I had shared over the previous few exhausting weeks.

Albeit not entirely inseparable, Dan and Maggie spent most of their time in each other's company, with me appearing every so often to join them on the beach or on one of their trips to plunge into the deep freshwater *cenotes* that littered the inland jungle landscape. We also, of course, visited the Mayan ruins at Tulum, perched over the impossible blue of the Caribbean Sea, the limestone, water and sand providing a layered contrast that was only bettered by the occasional palm tree leaning out seawards, framing the scene perfectly. Iguanas sunbathed on the steps of ancient structures, retreating into gaps in the masonry when a photo-hunting tourist loomed too closely over them. I listened as Dan gave his patter on the history of the Mayans and the architectural features of their buildings, which I could now recite by heart if there was anyone willing enough to pay attention to me. Maggie hung on his every word, clinging to his arm as they wandered among the stones. Dan grew into his role as oracle, provider of historical anecdotes and giver of information; Maggie, his muse, inspiring him to exaggerate his cringe-worthy tales even further.

Three became two and then became one and I was left on the periphery of this isosceles triangle of passion and contempt. While I lay staring at the ceiling of my simple beach hut, watching the canes mutate into writhing snakes, or as I walked along the shoreline lost in my own thoughts of theory and counter-theory – like a pathetic parody of Trotsky in exile – Dan and Maggie bought each other trinkets and jewellery; offerings to show their feelings when words were not enough. Soon, Dan was draped with strings of shells hanging around his neck; Maggie adorned with the earrings of jade that her lover had bought her. Dan was turning into a tanned, shoeless beach bum and I could visualise the perfect couple driving away in a VW campervan into the sunset on a long desert road, some cool guitar-based singer-songwriter on the radio, a dreamcatcher swinging from the rear-view mirror, Maggie with her *Jipijapa* palm leaf hat pulled down over her eyes dozing as her oversized feet were dangled rebelliously out of the window.

*

Our evenings were mostly spent in the company of other travellers and backpackers who'd holed up at the *cabañas*, the idyllic setting a perfect breeding-ground for long-stayers trying to forget where they'd come from or their impending return to embark upon a life of servitude to multinationals and mortgage lenders.

I really didn't dislike them as individuals. Most were kind-hearted, generous with their words, good listeners and had an enthusiasm for life that I could only aspire to. But en masse they moved as one and there was a strange hive mentality that simply gave me the creeps. They wore the same clothes, used the same expressions, had the same look in their eyes of surprise and satisfaction about who they were and what they were doing. Above all though, they asked the same questions. Constantly. How long have you been travelling? Oh, just a few weeks then? Where have you been? Where are you going to next? Have you been to such and such place or tried such and such thing? An amazing, life-changing, awesome, wicked, unbelievable, cool, pukka, blinding, sick, brilliant experience, depending on their background, age or country of origin.

I wanted to hang a sign around my neck with my answers. Ice broken. Job done. Leave me alone to smoke. I looked down at the cigarette that was burning in my hand, a trail of smoke heading in the direction of the jungle, pushed away by the sea breeze at my back. I stared at the brown stain between my index and middle finger and the filterless roll-up I was holding. When had I started smoking?

*

The restaurant at the *cabañas*, which sold simple meals by day, became the hub of activity by night, alternating loud, modern European and U.S. pop music with golden oldies from the sixties and seventies. Gone were the traditional *rancheras* and *corridos* that had been the soundtrack to our trip so far. Sometimes a guitar was produced and passed around and some famous singalong number was bashed out to the glee of the foreign revellers who, so far from home, found comfort in its familiarity and the feeling of belonging it gave them.

I observed the predominantly young crowd trying to outdo each other with stories of adventure inspired by the wanderlust they all shared, but most of all, desperately looking for a way to get into each other's underwear. One such hot and humid night, with Bob Marley soothing everyone's collective soul and fireflies glowing in the bushes around the campfire, I watched as Maggie took Dan seductively by the hand and led him away through the beach huts and down towards the sea. I waited until I knew I'd be at a safe distance to follow unseen, and then I slinked into the darkness into which they'd disappeared.

A half-moon tried in vain to steal the protagonism away from Orion, lying in an unfamiliar position to my European eyes. Dan´s theory of one people, one origin, filled my head and overtook my thoughts. I could hear him in my mind again, explaining in his patronising tone his answer to life, the Universe, and everything that lies between. He always had an answer to everything and was always, inexorably, echoing around in my head.

The moonlight provided enough illumination for me to see the pile of clothes they´d abandoned on the beach not far from the gently-breaking waves, which spilled onto the sand and eliminated any trace of footsteps that gave away their passage into the sea. The foaming water hissed as it receded but I could easily hear the pair of lovers giggling and splashing together, fingers entwined as they writhed around in the obsidian water.

I sat down far enough away to not be noticed, lit another cigarette and closed my eyes. I imagined them out there, the heat from their bodies protecting them from the night-time chill of the Gulf of Mexico. I could see the green glow of the bioluminescent algae moved by the rhythm of their bodies, heightening the sense of romance and sensuality. I could feel the soft skin of Maggie´s thighs under pale hands that had started to wrinkle, her breath mixing with mine, the warmth inside her tense body a sharp and exotic contrast to the chilly water that caused goose bumps to rise up on our skin.

I embraced her and watched her from the shore. I closed my eyes and tried to recreate her face. I couldn´t. It was blank. I didn´t know who she was, who anyone was. I opened my eyes again and stared out across the water. I don´t belong here. I shouldn´t be here, not now. Not with these people, doing these things. I stood up and brushed the wet sand off my body.

I wasn´t going to head southwards on our journey into Belize and Guatemala with this man. I wasn´t going to be led by the hand forever. I wasn´t going to be controlled as I always had been. It was time for

Dan and I to divide. To separate. My destiny wasn´t here, not with him, not with Maggie and her infinite legs; but instead, some two thousand kilometres away in the state of Guanajuato.

"*¿Cómo te llamas?*"

My name? I could be anyone right now, nobody would care, not this far away from people who really know who I am. I could start again, create my own history, personality, tastes. Be anyone I wanted to be. Be the person I´d never be.

"*¿Cómo te llamas?*" she repeated again, her smile had started to fade a little and worry crept into its curve.

"Max," I replied. There was a pause as she waited for me to continue. I glanced around at the interior courtyard in which we found ourselves, looking for inspiration.

"Archer," I said at length. "Max Archer."

"I´m Lina. Nice to meet you," my interrogator replied in Spanish. "Where are you from?"

"London." I didn´t want to complicate things.

"And how old are you?"

I answered all of her questions as well as I could. Questions that gradually got more challenging to find an adequate answer to with my limited ability in Spanish. Lina then gave me a sheet of paper with multiple-choice questions on both sides and an extra page to write a paragraph about myself, or something like that. She left me alone to do what I could. I set about my task without thinking too much about what I was doing, circling various options in front of me and scribbling something inane about my new self. Eventually, with the level test out of the way, I was free to go and explore the historic centre of San Miguel de Allende.

As much as I didn´t want to admit it, Dan was the reason why I was here. He´d told me about its rich history, described the steep cobblestone streets, sanguine red and ochre-coloured buildings, its courtyards and patios and the fact that it was a popular place for foreigners to learn Spanish.

I guess it was partly the blend of apathy, anger and hopelessness that I´d been feeling, combined with the fact that I´d struggled to understand and be understood during our trip so far – as well as the sense of inadequacy at having to ask Dan to do all the talking – that made me want to improve on my very basic level of Castellano. The experience in the *pulquería* too was in the back of my mind, as was the fact that I had the abiding feeling that all I was doing here in Mexico was drinking too much of too many different types of alcohol and wasting away what should really be the time of my life. What would I get out of this trip? At least Dan would use this experience we were having to further his future brilliant career. But me? I had to do something to stop my rot. So, I now found myself walking around the historic centre of a city that until recently I never knew existed, in a hitherto unknown state of Mexico that I would never have been able to find on a map in a million years.

The city´s skyline was dominated by the neo-gothic spires of the Parroquia de San Miguel de Arcángel, that reached up to the sky, its pink sandstone sinews bulging proudly out of the original structure on which they now clung. With its facade inspired by postcards of European churches and cathedrals, the Parroquia towered over the more diminutive collection of baroque and churrigueresque-fronted churches, mansions and palaces that made up much of the city´s attractive old quarter.

I marched up and down the many hills on which San Miguel de Allende sat, taking in as much as I could, delighted and surprised to be where I was, and at the same time slightly concerned that I couldn´t really remember getting here from the Yucatán peninsula. These kinds of things had been happening more and more frequently these days and although they were starting to worry me, I put my latest lapse into a room in the back of my mind, locked the door and set about exploring my current location.

I walked and walked around for hours before resting my weary body and bursting lungs at the El Mirador viewpoint, where I gazed out and observed the city below and around me. It looked as if it had been dropped from a great height, splashing its suburbs up the slopes of the depression in which it sat. The outskirts were littered with cranes and scaffolding as new housing developments were constructed in order to meet the demand of Americans attracted to its Old-World charm and a lifestyle they would never be able to afford in their homeland.

Back down on the streets and in the cafés of the old town I came across what I presumed to be some of the many foreigners living in the city, some with an artistic look to them; the majority over retirement age. They stumbled around the uneven streets, the slippery stones worn down from centuries of footsteps. They were swallows looking to escape the winter, silvery-grey snowbirds looking for a place to warm their ageing bones, but as they struggled up the steep curbs of roads laden with heavy traffic, I cringed at the thought of arthritic knees popping out of joint. *My* knees were hurting and I hadn´t even reached the age of twenty-five.

*

The language school in which Lina had had her first meeting with Max Archer had arranged for me to stay with a young family who lived in the Caracol neighbourhood, not far from the city centre. Emilia, Carlos and their two-year-old son Carlitos lived on the ground floor of a two-story building in an area at great risk of flooding in the summer months. The house itself was built around a covered porch area giving onto a small central patio garden with a semi open-air kitchen. The living room, which joined onto the sheltered outside space and garden, was where the vast majority of daily life took place. The bedrooms and bathroom were hidden away at the back of the house in almost perpetual darkness, the structure having been built into the side of yet another one of the precipitous hills that prevailed in the city.

Carlos, probably somewhere in his early thirties, worked for the local government as some kind of administrative civil servant and at first impression seemed to be a very decent human being. He was a quiet, softly-spoken man but from our very first meeting tried his best to make me feel at home, recognising his moral duty to talk to me about a variety of subjects so that I could improve my Spanish. His wife, Emilia, was somewhere nearer my age and a primary school teacher, although she'd taken time off in order to look after Carlitos, who spent most of his time chatting incoherently to himself or crawling around on dirty hands and knees in the small garden-cum-kitchen area.

They were humble people, if that adjective doesn't offend, and I felt both honoured and awkward to be staying with them. They'd given me the largest of the two bedrooms, which they insisted as a paying guest I should have. Emilia – and Carlos to a lesser extent – took turns to prepare the two daily meals that came with the homestay package; various combinations of eggs, black or refried beans, an occasional pork chop, chicken *enchiladas*, and spicy stews. The majority of the time each meal was accompanied with a delicious Aztec soup or chicken broth to start and all were invariably served with freshly-made *tortillas*.

After just two days in the bosom of my new family I felt at home. Emilia, who spoke much better English than my Spanish, did her best to translate what Carlos said to me when I didn't understand and I felt genuine warmth emanating from the family – the like of which I hadn't felt for a long time. I still hadn't begun my classes at the language school as it was an extra-long bank holiday weekend, so I took advantage of being around the house, playing with little Carlitos and chatting to Carlos and Emilia.

"I stop work because my maternity finished and we have only my father here," Emilia explained as I bobbed a giggling Carlitos up and down on my knees while she prepared lunch. "But he is very old and a little sick and cannot help a lot." She looked down at the dough for the *tortillas* she was kneading. "My mother dead and the family of Carlos live far from here in another city."

There was a melancholy in her eyes as she stared down past hands that were moving automatically in front of her spotlessly clean apron. I sensed a loss greater than that of her mother.

"We are not from here," she explained. "We come from León for Carlos work. Now we have Carlitos, I do not work." She looked lovingly at her son, who had a handful of dirt he'd taken from one of the many plant pots in the patio and was rubbing it gleefully into the front of his t-shirt. I felt I needed to say something.

"Do you like living here?" was all I could come up with.

Emilia smiled at me now, trying to disguise yet more sadness. "It has changed a lot. Now there are many people from United States that live here. The price of everything go up a lot. The houses, food, everything. Carlos has a good work but a tourist guide makes more money than him now. It has changed a lot."

I couldn't help but feel guilty. I was contributing to this inflated economy, forcing traditional middle-class families like my hosts further away from the city in which they live and work and making them look for extra sources of income in order to keep up with their ever-increasing rent payments. It won't be long before their landlord sells and more silver-haired snowbirds fly in.

As Emilia was putting the finishing touches to the stewed meat she'd been slowly cooking over the course of the morning, which had impregnated the house with a rich smoky aroma, her husband entered the patio through the gate that led onto the street. He was armed with bulging plastic bags full of objects that he'd been out to buy during the morning. He dumped everything in the living room, kissed his wife gently on her forehead – causing Emilia to blush slightly in front of me – scooped up his son, and ushered me to sit down to eat with them.

After enjoying the delicious *guisado* stew, which we stuffed into Emilia's home-made tacos, Carlos began to unpack the shopping he'd left to one side before lunch. Having my offer to help with the dishes politely refused, I decided that I'd go to my room and try to start the long road to speaking better Spanish by getting on with some exercises in the over-priced grammar book I´d bought at the language school.

In the darkness of my room, I began my journey, flicking through the first chapters, and soon started to realise that I knew much more than I thought I did. My confidence grew as I quickly and accurately rattled off pages dedicated to pronouns, articles, question forms and infinitives but soon my eyes, strained by focussing in the dim light afforded by the weak lamp beside my bed, obliged me to call it a day and I decided I´d be better off practising what I´d been studying.

Carlos had unpacked the contents of the bags he´d dumped down in his haste to eat earlier, and now the table under the covered part of the patio where we´d eaten was strewn with coloured paper, flowers, sweets and packets of food bought from a selection of bakeries and stalls in the city centre.

"Can I help you?" I asked in my best Spanish.

"Yes, please. That would be great," replied Carlos smiling warmly at me. He handed me a packet of balloons. "If you wouldn´t mind?" he asked politely.

I gladly took them, eager to join in with whatever celebration they were planning to have. Carlos went about carefully unwrapping the small packets of food.

Kneeling on a cushion on the stone floor of the patio, Emilia was busy cutting purple paper lace into different sizes, the sadness she´d shown earlier had disappeared from her face and she looked almost excited about what she was doing. Carlitos was active too, diving headfirst into a wooden box that had been dusted off and opened, desperate to play with the selection of toys that were visible inside.

I searched unsuccessfully for the word for birthday. "*Fiesta?*" That would have to do.

Emilia looked up at me from her task. "*Más o menos,*" she said serenely, looking over to the patio where her husband was now erecting a small decorated cross beside a shelf that until now had been obscured by plants. She put the scissors she´d been using down and walked past me to the cabinet in the corner of the living room that supported a huge number of framed photographs. She picked up one of the largest frames from its prominent position at the front of the gallery and handed it to me. I'd noticed the photo before, and although taken about what I calculated to be a year ago, I recognised Carlitos' cheeky smile at once. Sat next to the boy was another child of similar age and with a near-identical grin and facial features, which led me to believe that it must've been some cousin or other.

"This is Juanito." Emilia's eyes had reddened despite the party atmosphere they'd been trying to create.

I knew at once what this all meant now. The cross, the small candles that Carlos was now placing on the shelf outside, the bright orange marigold flowers. Emilia took the photograph gently from my grasp, walked slowly over to the cabinet and put it back in its pride of place. She then took another, this time with just one child as the protagonist, lying on his back smiling up at the person who'd captured him for all eternity.

The photo of Juanito was placed in the centre of the makeshift altar, which already had a selection of candles and marigold flowers in position thanks to Carlos. Emilia went about finishing the paper lace decorations, which she then placed in front of the shelf. I helped them put the offerings on the shrine and then tied the balloons I'd blown up around each side. Piles of sweets, chocolates and the toys that had attracted Carlitos like a magnet were also added to the scene. As I helped finish the altar I couldn't prevent myself from thinking about how honoured I was to be part of this and how surprising and inspiring it was to see my hosts' attitude as they remembered their baby boy. How they have faced, and embraced, a tragic death.

"Juanito is lucky," Emilia said, staring at the toy cars and action figures that were mixed among the other offerings. "He can enjoy the toys two months before Christmas, while the other children have to wait to play with theirs."

I didn´t know what to say. "I´m sorry for your loss." Again, I regretted my clumsy utterance as soon as it had left my lips. Carlos and Emilia turned and looked at me with surprise.

"Please don´t be," Carlos said kindly. He touched the top of my arm in a gesture of warm reassurance and looked earnestly into my eyes. "We´ve not lost our son. We´ve gained an angel."

*

I left the three of them alone in private. In spite of their warm insistence for me to stay, I wasn´t part of their real family or their stoical grief and so, careful not to step on any of the marigold petals scattered on the ground that would make it easier for Juanito to find his way home on this very special night, I slipped out of the gate and onto the street.

I walked the unlit alleyways of the Caracol neighbourhood close to the house, imagining the souls of the innocent children that had died who would soon be making their way back to spend the night with the family that missed them so dearly.

As many of San Miguel´s ex-pats recovered from their Halloween cocktail dinners and fancy-dress parties of the previous evening, I found myself in residential areas that most of them wouldn´t dare visit or even knew existed. I began to see small altars outside many houses, illuminated by fluttering candles and just like Juanito´s, full of sweets, chocolates, toys and balloons.

I wasn´t alone. A steady stream of people walked the streets as well, making their way to cemeteries armed with offerings; others were going to attend mass at one of the city´s temples of worship. More people I witnessed were preparing shrines for the following day, readying themselves to welcome those lost in adulthood, the same set-up with candles and flowers but the toys and other childish decorations were substituted with wine, *tortillas*, *tamales*, *enchiladas*, fruit, edible skulls and special seasonal breads and cakes. Families sitting outside their homes greeted me with a friendly *buenas noches* as they waited in calm anticipation to receive their lost relatives once more.

I was surrounded by ghosts. The ghosts of little angels taken too soon. How many people had lost a child? Why had they died so young? Could it have been prevented with better healthcare? A system that cared for the poor and listened to their needs instead of pushing them to the margins of society? These questions rattled through my brain, forcing a shard of pain into the side of my head.

I wound my way back down next to the ravine that ran past and often threatened my new home. I sat on the low wall opposite the house for several minutes and imagined what was to become of this tightly-knit family. Too many questions began to collide in my mind. Questions, right now, that I didn´t want to hear the answers to. I eventually got up and walked the few paces to the front door, opened it silently, and crept unnoticed in the darkness towards my room. From the patio I could hear Carlos and Emilia speaking softly, encouragingly, to their young son and his babbling speech as he responded to their verbal caresses. As if attracted by the orange flower petals myself, I approached the sweet conversation and the candle-lit patio, unseen in the depths of the living room.

The young couple had their backs to me and I remained undetected, observing their silhouettes as they cooed over their child. Emilia stopped speaking and as if sensing my presence, turned to face my direction. I froze and held my breath, not wanting to be discovered intruding on this most tender moment.

I couldn´t see her face but I could see that she was cradling something in her arms. I strained my eyes and could just make out a small head lolling to one side in the warm light and a bundle of arms and legs as Carlitos slept deeply. I slunk back into the pitch black of the living room, listening to Carlos´s low voice and the incoherent speech of a young child flow steadily onwards. Emilia continued to look blindly into the void where I stood. She didn´t say anything, but I knew somehow that she was smiling.

*

The next day I woke to a silent house, my hosts´ night-time vigil giving me the opportunity to escape before anyone else stirred. I walked the empty streets as one neighbourhood merged into the next, as the city slowly awoke from a dream. I wheezed on thin air as I climbed and descended the unavoidable gradients, strangely satisfied with the feeling of lactic acid in my thighs and calves, sadistically enjoying the complaints from the ligaments in my knees.

After a while, I had no other option than to rest and so made my way towards the Parroquia, always at hand, appearing suddenly at the end of picturesque streets when you were sure that you were far from its reach. I sat on one of the wrought-iron benches in the shade of the Indian laurel trees that made the El Jardín square such an attractive place to while away the hours sheltering from the relentless sun. I watched the street vendors set up their stalls, filling them with candy coffins, sugar skulls, skeletons on sticks and other normally macabre images that would attract both children and adults alike to part with their money. I massaged my aching calf muscles as I watched the preparations for the second day of the *Día de los Muertos* celebrations and the city itself come to life. My stomach soon reminded me that I´d left the house without breakfast, and so I heaved myself up from my resting place and decided to stop at one of the bakeries I knew was located on the route back to Carlos and Emilia´s house.

Like the stalls around El Jardín, the bakery had dedicated most of its display to the festivities and its shelves boasted a variety of similar items I´d seen being prepared on the streets. However here, most of the shelf space was taken up with different variations of *pan de muerte,* the baked bread in the form of human and animal figures which would be pulled apart like the bones of the dead. I´d seen these before in the majority of the altars, including little Juanito´s, so I decided I´d buy a selection of other pastries and small cakes that I could share with my host family in gratitude for making me feel so welcome and comfortable in my new surroundings.

I made my slow way home, leaving a trail of crumbs in my wake as I killed the hunger with one of the pastries I´d bought. As I let myself in through the front door, like the previous evening, I could hear voices again coming from the patio.

Someone had beaten me to it and the dining table was laden with a huge variety of the products I´d seen both at the bakery and on the stalls that morning. My small bag of goodies suddenly seemed inadequate by comparison. Emilia was pouring coffee into small cups that were laid out on the table in front of Carlos and an older gentleman who, judging by the shape of the bone structure of his face, must be Emilia´s father.

"Hello," he shouted across the room at me attracting everyone else´s attention, including Carlitos´, who´d stopped stuffing a piece of sugar candy into his mouth mid-air. "You must be *him*, then?"

"Please don´t shout, Papá. He´s not deaf," said Emilia, greeting me with a warm smile.

I walked over to the table and gave Emilia my paltry offering, which she quickly disguised among the feast her father had brought.

"I´m Max," I said, assuming I had no other option than try to survive in Spanish. It was sink or swim time.

"Juan Alfredo," Emilia´s father said, rising nimbly and holding out his hand for me to take.

We shook firmly, his hard dry hand testament to a lifetime of manual labour, his deeply-tanned and wrinkled face corroborating his years spent undertaking outdoor work in this harsh climate. His eyes burned brightly behind his mask of worn leather and ancient wood. What would he have done with another life, another opportunity in another place and time?

Carlos handed me a cup of coffee and a plate so I could join them for breakfast. I took the smallest cake I could find, hunger no longer a problem but not wanting to refuse their kind hospitality.

"This is my father," Emilia said, looking slightly embarrassed about stating the obvious but feeling obliged to do so all the same.

I grinned like an idiot, unsure what to say. I´ve never been good at speaking to older people, children neither for that matter. I found myself at a loss for words. Luckily Juan Alfredo wasn´t.

"So, you´re from the United States then?" he asked.

I hesitated. "Umm, no. I´m from England, actually."

"Better. There are too many of them others here already."

"Papá. Really, do you have to say that in front of Max?" Emilia complained, acting like a teenager ashamed and worried about what her father might say next. Juan Alfredo winked at his daughter.

"So, you´ve been having a look around the town then?" Juan Alfredo asked, addressing me again. "What do you think?"

I looked blankly back at him.

"Please speak more slowly, Papá. Max is still getting used to the accent here." Emilia asked her father, saving face on my behalf.

"You have been looking at the town, no? What do you think?" Juan Alfredo asked much more slowly and with significantly more volume.

"Very beautiful. It´s got a lot of history. There´s a lot to see," I answered enthusiastically. "I like it very much."

Juan Alfredo smiled wryly. "Well ..." he started. Emilia shot him a look across the table. He bit his tongue and changed what he was about to say. "What do you think about the *Día de los Muertos* celebrations, then? You´ve had a look this morning here, no?"

"He was here with us last night too," Carlos offered from the floor of the patio where he was now playing with his son.

"Ah," Juan Alfredo cast his electric eyes momentarily in the direction of the altar on the other side of the patio.

"I think it´s very beautiful and a ... umm, a beautiful way to remember people." I couldn´t express what I wanted to say. It frustrated me. They´d think I´m some kind of idiot with my simple thoughts and words. I had to improve.

"But it's changed. Too much." Juan Alfredo shook his head. "Here, in San Miguel, we don't go to the cemetery as we have no one there. But we wouldn't go anyway, if we did. Not these days."

"Why not?" I asked, keen to know why the mix of annoyance and melancholy had crept into his creaky voice.

"Because it's full of gringos taking photos."

"Papá," Emilia protested again. "Please be nice."

"It's full of foreigners taking photos," Juan Alfredo smiled defiantly at his daughter. "They crawl all over the place and don't respect us and our traditions. They think it's some kind of tourist activity. That's why I wouldn't go there on the *días de los muertos*. The people I love are with us all the time here," he pointed to the centre of his chest and then to his head, "in our hearts and minds anyway." He reached a dry hand across the table and took one of his daughter's, softly. "I know that even if I lose my mind, I'll carry them all with me in my heart. I don't need to put dead flowers anywhere to show that I still care."

Juan Alfredo turned to me again. "But it's changed," he repeated with more conviction this time. "People are adopting the gringo traditions. Halloween, *tricotri* isn't it? Rudely asking people for sweets, invading their privacy. Things like that. The old sugar *calaveritas* are disappearing and you never hear the *calaveras* being sung either. They used to be such a laugh, poking fun at the politicians and bigwigs." He stared ahead of him, thrust back into his distant past.

I was a little lost with the vocabulary but got the gist. I wanted to reply, I really did, but just couldn't think of what I could say to this living piece of history sitting in front of me. Dan would know what to say, what to ask, wouldn't he? Oh yes. The intrepid anthropology student and amateur archaeologist that he was. He'd take advantage of the situation in his quest for knowledge. If only he were here with me now. I tried to summon up something of him, to put myself in his shoes and act like he would if he were here. Juan Alfredo cut my train of thought off.

"We don´t need the parades either, with the music and dancing. It´s done for the foreigners, and the young people who just want to have a party and get drunk. It´s not what we used to do before."

Carlos and Emilia were looking at Juan Alfredo fondly, their silence indicating that they realised that things had changed dramatically for the old man. For them, it was a challenge to adapt and accept new customs and merge them with their own traditions, but for the elderly gentleman sitting and remembering his past in their kitchen, they knew it was almost impossible to accept and painful to remember.

*

After a lunch filled with small talk, misunderstandings and pleas of repetitions, I was exhausted. I excused myself and tried to switch off for a while in the depths of the darkness of my room. Through the door I could hear Emilia doing the dishes and cleaning the kitchen as Carlos and Juan Alfredo shuffled around the patio, dragging unknown objects here and there and speaking in low, hushed voices. Finally, as the sun sank behind the hills to the west of the city, I heard the front door open and close and the house was plunged into silence.

Juan Alfredo had sparked my interest in the parade now held as part of the *Día de los Muertos* celebrations and I was keen to see for myself what it was all about, even if it wasn´t the most traditional of customs these days. I emerged from my room and as I crossed the living space on my way to the front door, I noticed that there was a new addition among the plants on the patio.

Some of the pots had been moved to create more space next to Juanito´s altar and now there were two homemade shrines sitting side by side. In the centre of the second, surrounded by the same orange marigolds and candles, but with offerings more suited to an adult, was a black and white photo of a woman leaning into a pose that reminded me of a nineteen-fifties film star. I stared at the photograph for some minutes, trying to recreate in my mind the life of the owner of those deep dark eyes that would never have imagined they would look back into mine one day. A woman who would remain as much a mystery to me as I was to her. A woman who would always be carried dearly in an old man´s heart.

*

The night-time parade was full of colour, noise and crowds of people having a good time and I have to admit that although not really what I´d call "my thing", due to the close proximity of such a huge number of people, it was aesthetically pleasing all the same. There were of course a large contingent of foreign tourists and ex-pats, many of them with their faces painted like skeletons or zombies, trying their best to live the real Mexican experience without possibly really knowing what that seemed to be.

Brass bands marched through the streets, their trumpets screeching out off-key tunes and hordes of people in fancy dress joined in the procession that wound its way through the old town. There were the giant paper-maché figures of the *mojigangas*, painted in the form of the otherworldly *catrinas* and *catrines* with their white skull heads bowing down and their arms flailing around in time with the off-beat music. It was a colourful carnival atmosphere where cultures collided in an explosion of stereotypes and flash photography. It was another world away from the whispered conversations between the living and dead that were taking place behind closed doors in homes the length and breadth of the rest of the country.

I left the celebrations behind me and walked back to the Caracol neighbourhood, where I knew things would be more sedate. I sat on the low wall again that bordered the ravine close to the house and watched the fireworks that exploded above the spires of the Parroquia. It was a Disney-esque scene that I imaged would only serve to entice more people from other countries to come and settle here in their retirement, inspired by a holiday of revelry, tequila and friendly bartenders and waiters with their palms held out ready for the inevitable tip.

From my position I could see that the gate to the patio was open; a bridge of the continuity of life and death. It wasn´t my place or culture here. Carlos, Emilia, Carlitos, Juan Alfredo, Juanito. These people were not like me and I was – and would never be – like them. But right now, as the bangs of the fireworks echoed around the stone streets and grey blocks of the hastily-erected houses around me, and the candles of the makeshift altars flickered in the breeze, there wasn´t any other place in the World I´d rather be.

With the *Día de los Muertos* celebrations out of the way, it was time for me to get on with some serious studying. The language school I´d enrolled at was situated just a couple of cobbled streets away from El Jardín and occupied a large eighteenth-century house that used to belong to a wealthy Spanish family who´d made their fortune from the silver mines in the region before the building was supposedly lost in a drunken card game one evening in one of the city´s *cantinas*. After changing hands numerous times throughout the years and having been painstakingly restored to somewhere near its former glory, it was now home to several exhibition rooms and the largest centre of adult learning in the city.

I´d done as I´d expected in the level test and found myself in a low-level group that consisted of three students, including myself. I crossed the pretty interior courtyard where I´d demonstrated my poor control of Castellano the week before, smiling to myself at the arches that had inspired my invented surname. I made my way up the wide stone staircase in the corner of the patio and headed for the classroom to which I´d been assigned.

My two classmates were already there and grinned excitedly at me as I entered the room. Bob and Candy were an extremely friendly couple from Boston who were in the process of looking for a new home here in San Miguel de Allende in order to live out their dream. They made me feel welcome at once and I was genuinely pleased to be around them and their childlike energy, despite my unjustified prejudice towards their type. I was even more pleased to see Lina appear through the door and announce that she´d be my teacher for our thrice-weekly language sessions.

Lina was from the mountainous Asturias region in the north of Spain and had a contagious enthusiasm that was impossible to ignore. She explained to us in simple Spanish – dotted with the English vocabulary she deemed necessary for us not to get completely lost – that she´d lived here in San Miguel in her teens with her family when her father had been working reconditioning old mining equipment for resale. She told us with a passion that she´d fallen in love with Mexico, and the state of Guanajuato in particular, so once she´d graduated with a degree in Spanish Literature from Salamanca University back in her native Spain, she had absolutely no hesitation in returning to live and work here.

The first week of classes passed by quickly and it soon became clear that I was in the wrong level. I began to produce sentences far more complicated than I ever believed I was capable of and understood nearly everything that I listened to. It was, unnervingly, as if Dan had somehow possessed me with his language ability. I imagined that I must´ve passively picked up more than I thought while I was in his company. He did do the vast majority of the speaking for us after all. Or perhaps the short time I'd spent with my new family. Whatever the reason was, I found the class incredibly easy in comparison to my classmates, who could hardly string a sentence together no matter how much they laughed, smiled and gesticulated and how hard and willingly they tried. My mind wandered away from the tasks at hand and more often than not, I found myself being caught staring for longer than I should have at a bashful Lina as she gave instructions in her beautiful, clear, European Spanish accent.

I couldn´t help but be enticed by her and her scholarly manner, the way she read sentences out aloud, the movement of her lips, the way she held herself. She was as delicate as a hummingbird but her kind and gentle nature masked a strength that I gauged ran deeply within her like a seam of precious metal. A fortitude branded inside her, forged by what life had already thrown her way, but which had left her grace, generosity and enchantment untouched. She was the antithesis of the girls from where I´d grown up. A place now so far away from my present reality and circumstances that the materialism, high heels and fake tans seemed like scenes from some kind of bad soap opera I could barely remember. Lina was educated, mysterious and while only a year or two younger than me, conveyed a wisdom built on heartbreak and experience of life on more than one of the World's continents.

My friends wouldn't like her, no. They'd see her as too much of a challenge, too intelligent and therefore stuck up maybe, although I knew already that she'd never look down on or condescend anyone. Dan would like her, but not in the physical sense. She was the opposite to Maggie with her long gangly legs, green eyes and sun-kissed skin. But from where I sat at the front of the classroom, the windows open allowing a gentle breeze and the noise of the traffic on the cobbled stone streets to float inside, she was nothing else other than perfect.

*

On the back of Lina's recommendation, the school offered me private classes and according to the secretary in the office on the ground floor, Lina had volunteered to be my teacher once more.

Over the course of the next two weeks, I was as close to a model student as you could get. I undertook all of the exercises in our class with an enthusiasm that seemed to amuse Lina greatly and I tried as hard as I could to include as many new expressions and as much vocabulary as possible when we were speaking to each other. Her warm encouragement, and the profound attraction I was starting to develop for her, inspired me to push myself further each time we met. In the evenings, I ploughed through my grammar book, read as many newspapers as I could find, and with the aid of a borrowed dictionary from the language school's small library, I started to read the novel Pedro Páramo, which Lina had recommended and then lent me. I devoured the pages, travelling along the dusty road towards the ethereal town of Comala, immersing myself in the search for a father I never had, sharing the lives, loves and losses of the inhabitants and the power and unrequited passion of the eponymous protagonist as he longed for acceptance from his beloved Susana. I also spent as much time as I could talking with Carlos and Emilia and commenting on the news programmes that were often on the television while we were having lunch. I improved rapidly and not only had I now absorbed Dan´s level of Spanish, I´d now surpassed it by some distance.

During the third week of my classes with Lina I plucked up the courage to ask her if she´d like to have a drink with me after our lesson. The words had barely left my lips when her face lit up and she jumped upon my question.

"I´d love to, Max." Her dark chestnut eyes shone with emotion and she beamed at me from across the small table at which we sat. I could hardly breathe.

"Thank you," was all that stumbled out of my mouth.

*

One drink turned into two, which in turn became dinners in secluded patio restaurants and slow walks through the city centre under rose-pink evening skies. We began to meet in the *churrería* next to the school in the mornings too, left our classes in each other´s company in the evenings and often attended art exhibitions together that Lina was invited to by some of her other students. At the weekends we went to Dolores Hidalgo, Querétaro or other towns and villages nearby if we found out about an interesting festival or event that might be worth attending. Otherwise, we just stayed in San Miguel and simply strolled around El Jardín listening to the Mariachi bands that played their *rancheras* for a few dollars to the American tourists — or for even fewer pesos should the request come from one of their compatriots.

We talked about everything; life, travel, our families, our mistakes, hopes and dreams for the future. The only subject that wasn´t brought up was when I would eventually leave San Miguel de Allende. If someone asked me that right now, as I walked closely next to Lina, our elbows brushing together, both of us desperate for more contact but too timid to take the next step, I´d tell them that as long as the woman by my side is here, then I will never leave.

*

My life in Mexico was as stable as it could be. I was going about my studies as if it were a job I was trying hard not to lose, I had some kind of social life to speak of and someone special to share my time with. I felt whole, as if a part of me that was causing all my suffering had disappeared, been vanquished or simply just withered and died. Even the yellowish-brown cigarette stain between my fingers that had mysteriously appeared in the Yucatán peninsula had now vanished to a faint blemish. Life was good. So, although we hadn´t consummated our relationship with so much as a kiss yet, the next natural step, I suppose, was for Lina to meet my family.

"It´s very nice to meet you," Emilia said after giving us both two kisses on the cheek as she welcomed Lina into her home.

"Hello, I´m Carlos, and this is Carlitos." The obligatory kisses were given once more. From his position in his father´s arms Carlitos reached out and tried to grab hold of Lina´s hair, fascinated by the curls that were rare among the Mexican women he´d seen in his short lifetime. "Max has told me a lot about you," Carlos added.

Lina and I both blushed far too easily. Carlos avoided causing any more embarrassment and headed off across the patio to the kitchen to move some plates and cutlery around noisily.

It was Sunday and Carlos had been out early to the *tianguis* market that took over an unused patch of land twice a week by the west entrance to the city in order to pick up enough slow roasted barbequed lamb to feed at least twice as many of us. Emilia had prepared the ever-present tacos and the various sauces and vegetables that we´d add to the succulent meat. I appreciated the effort – and the cost – that was involved with their preparations and we enjoyed a fabulous meal. The afternoon stretched out as we whiled away the hours after the delicious lunch talking about Lina´s life in Mexico and Spain and the cultural differences that came up with such conversations.

Although I sometimes struggled with the speed of the dialogue between the three native Spanish speakers, each of them made sure that I wasn´t left out of any topic of discussion; Carlos and Emilia doing their best to ask me questions to involve me more and Lina using her linguistic background to reformulate anything that I missed. Carlitos on the other hand, was babbling away on the floor of the patio in front of the shelf that weeks before had been used as an altar for his deceased twin brother.

With half of the meat remaining but our bellies full to bursting, coffee was now being stewed in a saucepan on the stove, its aroma mixing deliciously with the smell of the barbeque lamb and the limes and coriander that were still left on the table. Carlos turned on the television, which out of respect to their new guest hadn´t been left on as it usually was as the background to our meals together.

As Emilia poured the coffee, we were greeted with an image of the sweeping arc of the Mexican senate with its giant national flag planted firmly in front – just in case there was any doubt it was a government building. The image quickly changed to the amphitheatre of self-congratulatory men in suits – and a paltry smattering of women – and a beaming bald gentleman with a thin moustache who looked more suited to a life of book-keeping than that of the President of the Republic of Mexico.

"They´ve passed it then. President Salinas must be a very happy man." Carlos was standing up watching the television; an indication that he considered this important news.

We were all watching it now, listening to the confirmation of the vote that had taken place earlier in the afternoon.

"Passed what?" I asked, my curiosity at what was happening getting the better of my ignorance.

"The TLCAN," replied Carlos, still eyeing the TV. "The free trade agreement with North America."

I could feel Lina bristle beside me for some reason. I turned to her to see if I could figure out what the matter was. "NAFTA, in English. The North American Free Trade Agreement between the U.S., Canada and Mexico," she said stiffly.

"About time too," Carlos added. "This will bring us into the First World finally. With no tariffs, we'll be able to punch our weight against the foreign companies, export as much as we want to the United States without any restrictions. Things will hopefully improve for everyone here at last."

From her position in the patio with Carlitos, Emilia observed Lina and I still sitting at the table with the limes, coriander and *jalapeño* sauce in front of us.

"I don't think it will be such good news for everyone, *cariño*," she said, addressing her husband affectionately but looking directly at us. Lina remained silent but a flicker of a satisfied smile appeared on her face at hearing Emilia's words.

"On the whole, it will," replied Carlos, still on foot. "I mean, of course, you can't please all of the people all of the time, but it's got to make things better for most of us, at least. I'm sure it will."

"I hope you're right, *cariño*. I really do."

*

We finished our coffee while Lina politely paid lip service to Carlos as he extolled the virtues of the free trade agreement that, in his opinion at least, would change the lives of the majority of Mexicans. Carlos wasn't exactly opinionated and he didn't force his ideas on any of us, but it was clear where he thought the future of Mexico lay, despite seeing and living the very real results of a global economy right here in San Miguel de Allende.

We thanked our hosts profusely for lunch and for their charming company and then we descended the hill down into the old town as I walked Lina back to her apartment. She was much quieter than normal and I knew that she was bothered by the news that we'd been witness to after lunch. She knew I was on the verge of asking her about it.

"I'm sorry Max, I know that you felt awkward there with them."

She'd stopped walking and was now looking at me sincerely. Her deep eyes had me under their spell. "I didn´t want to say anything because being from Spain sometimes I feel like I don´t have the right to tell people here how I feel about things in their own country. I´ve lived here for a quite a long time now, and I went to school here for a couple of years before too. I pay attention to what´s happening here as if it were my own country. I know Carlos and Emilia are very nice, but I´ll always be an outsider to a lot of people, you know?"

"You can tell me," I said, my body frozen by the closeness we shared. "You can tell me anything you think."

I was dying to hold her against me, thrust my nose into the hair on the top of her head while we embraced and just smell her for eternity. She stared up at me sensing my feelings, reading deep into my emotions, her eyes huge brown *cenotes* daring me to jump into the extasy of the relief from the tension that they promised. She touched me with a delicate hand in the middle of my chest, piercing my heart with the feathers of a hummingbird as she pulled at my shirt and brought my face down towards hers. I felt the soft coldness of her lips. Lips, alone, I´d kissed a thousand times, protecting the secretive warmth of her mouth. We fed on each other, embellishing our story, colouring it with our belief, our desire to create our own reality. We parted, the urge to open our eyes and confirm what was real overcoming the physical craving to continue our embrace to eternity.

Lina held me in her defiant, loving gaze, melting me with the white heat her eyes possessed. "OK. Do you fancy a couple of *chelas* then?" she eventually added brightly, breaking the deadlock.

My blank expression told her everything.

"God, how long have you been in Mexico? A *beer*, dummy. Come on." She took me by the hand and led me down into the centre of town. I didn´t really have a clue what was going on, but to be honest, at that moment, I didn´t really care.

*

Lina gave my hand a little squeeze and she slipped hers out of my sweaty grasp as we passed the unavoidable central square of El Jardín, busy as it usually was on a Sunday evening. I knew that she was conscious that despite the number of visitors the city received, it was still a small town, many people had a small-town mentality and should anyone see us walking hand in hand up Calle Hidalgo with lovestruck expressions on our faces, tongues would surely begin to wag.

We reached the intersection of Calle Insurgentes and Lina led the way across the road towards a low yellow building on the opposite corner. Its wild west saloon doors were a dead giveaway that it was a *cantina*. I remembered the places Dan and I had been to on a journey that now seemed a lifetime ago. I thought about the *pulquería* in Veracruz. That situation would never happen to me again, I swore to myself. Before I could hesitate any more, Lina pulled me through the doors and dragged me over to a table in a dark corner of the bar.

Cantina El Cucu was not exactly made for tourists and unsurprisingly there were none present as we huddled close together under a faded bullfighting poster from Castellón in Spain. There were few people in the establishment. Two men sat at the bar aimlessly watching a football match on a television bolted to a wall. Another man, who we'd passed on our way in, had his head resting on a table, seemingly fast asleep. A bottle of beer and a glass of untouched tequila or mezcal waiting patiently for him to regain consciousness.

The bar area itself was dominated by a huge nineteen-fifties refrigerator that the whole *cantina* seemed to have been built around, the enamel paint surrounding the handle worn away to the bare metal below. How many thousands of times had the appliance been opened and closed? How many Coronas, Dos Equis and bottles of Modelo had been extracted from its icy depths? Behind the wooden bar, antique shelves held a selection of spirits of which I'd never seen or heard before. Some had no labels at all.

Sitting in one corner behind the bar was a bearded man who was looking angrily at us. He rose reluctantly from his seat, peeling his arm away from where it had been resting on a shelf next to the metal box that served as the cash register. The wood had been worn down from years of supporting his forearm, or generations of forearms, while he and his ancestors listened and replied automatically to the drunken comments of their faithful clients.

He sidled over to us looking like we´d woken him from a bad dream. He glowered down at me.

"Hi Paco," said Lina. "How are you? And how´s Santiago?"

Paco´s expression brightened and he turned to face Lina.

"Oh, you know, things are slow here. Just surviving. Santi´s good, you know. Studying very hard. It´s an important year for him this one, if he doesn´t want to end up here, like his papá. Anyway, what can I get you?"

"A Corona, please," Lina answered.

Paco looked in my direction, his smile waning just a little. "And what about your friend here?"

"The same, please," I answered, as politely as I could.

"Do you want them *micheladas*?"

"No, thank you," Lina and I replied in unison, neither of us keen on having our beers laced with spicy sauce and covered in salt and lime. For us, it was an acquired taste at best.

As Paco went to fetch our drinks Lina explained that she´d given Santi private English classes earlier in the year, his father seeing how much foreign money was starting to flood in and keen for his son not to miss out on a golden opportunity. I stared at her as she spoke, the emotion of our first kiss still surging through my body. I fought to control the grinning idiot that had overtaken me and tried my hardest to concentrate on Lina´s words.

"I come here sometimes if I don´t want to bump into any of my foreign students. They´ll never dare come in here and I can have a beer in peace if I want to and catch up on some local gossip."

We waited for our drinks to be brought over and studied the old photos on the walls. I recognised some of the black and white buildings from the city centre, many of them now with a new facelift and the roads in front of them paved with asphalt. A shout of *GOOOOOOOOL!* suddenly blared out from the television as Pachuca Football Club scored against some other team dressed in red and white stripes. One of the men at the bar muttered something to his barmate, who nodded without replying. The sleeping man at the table by the door didn't stir. His loyal drinks would have to wait.

After Paco had brought our beers over, I leaned in towards Lina so as not to be overheard, although nobody seemed to be in any fit state to hear us and our secluded position and the loud TV made it an almost impossible task anyway. The desire to feel the warmth of her mouth again exploded inside me at our close proximity.

"So, what about earlier? With Carlos, I mean." I asked.

Lina let out a long puff of air. "I didn´t want to say anything at lunch and offend anyone, but NAFTA is a total joke. It´s going to make the poor even poorer still. Mexico´s going to be flooded with cheap imports from the United States and the country will become dependent on the U.S. to survive. We´ll completely lose our self-sufficiency. It will be a complete disaster."

She spoke with an inspiring passion and fury that I´d never seen before and it struck me that she´d just spoken using the first person to describe the people of Mexico that she identified with so much.

"This new *Salinismo*, that´s supposed to bring Mexico into the First World, completely ignores the plight of the indigenous people. It´ll take away their lands for macro-farming, leaving them with nothing but poverty, hunger and malnutrition. You'll see."

"Isn´t it supposed to modernise all of this? The farming, I mean," I asked, eager to hear her beautiful angry voice continue its vitriolic course once more. "That´s what Carlos told us, anyway," I added, shifting some of the blame for what I'd just said.

"It´s a joke," she repeated. She took a sip of her beer and composed herself. "Salinas and his corrupt party changed the constitution last year in preparation for this. They amended Article Twenty-seven, which redistributed the collective ancestral lands of indigenous people after the Revolution. Now, anyone can expropriate their property and foreign investors can come in and just take anything they like if it´s deemed in the best so-called 'national interest' for them to do so."

"Well, surely they´ll get some sort of compensation out of it, won´t they?" I dared.

Lina laughed out loud, which attracted Paco for one second before he was forced to listen to one of the barflies hold court about how the referee must be in the pocket of the president of one of the teams who were still playing on the screen above the bar.

"They´ll get nothing. And if they complain, they´ll end up in jail, or threatened, or worse. You know, the prisons here are full of indigenous people convicted without a proper trial, or even a trial at all. Most have no legal papers, anyway. Half the people can´t read or write and the majority don´t finish school, so what choice do they have when they have nowhere to grow anything to eat? If they protest, they´re beaten. If they stay silent, they´ll live on the margins of society forever. As long as Salinas and his PRI party cronies are in power, absolutely nothing will change. NAFTA or no NAFTA."

I was hooked on Lina´s discourse. If I could vote for her for something, I would. Mayor, President, whatever, I just wanted to hear her voice, see her lips move, the curls of her hair flowing with every furious movement of her head. I was biased, of course, but not just because in the dimness of the *cantina* I was falling in love with her, but the words, the content of what she was saying, the social injustice that she was laying bare to me was stirring something deep inside. I´d seen the old men and women sitting in squares in cities I´d visited, trying to scrape enough money together to eat. I knew that these people were living in another time and place to those that I´d seen in European style coffee shops in La Condesa. But until now, until this beautiful, passionate woman in front of me opened my eyes to the extent of their persecution, I was blind to the bigger picture. I didn´t realise what was really happening. I'd gawked at the Aztec statues, marvelled at Olmec and Mayan art, and taken photos of the colourful handicrafts in markets. I´d seen these cultures as dead, the images and artifacts I´d been witness to as things of the past, the people I saw begging on the streets remnants of a lost culture, the survivors of a dead people and not what they really are; living reminders of a time gone by, dressing differently from modern society, still eating and farming in ways that their ancestors did hundreds or even thousands of years before. They are the people of the corn. People who are forgotten, ignored, seen as inferior and brutally exploited, but they, their culture and their language are still very much alive and their struggle never-ending.

And I was desperate for Lina to tell me more.

Juanito didn´t just visit once a year, attracted by the toys, sweets and marigold petals laid out for him on November the first. He was here all the time. He was here in the middle of the night when I´d hear Emilia close the bedroom door softly so as not to wake Carlos and shuffle across to the sofa in the living room to talk to her child. He was here when Carlitos chatted away at thin air, offering the empty space in front of him a piece of whatever it was that he was stuffing into his mouth at the time. He was here with Carlos when he kissed his wife goodbye as he left for a job he´d applied for as an excuse to move away from the house in which his son had died. And he was here, ever-present in the eyes of his twin brother.

Ghosts had followed me my entire life in one way or another and in the comfort of this simple home in the heart of Mexico, it was no different. I'd learned to live with mine. And although Carlos and Emilia put on the bravest of faces, they were still struggling to come to terms with theirs.

They filled their days with the tasks of the middle-class Mexican family, hiding their grief in the mundane and living their emotions and dreams through their surviving son. They did their best to make me feel like I was part of their family, which they achieved almost from the very first day I slept under their roof. Emilia went above and beyond the role of host mother, preparing food that I´d be more than happy to eat at any restaurant in the city and Carlos eagerly encouraged my participation in conversations as often as he could.

With Carlos´s willingness to involve me when watching the news on television, not only was my level of comprehension and fluency in Spanish improving rapidly, but my understanding of the political situation in Mexico too was becoming deeper day by day.

One evening towards the end of November, with the TV flickering away in the background as I cleared the table after dinner – having won my battle with Emilia to assist her with the dishes in the kitchen – my attention was attracted by Carlos, who´d turned up the volume and was standing in front of the screen, arms crossed and absorbed in what was being said.

He was staring at a man with tanned skin, thick black hair and a well-groomed moustache, who was surrounded by reporters thrusting microphones into his face. He looked determined, satisfied, and with an air of a man who knew where he was going and how he was going to get there. I went to stand next to Carlos.

"I accept … I accept with the enthusiasm of a Party man, the support that you give me today; the one that leaders, directors, militants and sympathizers of the Partido Revolucionario Institucional give me for my candidacy for the Presidency of the Republic."

The crowd he was addressing roared their approval. The speaker soaked up the glowing admiration.

"I do it … I do it convinced and I also do it deeply moved. The fact that women and men with whom I share ideals, with whom I share purposes, have decided to propose me to be the candidate of the Partido Revolucionario Institucional for the Presidency of the Republic, is for me, the highest honour."

I listened to his perfect intonation, the way he emphasised each point he was making, leaving his listeners hanging on his every potent word. He grew into his role, allowing himself to smile at the encouragement he was receiving from his supporters.

"I am heir … I am heir to a culture of effort, and not of privilege," he continued. I have to admit that he was a good speaker. I glanced at Carlos, who was rubbing his chin, deep in thought, his expression hard to read as he listened intently. Whatever he was thinking, it was clear to me that he considered what we were listening to of great importance for the country.

"I belong to the generation of change. The generation led by Carlos Salinas de Gortari." An enormous cheer erupted from the party faithful at the name of the outgoing president.

"The generation headed by Carlos Salinas de Gortari, who led the project that I believe in and share. That of the great reforms of the Revolution."

I thought of Lina and what she'd told me about Article Twenty-seven. Was this man responsible for part of the reforms that she'd passionately told me are so unjust to the indigenous population?

"He'll shake things up a bit." Carlos spoke over the presidential candidate, who was now underlining the importance of nationalism and sovereignty and where he believed Mexico's future to lie. "He's no oligarch like a lot of the others. It's good to see a fresh face like his in the old party at last."

"He speaks very well," I answered, not really knowing what else I could say at this point.

"Well, let's hope he'll bring everyone in the country together. It's been divided for far too long." We both turned round at Emilia, who'd added her opinion from the kitchen.

"He's been doing that already for the last couple of years, no?" Carlos said, his attention back now on the speaker on the TV.

"As the Secretary for Social Development? Whatever that role really means. But what's he actually done, *cariño*?"

"Funding for rural communities, infrastructure ... modernisation of agriculture," was Carlos's confident answer, his eyes still fixed on the television set.

Emilia raised her eyebrows at her husband's back, wiped her hands on her apron and went about cleaning up Carlitos, who had chocolate smeared all over his face. I could see that she was doing her best to hold her tongue and respect her husband. I only wish she had the courage to give her full opinion and not abide by the social norms that still dictated family life in the country. Carlos was a decent, liberal man, had virtually no vices and clearly loved his wife, but although they had an educational level above the national average and considered themselves modern Mexicans, there was no hiding the fact that Emilia was still in the kitchen and Carlos in front of the television.

I smiled supportively at Emilia as Carlos stared intently at the unfolding events. I stood side by side with Carlos as the candidate's speech dragged on. My legs ached as we heard promises to build a fairer, more inclusive Mexico, where the Partido Revolucionario Institucional would spend public money in the best interests of the Mexican people. We heard how everyone, at all levels of society, would have the opportunity to build themselves a better, brighter future with the backing of a strong and internationally significant economy and the much-vaunted Free Trade Agreement. I wanted to sit down but I stood, arms crossed like Carlos listening to the electoral spiel continue.

I was starting to drift away from the words, his voice and repetitive promises somehow soothing me into a state of relaxation. I swayed on my feet as he came to the end of his speech after nearly half an hour, yearning to fall back into the comfort of the sofa. The crowd were lapping up his every word and chanted his name and catchy political slogans between the pauses in his discourse as he wound up his acceptance for presidential nomination.

"We're going to win! Solidarity!" his supporters repeated.

"With the strength of our party, we are going to win. We are going to win the future for Mexicans! For our children, for our families, for the well-being of each and every one of our compatriots. A future of better freedom, of more democracy. A future of greater social justice, a great and certain future for the nation. Vamos por más progreso para México! Viva Carlos Salinas de Gortari! Viva el Partido Revolucionario Institucional! Viva Mexico!"

Grand applause and cheers greeted the end of the speech. Carlos was moved by the words; I was impressed by their delivery. As I sat down to finally rest my aching legs, the smiling face and eloquent words of Luis Donaldo Colosio Murrieta reverberated around my head. A voice and a smile that would be imprinted once more in my mind three months from now, sitting and waiting in a prison cell somewhere in the north of Mexico, surrounded by desert, my fate – and that of the country – balancing delicately in my hands.

My days in San Miguel de Allende passed by in much the same way as they´d done over the previous weeks. I strove ever harder to better my Spanish, I was well and truly part of my host family, and my blossoming relationship with Lina was filled with long conversations over coffees, *chelas* and romantic dinners. I wasn´t looking inside myself or anything like that but somehow I was finding my place in the World, recuperating the story of my life, putting my arms around the happy little boy I´d abandoned years ago. For once, my life was heading in a direction that I wasn´t trying to fight against and I gladly yielded to the flow in which I found myself pleasantly drifting.

In the week after Colosio´s acceptance speech I started to notice campaign posters going up beside the main roads on the outskirts of the city. *Unidad y Esperanza,* many of them proclaimed, promising Mexico the unity and hope that it so dearly needed. His smiling face and bushy moustache were everywhere too, seemingly watching me to see if I would, one day, manage to escape San Miguel´s clutches. He was there on the road outside the Tuesday market, spying at me from fences that enclosed land earmarked for new development, his sharp eyes following me from billboards in front of the bus station. But apart from his intense stare checking me in and out of the city, everything remained more or less the same. Everything that is, except my classes with Lina.

Gone were the exercises about gerunds and infinitives, the subjunctive and tricky irregular verb forms. The listening comprehensions from text books went out the window too, replaced by recorded news stories about NAFTA and its consequences for the poor. Instead of the rather sterile readings which told of the food and customs in various parts of Mexico, we now discussed articles about such things as worker´s rights and the current situation of women in today's society.

"You know, nineteen ninety-three is supposed to be the *International Year of the World´s Indigenous People,*" Lina said vehemently, her hand resting on the copy of *Mundo Obrero*, the socialist bulletin that a friend had sent her via airmail from Madrid. "And yet they still face marginalisation and violent brutality at the hands of the police and the military while they´re stripped of their lands or forced to relocate. They suffer assimilation policies from their government and if they dare to stand up for their rights, their protests are criminalised. They´re powerless and have no voice in our world."

I watched her pace backwards and forwards in the classroom, looking at me intensely, making me feel guilty to be white, European, privileged and male. I could listen to her forever. Lose myself in her maelstrom of justice and injustice.

"Women suffer the most, of course," she continued angrily. A shadow fell into the room as someone passing by on the corridor outside stopped briefly near the open door. Lina carried on, unaware of the potential eavesdropper. "You know that something like one in three indigenous women are raped during their lifetime. They´re married off when they´re just children themselves and face a life of slavery to their husbands or whoever it is that owns them."

I would never do this to you Lina. I´m sorry. I love you.

"Here in Mexico, where abortion is a crime, women are beaten by their husbands – many of them victims themselves – alcoholics, working for little or even no wage to survive." Lina wiped a loose curl that had dared to interrupt her vitriol away from her face. "Many women get up at four in the morning to make *tortillas*, care for children, look after animals and do all the other tasks that need to be done around the house. And then there´s those that work – or are trafficked into working – in the appalling sex trade here."

Out of the corner of my eye I glimpsed the shadow at the door move slowly away down the corridor. I quickly forgot the momentary distraction and focussed back on my beautiful, angry girlfriend. I should say something. Make this more of a two-way thing. Get involved for once. Come on. My passivity angered me.

"It looks like it´s changing now a bit here though, doesn´t it?"

Lina looked at me incredulously, her passion beating down any tender feelings that she had for me. But I took solace in knowing they were there all the same, lurking somewhere in the depths of her subconscious. Thankfully.

"Are you fucking kidding?" she said. It was out of place for her to swear, especially in her workplace. "How do you come up with something like that?"

"Umm ... the new, umm, candidate for PRI. Colosio, isn´t it? He was in charge of social development before. He´s done some good things ... apparently."

Lina smiled at me. I wanted to think that it wasn´t condescending and she was just setting the record straight to someone that really didn´t have a clue what he was talking about. Dan would though. The travelling, civilising hero coming out of disaster, bringing knowledge from his superior ancient culture. No ... shut up. Get out of my head. I barely knew you before we came here and now you pop into my mind whenever I need an intelligent comment. Drilling holes into my skull with worms, filling it with bees. Inside, buzzing. Just get out of my head. Go.

"It doesn´t matter who the figurehead is. Who´s been put in charge. The party is corrupt to its rotten core. It´s been in power for seventy years, you know. God, it´s practically a dictatorship. Oh, a good one though, a perfect dictatorship as it´s camouflaged as something else. It disguises itself as something that resembles a democratic party." She laughed, although there was no humour in her eyes. Just fire. "They blatantly rob the vote too," she cut me off as I was making a gesture to interrupt her. "Ballot boxes go missing, there are threats of violence, people that have been dead for years suddenly resurrect themselves and vote for the party. In some places they get one hundred percent of the vote. It´s a bare-faced crime."

"But Colosio´s been working hard to make things better for the poor people, the indigenous groups, people like that."

Lina didn´t interrupt me now and sat looking at me compassionately for a moment. There was no malice towards me, just pity and then tenderness once more. She knew me well enough to know that I was just repeating second-hand what I´d heard elsewhere.

"Funding´s been given to some of the poorest areas in the country, hasn´t it?" I added nervously, clinging to my one line of argument, although I had no idea why I was still trying to add anything at all. I grew smaller.

"Infrastructure, you mean?"

I nodded meekly, ready for the counterattack.

"Roads have been built, yes. I admit that. But roads into jungles so multinational´s like Coca-Cola and Nestlé can steal water, Bayer and Monsanto can strip the land of its natural resources and petrol companies can fill their pockets. Oh, Colosio´s won the people over with his charm and promises of a better life alright. He´s given machinery to coffee growers and organised bank loans to subsistence farmers. Fantastic. If only there was electricity to power the machines. And don´t get me started on loan repayments from people that don´t actually earn any money."

Her cheeks were flushed and I could see that her forehead had started to build up a fine layer of sweat. I stood up and opened one of the windows that at once let in a refreshing evening breeze and accompanying traffic noise from the cobbled streets below. We sat down in unison at the same table, our hands almost touching. I wanted to take hers in mine, somehow tell her that everything would be alright, say something beautiful to calm her nerves and bring an end to the injustice that she raged against.

"Some regions don´t even get any funding at all," she continued softly. "It´s been taken away from them as an act of revenge." I didn´t need to ask what for. "For protesting against the land grabs, the evictions, the abuses, for forming a group that will finally stand up for what they believe in," she continued, trying to control her emotions. "A group that will fight against all the injustices, fight for drinkable water, education, the health care that is so desperately needed so that children don´t die from curable diseases."

I thought of Juanito. Why had he died? Could it have been prevented? I will never ask. I will never know.

"In the south-west in Chiapas though, they´ve started to fight back. With education, organisation, and now with arms."

A shiver ran down the left side of my body leaving the hairs scattered along my forearm erect. My attention was caught truly and firmly by this new information. A revolution? I needed to hear about this new development.

"Earlier in the year a *guerrilla* camp was found deep in the jungle by the army. The government had no idea what was going on, no idea that these poor, uneducated people could organise themselves in such a way. No idea that these *campesinos* had the balls to stand up and fight like this."

I was wrapped in what Lina was saying but was distracted by the shadow that was back at the door again, larger this time and I sensed that there were now two people listening in on us.

"Lina, I think we should–"

"So, the government abandoned Chiapas. I mean, they flooded the area with troops, but they´ve tried to largely ignore – or cover up – the *guerrillas´* campaign. I guess they don´t want to create an international scandal before the Free Trade Agreement by going in and massacring a whole load of ethnic people, do they?"

"Umm, I think it´s better if we–" She took my hands in hers and looked deeply into my eyes. I was helpless.

"So, whoever´s told you that this Colosio is a good man might be right. But I can tell you that his party is a monster. A hydra. If you cut off one head, another more evil one will grow back in its place. And it must be stopped."

I´ll do it. I´ll do anything for you. Just tell me what I need to do, was all I could think as I was captivated by Lina, her soft hands caressing mine. I ignored the world around me, shutting out the noise from the traffic outside, the breeze that had blown the papers and articles off Lina´s desk, and the dark shapes that were still silently listening near the open classroom door.

*

I watched the bubbles twist and writhe together as they fought to be the first to reach the surface. They collided and bounced off each other in a race to exist no more. I imagined each one of them to be a tiny commuter, elbowing other people out of the way as they rushed to work, falling over themselves for a seat on a packed underground train that would take them closer to a retirement slumped in their favourite chair. Large glass of wine in hand. Just sitting. Doing nothing.

Before my imagination could continue its downward spiral, I was interrupted by Lina´s melodic Spanish accent as she sat down heavily next to me.

"Quit playing with your ear, you´ll wear it out," she ordered.

I did as I was told and stopped my involuntary fidgeting, coming back into the real world and welcomed Lina with a loving smile.

"What are you doing?" She kissed me softly and quickly on the lips while Paco´s back was turned as he disappeared into his enormous refrigerator to grab Lina a Corona to accompany mine. He may be gone for some time, I thought.

"Umm, nothing," I replied. Lina looked at me and then at the half empty beer that I´d been engrossed in when she´d walked through the swinging wooden doors of the *cantina*. She frowned. She must think I´m not right in the head. Try to act normal for once, will you? I tried.

"Apparently, there´s an exhibition of etchings at El Nigromante if you´re interested. We could go and get something to eat afterwards, if you fancy–"

"Sorry honey," she interrupted, raising her hand gently to quieten me. She was looking at the television above the bar. "Could you please turn it up a bit, Paco? Thank you."

"By your decision, today, for the first time, I take the floor as Candidate of the Partido Revolucionario Institucional for the Presidency of the Republic."

Here he was again, his confident smile and moustache following me from every angle. There was no escape.

"Many images accompany me at this moment, but the one with the greatest meaning, the deepest and the one that most demands of me is the look of hope of our children, of our young people."

Lina was watching and listening with her lips pressed thinly together, ready to pass judgement on what she was witness to.

"Democracy and justice are ways to enhance the Nation."

Colosio continued in his hypnotising manner, addressing a flag-waving public spread out before him in the foreground. Behind him the other party members sat. I recognised the shining head and pencil moustache of the President looking on proudly at his protégé.

"The government with which Mexico will close the century will have to begin its administration with a stronger economy, with a more vigorous state, a more participatory society, self-confident. Actions of change have been carried out, both in economic structures and social practices. And these have been the most important in our modern history. So, we now have the tools to face the future."

"What kind of future do the poorest people have now, *cabrón*?" Lina hissed more loudly than she should've. "We know what tools Bush has given you. You've pushed your own people under a bus." She stared angrily at the screen, sneering as the speech continued unabated.

"The Free Trade Agreements with the countries of North America and Latin America, as well as the commercial arrangements that are outlined with other regions of the World, what they do is provide certainty, provide clarity to our commercial relations. There are favourable conditions to increase competitiveness. We are facing new opportunities; we want concrete benefits for Mexico in economic globalization. We will gain them by competing."

"I can't listen to this." Lina turned to me again. "What were you saying about some exhibition?"

Colosio continued to distract us in the background. *"Before you all, I also affirm my commitment to democracy."*

"Liar! There is no democracy in this country!" Paco, who'd been watching quietly from his chair behind the bar, his right arm planted in its usual place, broke his habitual deadpan silence.

"I affirm it categorically: the PRI does not need – nor do I want – a single vote outside the law. We will work so that these elections are an example of democratic practice," Colosio promised, as if in response to Paco's accusation.

The place was suddenly full of chatter as the drinkers at the bar began to chip in with their opinions, as if debating an offside decision in one of the football matches Paco frequently had on to please them. Rising from the dead, the man who may very well have had his head planted permanently on the table since our last visit joined in too.

"*Hijo de la gran chingada* of a politician."

"He´ll change things around. Give him a chance, *güey*."

"They´re all the same. Thieves, all of them. And the banks too."

"What are you saying? He´ll make a great President. He´s just what Mexico needs right now."

"Can´t be any worse that what we´ve had for all these years."

I knew Lina wanted to jump in and tell them all what she thought too. Bombard the innocent drinkers with a multitude of facts and figures that would make them feel ashamed to be sitting here drinking beer after beer, their pot bellies full, the hunger suffered in many other parts of their country a stranger to them as they counted the tourist dollars. I squeezed her hand affectionately. Thankfully she got the message and we sat in silence as Colosio wound on and on, accompanied by the comments of the regulars at El Cucu.

The camera panned away from the presidential candidate and focussed on the men in suits sitting behind the speaker as Colosio promised transparent finances, clean elections and an external audit of the electoral register by independent observers. There were not many supportive smiles from his colleagues.

"Ha, look at them, sharpening their knives already. He won´t last long there," Paco said as he smeared thick salt crystals around the edge of a glass. "The sharks will get him before he can clean out the rot among the *priístas*. You´ll see. The sharks will get him."

The speech dragged on and the barroom comments fell away as the punters ran out of their favourite one-liners. Lina and I sat listening silently too and soon I fell into a similar daze that had overcome me as I stood shoulder to shoulder with Carlos little over a week ago. Lina was still attentive though, and I knew that she was absorbing what she was hearing so she could repeat it to me later or use it tomorrow in class and present her counter-argument as eloquently and bitterly as she could. I was looking forward to hearing her voice already, riding on the sweet waves of social injustice once more as she spilled out her feelings to me.

Back on the TV above the bar, Colosio was keen not to leave anyone in the country feeling left out. He promised that the rural communities would be connected with new infrastructure and technology. That train networks, ports, roads and hydraulic projects would be implemented. At the same time the environment and natural resources would somehow be protected, indigenous people would be given more opportunities and the marginalised in both the countryside and the cities would receive the full support from the government to improve their lives.

"Let us remember, friends, that the world in which we live was not inherited from our parents, it was lent to us by our children."

Bravo, maestro! Farmers, workers, professionals, university students and professors, teachers, technicians, businessmen, manufacturers, salespeople, service industry workers, civil servants, country folk, women and young people all got a worthy mention. Colosio began winding up to the grand finale of his speech as he endorsed the heroes of Mexico´s revolutionary past too.

"To Hidalgo, with his passion for Independence. To Morelos, and the Feelings of the Nation. To Juárez, with his faith in sovereignty and the law. To Madero, and his democratic ideal. And to Zapata, with his call for social justice.

"Come on, my friends. Let's undertake this campaign with the proposals of the Mexican Revolution for our time. With our strength, with our organization, with pride, with dignity, we are going to go all the way. Vamos por más progreso! Vamos por el triunfo! Viva el Partido Revolucionario Institucional! Viva Carlos Salinas de Gortari! Viva México!"

Viva! Goose bumps crawled down my arms. I wanted to shout something. Anything. I didn´t know why. I didn´t care about what he was saying really. I just wanted to feel the passion. Any passion. To feel so strongly about something that I´d give my life and soul to fight for it, just as he was doing. Lina had that passion. She would wage war if she thought that there was a chance for justice in this world. She´d done this to me. She´d woken something inside that had been lying there latent, nullified by an apathetic, nihilistic life and upbringing in a comfortable and safe western country. I looked at her from across the table, she looked back at me and we understood what we had to do. There would be no going back. We were committed, one to the other, and we would make the World a better place. Together.

*

Our arms and legs brushed against each other and I could feel her skin flinch and then shiver as I ran my fingers down the soft skin of her silky back. In the darkness of her bedroom our two worlds collided and we twisted our naked torsos together as we made love for the first time. We stole the breath from each other's mouths, no words could be spoken. We were in this together until the end, her passion now part of me forever, my soul entangled with hers caught by the barbs of our mutual desire. I had no name. She had no name. We were the space between the stars. Black sky, black earth. We were one.

The clock on the wall was partly obscured by the wicker baskets on the shelves that served as rustic decoration but I could see that she was already half an hour late. From our usual table in the window, I looked out towards the Iglesia de San Francisco with its sandstone facade and bell tower, the tiny cactus growing defiantly in a small crack at the base of its dome a constant reminder that life can and will prevail. How many times had we sat here over the last few weeks, drinking *café con leche* and eating sugary *churros* before our class? Lina nostalgically enjoying the tastes of her once native land. As I sat there, I envisioned her walking quickly across the small tree-lined square in front of the church, waving at me as she pushed a bouncy curl out of her eyes, an apologetic look on her face for being late. Our sleepless night together a perfect excuse for her to arrive later than usual.

I finished the dregs of my lukewarm coffee, the limp *churros* barely touched, and made my way over to the language school a few metres further up the sloping street. She must've been running late and gone straight there. She's a diligent girl. She must be there, preparing something for our class or some engaging activity for one of her other groups later on. Something that she knows her foreign students will like. She must be.

I climbed the large stone staircase that hugged the corner of the patio and then entered the classroom where our budding romance had begun. There was no sign of Lina. The books and folders that she used for her classes were still neatly lined up in the bookcase next to the blackboard. The blinds covering the windows down. I waited for another half an hour.

Maybe she'd fallen asleep after I kissed her gently on her forehead as she lay in bed while I made my way home for a fresh set of clothes. I descended the stairs and hovered in the secretary's doorway until she noticed that I was there. No, she hadn't seen her. Hadn't received a message either. She must've overslept or be feeling unwell. I decided I'd go back to the apartment where I'd woken this morning from the few precious moments of sleep as black night became blue day. I knocked softly at first but then soon found myself banging my fist on the door to her first-floor apartment at the lack of an answer. Nothing.

The rest of the day was a hurricane of increasing panic. I went to all the places that we usually spent time together in the hope that she would be there at one of them, maybe with a group of students whose insistent invitation she just couldn´t refuse. Nothing. I went back to her apartment and again banged on the door until my knuckles and the side of my hand were red and sore.

The day consumed the passing hours. Paco hadn´t seen her at El Cucu, nor had the secretary at the language school, who was now looking increasingly worried herself about my state of alarm and the fact that Lina hadn´t appeared for her afternoon classes either. The director of the school had only made an appearance briefly that morning so I had no one else to ask.

I ploughed the smooth streets again looking for my love, looking for a familiar face that I recognised to ask about her disappearance. Nothing. Exhausted, and with no other recourse left, I trudged back to the house in Caracol. Maybe she´d left a note there. Left a message with Emilia or Carlos. *Something.*

Night fell, and with it her absence brought a black hole that sucked me into a pit of uncertainty, tensing my muscles and folding time in on itself. I waited for the grey glow of dawn to emerge out of the restless night and then left the house.

The streets were empty in the Caracol neighbourhood but here and there I could see lights coming from homes as people prepared themselves for the day ahead. I passed through the centre of the city and more people started to appear, sharing the changing light with me while grey turned to pink to blue. Lina´s apartment was in perpetual darkness. Nobody was readying themselves for the day. Nobody answered my insistent knocking and pounding.

Throughout the morning I retraced yesterday´s steps adding a stop at the police station where they listened politely and took a few cursory notes but insisted that I should wait another day or two to see if Lina showed up. These things happen, I was casually informed. Carlos unselfishly managed to get the morning off work and did the rounds of the local hospitals. Nobody matching Lina´s description had been admitted. I called the Spanish Embassy in Mexico City numerous times. Nobody answered the phone.

Back to the school I went again at the hours when Lina was supposed to have classes. Again, the flustered secretary had no news and again the director was out at a meeting somewhere. My mind starting inventing stories and hypotheses and I couldn´t help thinking about the shadows in the corridor that had stood listening through the open door of Lina´s classroom. What had they heard? Who the hell were they and why had they found our conversations so interesting to linger there in such a way for so long?

Back again too I went to Lina´s apartment, my ear pinned to her door, listening for any signs of life.

"Can I help you?"

I turned my head to see the landlady who lived in the ground floor apartment. We´d greeted each other several times over the weeks as I´d paid visits to the apartment above.

"Oh, hello," she said recognising me. She must´ve heard me over the course of the last twenty-four hours as I rattled the door on its hinges. She hadn't appeared before. Why not? Had she been avoiding me for some reason? She looked both puzzled and pre-occupied at my presence and dishevelled appearance.

"Have you seen Lina?" I blurted out, knocking her backwards with my forthright words.

"Umm, no. Not for a day or two, I think." She frowned. "Has something happened? Is she OK?"

"I ... I don´t know," I stuttered. "Have ... have you got a key?"

The apartment lay in semi-darkness, the curtains tightly drawn. I turned on a light and looked around, the landlady lurking behind me in the doorframe, not trusting one hundred percent my motives for being there. I scanned the open-plan living and kitchen area, looking for a clue as to what might´ve happened. Nothing was out of place, no sign of a struggle. What was I expecting? I don´t know. I checked the bathroom, an arch of blood splattered against white tiles flashed into my mind, but of course there was nothing there either. Footsteps followed me at a safe distance from the living room.

I entered the bedroom, where we´d made love just two short nights ago. Lina´s clothes hung on a rail. I wasn´t really familiar enough with the rest of her possessions to know if anything was missing and with the landlady hanging around suspiciously I wasn´t about to go rifling through drawers and cupboards to see if her passport was here. That would have to wait. I´ll come back and break the door down or something when I know that this woman isn´t at home and possibly spying on me from the apartment underneath.

I looked at the bed. I remembered how we´d become one mass of skin and fluids, our minds and bodies in tune, flowing back and forth like waves lapping the shore. Something wasn´t right. Something was different. The bed was made. Lina never makes it, she just pulls the covers haphazardly over the mattress, creases and folds ignored. But now it was neat. Pulled tightly at the corners, the pillows fluffed. This wasn't right. Something was wrong. Something had happened.

In the dim light of the bedroom I could see that there was something on the bed. Sitting in the middle was a large brown envelope. There was no name written on it, nothing to indicate what was inside. I glanced over my shoulder expecting my chaperone to be glaring at me but her attention had been captured elsewhere and she was busy checking on something in the kitchen. A dripping tap perhaps? I don't know, and didn´t care. I grabbed the envelope. It was light and contained papers or something similar. I folded it in half and stuffed it down the backside of my jeans, hoping that I hadn´t been observed. I turned around just as the landlady reappeared, suspicion rising on her face.

I quickly thanked her and trying not to burst into a run, made my way out onto the street, the brown envelope burning into my thoughts and scarring my back. I wanted to rip it open right there, solve the mystery of Lina´s disappearance. But not here. Not now, in public where prying eyes could see what I was doing. I knew I was already a suspect. I´d seen the way the police had looked at me. The landlady too. I walked as fast as my legs and the orography of the streets allowed. When there was no one around I ran, stumbled and lurched my way back to the Caracol neighbourhood, to my temporary home and the refuge of my room where I´d open that damn envelope that was searing its plain brown image into my mind.

I reached the sanctuary of my bedroom and pulled the thing out. Why hadn´t I opened it before if I thought that it was a clue to Lina´s whereabouts? What´s the matter with me? No, I did the right thing, people were probably watching me. Why would I give them extra motives to distrust me by seeing me stealing something from a potential crime scene? I held the envelope in my hands, too heavy for a letter, and ripped it open. A thin newspaper flopped out onto the floor. I picked it up and stared at the cover.

Large letters informing me that the publication was called *El Despertador Mexicano* headed the page. Under this, in smaller font, *Órgano Informativo del EZLN México,* explained who´d been responsible for publishing the bulletin.

EZLN. I´d heard Lina mention those letters before. I couldn´t remember what she´d told me it stood for, or who this group was but bells started to ring that it had something to do with the Chiapas region. Next to the issue´s name was a simple black and white drawing of a man in a large hat. His bushy moustache, belts of bullets strung across his chest and my visits with Lina to as many museums as possible told me that it was a depiction of the revolutionary Emiliano Zapata. The title below read: *Declaration of the Lacandon Jungle – Today we say, ENOUGH!*

I ignored the article on the front page and started to frantically flick through the rest to see if Lina had slipped a note inside. Nothing. I stared at the headline again and thumbed the pages more slowly this time in case she´d written a message for me somewhere inside. In code perhaps. Something only her and I knew. I scanned the first few pages, paying little attention to what was written until a black and white photograph stole me away from my task.

A group of soldiers, men and women of varying heights, were marching in formation in a jungle, rifles held across their chests, faces blotted out. Above the image were the capitalised, bold words: LIVE FOR THE COUNTRY OR DIE FOR FREEDOM.

What was this all about? I started to read the article next to the photo as quickly as I could, translating with relative ease after my recent intense practice, my lips mouthing the words as I ran my finger down each line.

Mexicans: workers, peasants, students, honest professionals, Chicanos, progressives from other countries. We have begun the fight we need to meet the demands that the Mexican State has never satisfied: work, land, shelter, food, health, education, independence, freedom, democracy, justice and peace.

It, she, was talking directly to me, *at* me, demanding my full attention, begging for it.

We have been walking for hundreds of years asking for and believing in promises that were never fulfilled, they always told us to be patient and to know how to wait for better times. They recommended prudence to us, they promised us that the future would be different. And we already saw that no, everything is still the same or worse than what our grandparents and parents experienced. Our people continue to die of hunger and curable diseases, plunged into ignorance, illiteracy, and lack of culture. And we have understood that if we do not fight, our children will go through the same thing again. And it is not fair.

Necessity was bringing us together and we said ENOUGH. There is no longer time, nor encouragement to wait for others to come and solve our problems. We organized ourselves and we have decided to DEMAND WHAT IS OURS BY TAKING ARMS, just as the best sons of the Mexican people have done throughout their history.

I paused. These people must be the *guerrillas* Lina had told me about. Has she left this for me? She must´ve done, it was on her bed. The bed where we´d slept together hours earlier. It was a clear sign. But what does all this mean? I carried on reading.

We have started fighting against the federal army and other repressive forces; We are thousands of Mexicans willing to LIVE FOR THE COUNTRY, OR DIE FOR FREEDOM in this necessary war for all the poor, exploited and miserable of Mexico and we will not stop until we achieve our goals.

A shiver ran down my spine and the hairs on my arms stood to attention once more as they had done when Lina had first opened my eyes to the possibility of armed rebellion. These people here, whose words I was reading, whose images I was observing, will give their lives for something. Again, I felt ashamed of my heritage and burnt with guilt over my own privileges. But through this haze of self-loathing, I was starting to realise what I had to do; what Lina had inspired me to do. What Lina was now telling me to do.

We urge you to join our movement because the enemy we face, the rich and the State, are cruel and ruthless and will not limit their bloodthirsty nature to finish us off. It is necessary to fight them on all the fronts of the struggle and hence your sympathy, your solidarity support, the publicity you give to our cause, the fact that you make the ideals that we demand your own, that you join the revolution raising their people wherever they are, be vital factors until the final triumph.

I´ll join your revolution. I´ll rise up with you.
But what about Lina? I have to find her.
If she were here, she would´ve contacted you. She´s gone.
I´ll find her. Whatever it takes.

How?
I'll search the face of the Earth. Asturias, Salamanca, anywhere.
She won´t be there.
Where is she then?
Chiapas.

All my life I´ve been running from something, searching for something I can´t touch. Something intangible. Something I never knew existed, something that lay dormant inside, part of me, terrifying me. Another being trapped within, scaring me to death. I´m not like the others, no. I never was. Never have been. Now. Now I´m here. It´s different. I´m flying on the back of the plumed serpent. I´ve tamed him, beaten him down, sunk my claws deep into his scaly flesh and now I´m coming for you. I´ll bring you to your knees and bury you with fire. A fire that will scorch the Earth and give it back to those that rightfully own it. Green shoots will rise from the burnt land. A new landscape, a new system. No more hiding. You can´t hide behind your armies and your bureaucracy. I´ll dance on your fucking graves motherfuckers. Know who I am. Know I´m your enemy, just look me in the eyes. Fear my blackened war paint. See me. Feel me. I´m coming for you. Know who´s going to hunt you down. Hear my voice in your ears, the hiss of the serpent now become the roar of the jaguar. Feel its teeth sink into your world, rip its rotten core out, suck the blood from your economies, leave you limp and powerless. I´m dreaming of the dead, seeing their ghosts come out of the mists, out of my smoke, out of the dark crystal. Out of the emptiness beyond the mirrors. Be afraid of what we can do, what we´ll achieve together. One by one you´ll fall like dominoes. We´re going to wake this imperfect world up, shake it to its foundations. Destroy it and start again. There can be no creation without destruction. Know that, fear that. The ground you build your castles and ivory towers on will ripple with our resolve. Nothing can stop us. Markets will crash. Your bones will be crushed. Nature will heal, deep cuts will scar. We´ll resurrect the past, the spirits, forgotten languages, our structures, our communities, our hope, our will, our love.

People have come and gone from my life. Friends, family, lovers, and now Lina. But Dan was ever-present. He was with me as I rode down the spine of the country, past cities already visited together, past recently forged memories. He was with me as I bought packets of sugary sweets and fried *totopos* from the vendors that boarded the bus at every stop it made on its crawling journey. And he was with me as much in my waking hours as in my dreams. I barely knew who he was a few weeks ago and yet here he was, part of my consciousness, guiding me towards the Mayan ruins of Palenque when I knew I really should be heading for the mountains or jungles of Chiapas in search of Lina, the EZLN or the *guerrilla* camp that I naively imagined would welcome me with open arms and where my love would be impatiently waiting for me.

I had no idea why we hadn´t tried to get to Palenque before. We´d been just a few hours away when we´d caught the bus from Coatzacoalcos to Campeche but for some reason we didn´t make the short detour to what I imagined would be another anthropological highlight for Dan. Perhaps his disappointment at learning the fate of the colossal Olmec heads had put him off. Or, like me, maybe he was following a voice inside his head that he just simply couldn´t ignore. A buzzing. A longing. Loss. Whatever it was, he hadn´t shared it with me, but now he´d made amends and had guided me here against my will – better late than never – to visit this place on his behalf.

I stepped off the bus, tired and unwashed after two days travel. My body ached and I was pleased that I´d now be able to stretch my stiff legs. I wasn´t where I wanted to be though, where I *needed* to be. Dan was to blame for this, as ever, although I was now on the fringes of the western jungle of Chiapas, closer to my goal. Closer to her? OK, we´d go to the ruins if that´s what he wanted for us, but first I´d do something that *I* needed to do here.

But I felt sick. Lina´s absence was a ball of molten rock dragging my organs out of my body, destroying them and turning every cell in my body into cancerous desperation to be with her. I had no choice, I had to continue. I closed my eyes, took a deep breath and got on with what I had to do.

I wearily collected my backpack from the belly of the bus. It was lighter now after leaving San Miguel in such a hurry, only stuffing in what I considered essential for my trip. I reached inside and pulled out the precious crumpled envelope that Lina had left for me. If only I had the photo that Paco had taken of us in El Cucu instead of just *El Despertador*. I was delighted that Lina had insisted that she wanted it so much. Proud that it was pinned to the wall above her bed, with me the last person she´d think about before closing her eyes at night; the first person she´d see in the morning. But I needed it now. Needed it to show the people here. Show them who I was really looking for. A face that might warm hearts and jog memories, and not only look for the organisation that had produced the pages I now held; the group that may now hold the key to finding the delicately powerful woman who´d changed my life. However, these sheets of printed paper were all I had. I swung the backpack over my shoulder and left the crowded station.

I could tell immediately that the population of Palenque had a much higher percentage of indigenous people than other places we´d visited. Dark-skinned men and women sat by the sides of the roads, in doorways, or walked slowly along the dusty streets outside the station. Men wearing large cream-coloured cowboy hats looked at me distrustfully and women with pink shawls draped over their shoulders crouched on the pavement selling sweets, homemade snacks and small handicrafts. I supposed I was in the right place, or at least on the right track. I scoured the scene and eventually chose to approach a friendly-looking middle-aged lady selling boiled corn cobs. Had she seen Lina? I pulled out the copy of *El Despertador* and showed it to her, not really sure if this was the right way to go about doing things.

"Excuse me? Do you know where I can find the EZLN?" I asked politely. "Ejército Zapatista de Liberación Nacional?" I added. She looked away as if she hadn't heard me. Deaf ears. I tried again with two men who were leaning against a wall smoking, their hours merging into days. They glared at me angrily through blood-shot eyes and again said nothing. Unperturbed, I continued to dare to ask people in the area around the station, showing them the article on the cover of *El Despertador*, and every time I was met with a brick wall of silent anger. OK Dan, you win, let´s go. Your turn.

It was an hour or so´s walk to a campsite close to the ruins and with the afternoon casting longer and longer shadows across the roads around the bus station, I decided that it´d be best to head in the direction of where I´d planned to sleep that night. I squinted into the low sun and adjusted my backpack so it was more comfortable for the journey ahead. Shit! What the hell was that? A hard thud smacked into my head somewhere around my right eyebrow. The pain soon followed, radiating out from the source of the blow. I bowed forward with the agony and instinctively clutched at the guilty spot on my head before pulling my hand away to reveal a patch of blood on the palm. I looked around me, I could feel the warmth start to trickle slowly down my face. It was as if all eyes were drilling into me, willing me to leave this place. There were no sympathetic looks. Would more stones soon be cast my way?

I was exposed out here. I soon noticed that unlike other towns and cities, the police were conspicuous by their absence, which struck me as odd due to the numerous army checkpoints that we´d had to pass through in the region to reach Palenque. I´d passed their brief interrogation by posing as an anthropology PhD student undertaking research for my thesis. It was useful to have Dan around sometimes, I had to admit. Max was in control now though and judging by the welcome I´d received here in the west of the town near the bus station, I thought it high time I started my hike out towards the ruins before anything else could happen to me.

The cut on my head didn´t bleed a lot but I was left with a stinging pain that reminded me to pick up the pace and get to the campsite I´d read about as quickly as I could. The late afternoon was cooling fast as the sun disappeared behind the treeline on the horizon but despite my backpack being lighter than when I´d arrived in the country, the humidity made sure that soon not an inch of my clothing was left dry. Eventually, with a little dull light left in the sky, I arrived at my destination and was quickly allocated a simple *cabaña* by the overweight man working there, who eyed my wound with indifference. He´d seen worse no doubt.

My lodging sat at the edge of the dense jungle, a back breaking hammock and mosquito net the only visible furniture inside. I flicked on the light switch and a bare bulb burst into life as I settled in. The whole place was at once filled with a variety of moths and bugs that forced me to hunt for the small torch I´d packed what now seemed like years ago back in England. I turned off the light and with the aid of a weak, battery-powered beam, I went back to the little hut which served as the site´s reception, where I´d seen a small sign informing people that snacks and cold drinks were available.

I sat down on one of the cushions scattered around a huge wooden cable reel that had been sawn in half and sipped on the ice-cold beer I´d just bought. Insects buzzed around the lights, while others in the darkness beyond screamed their constant electric night-time calls. I smacked at something that had started to feed on one of my legs, attracted to my virgin flesh; a rare vintage brought in from a faraway land. A shadow appeared close by. I looked up to see what was possibly the tallest man I´d ever witnessed. Standing at what must have been nearly seven feet tall, this strange specimen was smiling erratically down at me.

"Hey man," he said. "Do you mind if I join you?" He beamed at me, seemingly desperate for company. His dark grey clothes were baggy to the extreme and covered a skeletal frame in need of nourishment, his shorts longer than any trousers I´d be able to wear. He had a beer in his hand and an idiotic grin hovered above a shaggy goatee beard. What could I do?

"Sure," I answered unenthusiastically.

Strained pleasantries and introductions aside, Pete, from somewhere near a place called Whitehorse in Canada, got quickly to the reason why he was now sitting with me swatting away mosquitos around a table that used to hold half a kilometre of heavy-duty electrical cable.

"I´m looking for the truth man. The reality of life." He let out a long cloud of marijuana smoke and held out the joint he´d produced from an enormous pocket on the front of his combat shorts. I refused politely with a firm shake of the head. I needed to remain sharp.

"It´s out here." He swept his hand like an emaciated farmer sowing seeds as he gestured towards the jungle. "I´m going to find a shaman, you know? Magic plants are here somewhere and they hold the key to our existence man. Cactus." He took a long puff of the joint. "Vines," he added, as he let it out.

"Ayahuasca?" I ventured. I was met with a blank look. "Vines, yes. Anyway, there should be something like that around, I´m sure." I wanted to get away from this guy. Away from his innocent ignorance. I had to sleep. To get the ruins out of the way and then find the EZLN army. And Lina.

"I´ll go on a journey, man. You know, find out what it all means. Find the answer to everything." He smoked a bit more. "And you, man? What are you doing here?" Pete trapped me here for a little longer. A bug caught under a glass.

"I´m here to see the ruins," I half lied.

Pete frowned. "Ruins, man?"

There was no possible way in the world that this giant beanpole of a man didn´t know that there were some of the finest Mayan ruins about a twenty-minute walk away from where we both sat.

"How long have you been here?" I asked. I tried to hide my incredulity and reserve passing judgement on this guy. He was here, he'd made it this far at least and survived. He must be a trailblazer to the good ol' folk back in Whitehorse, wherever the hell that was.

"Umm, I don't know. A week ... maybe two." Pete counted them out on elongated fingers that could've been painted by El Greco.

"I'm going to visit them tomorrow. Why don't you come along with me?" No. I was stunned. What the fuck had I just said? It wasn't me, it was that prick Dan in my head again, making decisions for me. Planting words in my brain. Leave ... me ... alone.

"Ah man. That would be awesome, thanks." Pete smiled a goofy smile at me as I stood up, abandoning at least half of my beer, the can dripping condensation onto the dark wooden surface of the table. Pete got to his feet too, genuine joy etched on his face, waiting for a handshake or a hug or something.

"Goodnight," I said abruptly.

"Night, man. See you tomorrow," Pete replied to my back as I was swallowed by the night on my way back to my *cabaña*, a needle-like pain above my right eyebrow and the shrill sounds of the insects reverberating around my sore, confused brain.

*

There were two of me. Which one could I trust? They appeared the same but each had a different look in the eye. The broken piece of mirror nailed to a tree spilt me apart, razor in hand. I stared at the four-eyed monster. Was it incomplete? No. I am already complete but just divided. I needed to find my real reflection in the pieces, convert into what I truly am. I gazed at the images. Black bags pulled my face downwards. I'd look better with a beard. That would mask some of the anguish that had taken over my features. I put the razor down on the tiny sink under the broken glass. Pain again, this time in my foot, excruciating. Fire ants were swarming over me, attacking the intruder who'd invaded their land. They had every right to. Who was I to be here disturbing their community, destroying their home? Invading. I bore the pain as long as I could, feeling it creep up my calf and shin. I deserved it. I wanted them to punish me for being here, for forcing myself upon their way of life and their habitat, but I could tolerate it no more and brushed the ants off as gently as I could.

I stood away from their nest and watched them gradually restore order again, carrying off their dead, each one of them stopping briefly to communicate with every other ant they came across during their task. If only we could be more like them. My old life, where the people you pass on the street hang their heads or look the other way to avoid communication at all costs. Even in the countryside, with no other people around they do their best not to have to make eye-contact should you be passing them on a footpath. We don´t deserve to be the dominant species on the planet. Our time will eventually come.

*

Pete was already waiting at the cable reel and greeted me with a wide smile. I could see he was relieved that I´d kept my side of the agreement given how quickly I´d disappeared the previous evening. We were soon walking along the road to the ruins, Pete towering over me, babbling on about the purification ceremonies he´d seen in other parts of the country. *How they just cover the people with smoke, man.* I answered politely, keen to get this out of the way, to placate the voice in my mind at the same time too. Tick the boxes and get the fuck away from here as quickly as possible.

*

The ruins of Palenque resisted the encroaching jungle and the snaking vines that tried to carry the stones off into the dense forest. The site was an open window into the past, present and future, its steep terraces and platforms supporting temples and towers with intricate reliefs that told stories of gods, warriors and governors. It was in constant movement, pushed and pulled by the angry vegetation that one day would have its revenge. Iguanas, toucans and thin green snakes were the real owners of this land. Jaguars too; the guardians of the night keeping the delicate balance of the food chain in order. They knew all that set foot in their domain.

The lost world cries of howler monkeys pierced the air, mimicked by the excited screams of children scrabbling over the Mayan structures. Fathers with Colosio style moustaches and mothers in pastel clothes took it in turns to film their offspring with bulky video cameras. I didn´t hate them anymore. They, like me, are simply a product of their environment. They don´t each have the individual blame for Earth´s lurch towards its dark future. We were here sharing this moment, this little piece of time that would never be repeated. We´d take it back to other places in the World, to different continents and repeat it to others willing enough to put their petty envy to one side for a moment in order to listen to our small achievements. I´d be in the background of their shaky video. People would comment about my lanky travel companion. We´d be part of their lives forever.

I dragged Pete as quickly as I could around the site, stopping very infrequently so he could take a photo or two – probably the only way he´d be able to recall later on the places he actually visited on his path to enlightenment. My camera was still at the bottom of my backpack in my *cabaña* at the campsite.

We crawled through the depths of the pyramids, past black spiders the size of fists that scurried away from us as we approached. I felt something in my hand. I flinched, but it wasn´t a spider. It was Dan´s guidebook on Mesoamerican archaeological sites. What was I doing with it? Surely he´d need it wherever he is now. On his netherworld journey, snaking his way down to Tikal, Copán, or some other site that he´s probably at this moment explaining to some impressionable female backpacker that would be charmed by his intelligence and intrigued by the huge scar on the side of his head.

We arrived at a dimly-lit annexe deep inside the Temple of Inscriptions. My guidebook was open at the page that told us that this was Pakal´s tomb and he´d ruled over the region from the age of twelve for seventy long years. Like the Partido Revolucionario Institucional. Pete and I stared at the beautifully-carved sarcophagus lid, which told the story of the ruler´s life, family and ancestors along its sides. The top of the large slab depicted Pakal´s rebirth into the eternal life, carried by the cosmic tree up into the sky where the supreme creator Itzamnaaj awaits to help him fulfil his destiny.

I suddenly couldn´t breathe well, my chest was becoming tighter and tighter. Air sucked from my lungs. I felt the walls closing in on me in the confined space of the passageway under the pyramid that was built around the great overlord´s tomb. The black spiders were getting closer and would soon be crawling all over my skin, entering my mouth and ears. Pete was leaning over me, crammed into the suffocating space beside me, grinning at me, baring his fangs. What the hell was I doing here? I had to get out, climb my cosmic tree, find my own god and fulfil my destiny while I still had a chance.
And so, I ran.

*

Back at the campsite Pete chatted excitedly, seemingly oblivious to my panic attack and inspired by our morning together at the ruins and my subtle encouragement to finally go in search of the shaman that would take him to another level of awakening. I sincerely wished him the best of luck and then hid myself away in my *cabaña*, out of sight of other potentially lonely travellers looking to pounce on their unsuspecting victims.

I pulled out the crumpled *El Despertador* from its envelope in my backpack. I closed my eyes and saw Lina´s delicate fingers holding the same page as I now held in my own dirty hands. Our fingers brushed together and I felt static electricity surge between us. Desire swept through my body. I opened my eyes again. EZLN. EZLN. I´d wasted too much time here paying attention to what Dan wanted; to what other people wanted. I could fill him in another time about the Temple of Inscriptions and Pakal´s tomb, but right now I needed to find Lina, find the EZLN and join their fight, crush globalization and save the indigenous people of Chiapas.

I walked towards the city centre along the same road that I´d taken the previous night with my head stinging with the pain of the rock that had recently been thrown my way. Without my backpack it was a much easier walk, despite the heat of the day. I stopped occasionally when I came to a stall selling fruit and hot corn cobs or a makeshift shack that passed itself off as a small shop, asking the people there again about the EZLN. Again, like the thick undergrowth of the dark jungle, I was met with an impenetrable barrier.

When I finally reached the bus station I stopped and scanned my surroundings, looking at the faces of the people who were staring back at me, seeing if I could read into the eyes of the rock thrower from yesterday afternoon. I noticed at once that there were more police around today, and a largish contingent of soldiers too, stopping and searching people as they got off the numerous buses that pulled into town, throwing people´s bags and sacks to the ground after each unsuccessful search. There was suddenly a surge of movement among the crowd, some kind of commotion coming from inside the station. I recognised the voice at once, pleading with the police to let him go in his hippy-inflicted Canadian accent.

Two heavily-armed policemen all of a sudden barged through the growing throng of people outside the station and headed towards a police car with flashing lights that was parked outside, surrounded now by a group of increasingly angry onlookers. A tense situation was beginning to unfold. Behind the first two policemen were two more, comically short compared to the giant suspect that was sandwiched between them with hands cuffed behind his back.

"I didn´t do anything, man," Pete whined in English. "They're not mine. I don´t know how they got there. I really don´t. *Por favor*." He looked around as if searching for help and then he saw me.

Don´t do it Pete, please. He was on the point of calling out to me but the wind was forced from his body as he was doubled over by a fierce blow from one of the policemen´s night sticks. They bent him over, breaking him in half as they bundled him into the car. I slipped away as quickly as I could, escaping the stare of one of the officers as he scanned the area where Pete had been looking just seconds before. It was time for me to leave.

*

I was back on the road that linked the ruins with the city again and I felt incredibly exposed. The fruit and corn sellers gave me the evil eye as I passed them once more. If only a taxi would pass by. I don´t care how much it costs, I just want to get out of here, get on a bus and head for San Cristóbal de las Casas, into the jungle, the mountains, or wherever. I was buffeted by the force of the displaced air as cars and trucks sped past me, not slowing down, too close for comfort. They were doing it deliberately; I knew they were. Making me feel even more unwelcome than I already was here. Maybe I could hitch a ride with one of them. I don´t know, it could be dangerous. A bad idea. But I was vulnerable out here. On my own. Just me. That´s a first.

Everyone in the area knew what I was looking for and I had no idea what Pete might´ve told the police about me. I desperately had to get a move on and escape this area as quickly as possible. I heard a car pull up behind me. Don´t look. They must be buying something from one of the stalls, it´s OK, just don´t look at them and give them a reason to question who you are and what you´re doing here. Or throw another rock.

Everything then happened so quickly. Footsteps running, my arms pinned beside me, a sack shoved over my head. I didn´t struggle. I let them take me. I couldn´t fight against them. Their grip loosened against my acceptance and they helped me gently into the car that had stopped behind me. The doors closed and we were away. I didn´t say anything, I´d wait until we got to the police station. I´d explain everything about Pete, that we´d only just met yesterday. That I´ve got nothing to do with drugs or anything like that and I was just a tourist. EZLN? No, only looking for a photo of them, or something. I´m doing some research. Something like that. I´d ask for a lawyer, yes, a phone call. Just calm down now, it´ll be alright. Breathe.

Nobody said anything and we continued our journey to the city´s police station. How many of them were there in the car with me? Four, like when they arrested Pete? They didn´t put anything over his head. I guess he was just too tall. I rubbed my hands together nervously. They were not bound, no handcuffs. The time passed by. The silence was uncomfortable, the journey becoming too long to be going to the police station in Palenque.

I cleared my throat. "Umm, where are you taking me?" My question was predictably unanswered. I´d be wasting my breath asking anything else. We rattled away on our magical mystery tour, a cold panic growing inside the pit of my stomach, clutching at my windpipe, shortening my breathing with every unseen metre and each second that passed.

One hour, at least. Then what I imaged to be two or more. The windows of the car were open and the air gradually became cooler and more humid, unfamiliar. I could smell the damp vegetation around us infused with smoke from wood fires. The roads grew more winding and our speed dropped as we negotiated the bumps of potholes and hair pin bends along our way. We slowed to a virtual standstill and made a sharp right and the environment quickly changed again.

Travelling now on our new path, the vehicle´s suspension started to creak and complain as we left the paved surface of the main road and began the next leg of the journey down what could only be a dirt track. Through the criss-cross weave of the material of the sack that I still had covering my head, the light changed to a dark green as we drove deeper into the dense forest. Still nobody said a word. The panic inside me lessened and my mind began to wander. Was the sack I´m wearing made of the fibrous agave from Mérida? What kind of four-wheel drive vehicle are we in? A Hilux? What colour? Red, I reckon. Most are in these parts. Are they going to kill me? Dump me here?

We bumped and bounced our way for what seemed like an eternity until the land smoothed itself out and we finally ground to a merciful and worrying halt. The doors were opened and I was gently pulled outside into the cool fresh air that welcomed us. Around me the buzz of insects and the clucking of hens. But I wasn´t given the chance to get my bearings and enjoy the rural sounds, instead being swiftly – and carefully again – led into a building of some sort close by. As soon as I´d been ushered inside, the door was closed and I heard a key turn in the lock behind me. I stood there for some minutes, not knowing what to do, what to think. Eventually, I plucked up the courage to pull the sack off of my head. I looked around. I was alone.

The room was simple. Its one window was far too high and small for me to squeeze through and escape. It did though, provide just enough light so that it wasn't necessary to switch on the one bare bulb that hung from the ceiling. I knew that there would be an army of insects lurking somewhere just waiting for their chance. There were two wooden buckets in one corner of the room, one with fresh water and the other empty. In another corner there was a thin mattress with a neatly-folded blanket and pillow. Everything looked clean – even cleaner than some of the places that I'd paid to stay in recently. In the middle of my cell there was an uncomfortable-looking chair and a small table, on which lay a sheet of plain paper and a pencil, which had been sharpened – of course – with a knife or perhaps by someone skilled at using a machete. I walked over to it and picked up the paper. I turned it over, the other side of the sheet was blank too. It was for me, for my confession. But what do I confess to? I stared at the page, at the words I should've written to Emilia and Carlos. I saw my own handwriting thanking them deeply for the kindness that they'd given me, the moments of tenderness and loss they unselfishly shared with me. The gift of time they'd sacrificed in my darkest hours of need. The words I hadn't written, the thanks I never gave faded into a spectrum of colour, spinning inward on themselves until they were consumed by the pure white of the paper on which they were unwritten. I will never forgive myself for the blackout. Never feel a love like that for another family ever again.

I sat down on the creaking chair and studied my surroundings further. How had I got here? What had I done? What had *been* done? There was nothing I could change. Nothing I could do. Nothing except wait for what was to come.

*

The afternoon passed by and nothing happened. I sat at the table, I lay on my surprisingly comfortable bed, I stretched my aching muscles and I paced around my cell, listening to the faint hum of the jungle outside and the occasional call of a rooster in the distance. How long will they keep me here? What are they going to do to me? To be honest, I didn´t care. This was where I wanted to be, wasn´t it? This is where I needed to be. I´d found the EZLN – or should I say they´d found me – and sooner or later someone from their army would be here to do whatever it was they were going to do with me. I wasn´t worried. I felt closer to Lina. And the clean bed linen and preparations for my arrival told me that I probably wouldn´t end up with a bullet in the head, at least not here, not yet. I picked up the pencil and stared again at the blank page that had been left for me. I knew what I was going to write, who I was going to write to.

Knocking at the door ripped me away from my thoughts. They´ve got a key, why don´t they just open the door? I´m the prisoner, aren´t I? The knocking repeated more loudly. I cleared my dry throat.

"Come in."

I heard the key being inserted in the lock. Then there was a pause. It didn´t turn and the door remained locked.

"Can you please put the sack over your head, if you don´t mind?" asked a polite voice in Spanish with a Mexican accent I wasn´t accustomed too. It was clearly different from the Yucatán or Chiapas areas; accents that were complicated for me, to say the least, to understand very well.

I looked at the bag that had blinded me during the three-hour journey here. "OK," I replied, taking it and blotting out my vision after I´d made myself as comfortable as possible on the rickety wooden chair. "Ready," I said cheerily.

My voice sounded ridiculous in my current predicament and why I chose to respond in that manner was beyond me, but there was something in the soft delivery of the request from the other side of the door that put my mind at ease. I heard the key turn and then someone enter the room. Footsteps coming in my direction. My body tensed for the first time here fearing the interrogation was about to start but then

I heard various objects being placed on the table and the unmistakable smell of corn *tortillas* mixed with what could only be stewed black beans. My stomach woke up and growled in anticipation.

"I don´t know if my English is good, but I can try to talk in your language if you wish." My captor´s English was clear and calm.

I was taken aback by the offer but for some reason answered in Castellano. "It´s fine, we can speak in Spanish. I can understand." It wasn´t defiance or anything like that. Instead, there simply must be something seriously wrong with me as all I could think about was using this man as another opportunity to practise.

"As you wish," the man replied, switching back to Spanish. I could almost imagine him shrugging his shoulders at my indifference to his perfectly-pronounced generous offer.

"Please, go ahead, eat. I´ll come back later."

With those words, he left me alone again and closed the door. I heard no key turn in the lock.

I quickly took the sack off my head, hunger hastening my actions. On the table in front of me were indeed the *tortillas* and beans I´d smelled before, accompanied by a small amount of steaming scrambled eggs. There was also a large bottle of water. Beside these provisions was a long piece of material that I could only assume I´d have to use as a blindfold the next time my host knocked politely on the door.

I gulped down half the water in seconds but I ate the food as slowly as I could, savouring each mouthful of the simple meal, wondering why I was being treated in such a way after having been kidnapped in broad daylight by the side of a busy road.

Several minutes after finishing, there was the predicted knock at the door. I tied the blindfold around my head.

"Come in," I said as before. "I can´t see anything," I added, not knowing the word in Spanish for the strip of cloth that was now obscuring my vision. I heard my host approach, expecting him to remove the dirty plates but instead he put something down on the floor on the other side of the room and then the crumple of sheets told me that he´d sat down on my makeshift bed. There was then the unmistakable *chisp, chisp, chisp* of a lighter which was quickly followed by the strong smell of tobacco smoke. A long period of silence followed, in which I could hear my jailor – or whoever this man was – sucking on a pipe of some sort. He must´ve been studying me, checking me out, wondering who this person was that he now had under his care.

"What are you doing here so far from home?"

The words took me by surprise. The silence, smoky air and food in my stomach had sent me into a comfortable daze. He knew full well what I was doing in Chiapas.

"I´m an anthropology student. I´m only here to see the ruins and learn about the different cultures." The same lie I´d told to the soldiers that had stopped the bus at the road block wouldn´t work here, but what else could I say? There was another long silence again, more smoke, the faint noise of insects outside.

"Why are you looking for the EZLN?" asked my roommate in the same clear, calm voice he´d used when speaking English. Lina´s alluring eyes and rebellious curls burst into my mind. Time for the real truth now then.

"I´m, umm … looking for someone," I replied, my voice breaking as I unsuccessfully failed to hide my emotions.

"And who exactly are you looking for, my friend?" the man asked, his interest clearly sparked. "Someone in the EZLN?"

No. Possibly. I don´t know. Someone who broke into the abandoned part of my soul. Someone who turned on the light in this isolated and frightening place I dared not venture. Someone brave enough to blow away the filth, the mould, the creatures that had occupied this desolate landscape. Someone who loved me. Someone who taught me how to love.

"She's Spanish. Pale skin. Curly hair. Her name's …" I let out a long puff of air. Her name. If I say her name all of this will become real. I was terrified. "… her name's Lina."

The man remained silent. Why? Did he know something? Please tell me something. Anything. Sharp pain radiated around my body, my mind. The epicentre of the agony in my chest.

"I'm sorry. I haven't seen anyone like that. If I do, I'll tell you."

I believed his promise. I've no idea why, but this man that had just entered my life, this man that was holding me captive – probably at gunpoint – sounded undoubtedly sincere.

"Why here? In this part of Mexico. And why the EZLN? What do they have to do with the person you're looking for if you don't mind me asking?"

El Despertador. If I had that here, I'd show it to him, explain what had happened in San Miguel de Allende. He'd believe me, I knew he would somehow.

"Because I want – she wants – to help the indigenous people here in Chiapas. We want to join your fight for a better life for them. Together." There. I said it. You decide whether to believe me or not. Now either let me join you or kill me. Dump my body unceremoniously in the jungle and leave me to the ants and insects, they'd know what to do with me.

"And what does a skinny young man from England, in your condition, know about what's happening in Chiapas?"

What does he mean in my condition? What condition am I in? No matter. He knew where I was from. Had Pete told him? No, impossible. I was definitely not in a police station. Pete was long gone and left to his own self-inflicted fate.

"I know that multinational companies are illegally taking away the land from the indigenous people. Natural resources too. They're building roads and electricity networks for themselves and forgetting about the people." I paused. What else had Lina told me? Come on.

Think. This could save your life. "And bank loans which they´ll never be able to pay back. Umm ... they´ve no way to protest and if they do, they´ll end up in prison, or worse." That borrowed speech would have to do for now.

"Let me tell you a little bit more about Chiapas, my friend." There was more puffing on the pipe and a *chisp, chisp, chisp* until the tobacco ignited and the smoke around me intensified. "The multinationals you tell me about are indeed taking what they want. PEMEX, for example, is sucking the oil and gas out of the land, land that is – in theory anyway – supposed to be controlled by the local *ejidos* councils and the indigenous groups here. The very land that was ceded to them during the Revolution."

"Until the government scrapped Article Twenty-seven, no?" Thank you my sweet Lina, wherever you are.

"Yes, that´s right. I´m impressed. You´ve obviously been doing your homework, my friend."

Through my blindfold I tried to imagine the face of the man sitting and smoking on my bed. Right now, I believed, and hoped, that he was smiling. Anyway, we were talking more or less on the same level, about the same things. Like peers. I felt safe, for now.

"These companies take what they want and leave behind nothing but destruction, environmental damage, alcohol abuse, prostitution and poverty. Coffee is sent to other countries. Right now, somebody in Beverly Hills is probably drinking coffee from here for five, ten dollars, I don´t know, and it´s the foreign buyers that reap the rewards, the farmers are left with next to nothing. With cattle and logging it´s the same story too. You know, Chiapas is one of the richest places in Mexico. The natural resources are unrivalled in most parts of the World. It produces more than half the hydroelectric energy in the country, yet one third of Chapanecas have no power in their homes and half have no drinking water, despite the blessed rains that fall on this beautiful land.

"Corn, tamarind, honey, sorghum, avocadoes, cacao, all are cultivated here. Giant cedar and mahogany trees are felled for foreign profit. But the people receive nothing in return. Ninety percent are on a pittance or no salary at all. Three quarters don´t finish primary school. When you walk through the villages it´s common to see young children bent over under the weight of the bundles of firewood they carry on their backs or washing clothes in dangerous rivers. The children don´t exist. Nobody exists. People die here without ever being born. They die with no place to go."

He paused before continuing. I didn´t know if it was for dramatic effect for my benefit or if what he was explaining to me had affected him deeply. Whatever it was for, it had me captured and gripped by what he was saying, temporarily forgetting my own plight – but not Lina, she was in the forefront of my mind. She was there with us, listening, observing through my eyes, my senses.

"A million and a half have no access to medical services, more than half the population is malnourished, up to eighty percent in some areas of the Highlands. With the PRI in power there are no plans for any healthcare here. Do you know that fifteen thousand indigenous people in Chiapas die each year? Adults and children – anyone – from respiratory infections, malaria, dengue, tuberculosis, parasites, cholera. The treatment they have is nothing more than a few herbs and wet cloths. How many people in Britain do you know have died of these things that I mention?"

It was my turn to keep my silence and ruminate on what I´d just heard. I was already aware of most of the things that I was being told but captivated by the way they´d been reeled off with a perfect mix of passion and tranquillity. He knew, and believed, in what he was saying and with every word I was more and more entwined in the cause being laid out for me to understand.

"I just want to find my friend and help the people in Chiapas fight for their rights, that´s why I´m here. Why I´ve been looking for the

EZLN," I said meekly, filling the gap in the conversation that had been left for me. As if they'd take this mighty warrior into their ranks.

"And what do you actually know about the EZLN? If you don't mind me asking? We do know you've been looking for them, haven't you? Not just for your friend. Lina, wasn't it?"

I felt cornered, nervous about giving the wrong answer, suddenly thrown by my love's name parting the lips of the unseen man sitting next to me. "Umm … They're going to fight against the Mexican government with an indigenous army. It's … umm … going to take control of Chiapas and govern it with the people who it rightly belongs to. And I want to help them do it. Join their war."

"You know," said my captor, who'd opened some kind of clasp and was now fumbling around with what was inside the thing he'd just undone. "You're actually mistaken. The EZLN doesn't want control of anything. In fact, they're repulsed by the idea of power. They're just helping the people defend their rights, providing a voice, giving them justice, freedom, dignity."

A quiet tapping sound interrupted his discourse and a short while later the familiar *chisp, chisp, chisp* was followed by a cloud of invisible smoke as fresh tobacco was burnt.

"They aren't separatists, fanatics or terrorists. They love the flag, love Mexico, it's true, but they want to fight for a Mexico that's not a disgrace to live in. A Mexico where people can work in peace without worrying about what's going to happen to them. Without fearing for their lives or those of their loved ones. Where it's safe for women to walk the streets without being assaulted, kidnapped and raped, where children are not prostituted by corrupt officials, where the media can speak freely without fear of reprisals about what they broadcast. A new civilization. A new way.

"The fight is not just here in Chiapas though, my friend, not just for the rights of the indigenous people. The fight is for universal rights, not limited to one country, one region or one group of people. It's not about the right to be equal, it´s about the right to be different. It´s about the right to exist, no matter who you are, where you live or where you´re from."

I knew that he was staring at me, judging me. I had no answer to the words I was hearing. I longed for more, to hear his melodic voice carry me away. This is what I´d come here for. In part.

"The EZLN are not the answer to everything. You must realise that. They´re just a bridge between the people and the government. And of course, they´re not a political group either. Heaven knows there are enough political parties already. They´re just an armed movement doing politics, that´s what they are. But, you know, in the end, war is incompatible with democracy. Armed groups, the military, shouldn´t ever govern, including the EZLN. If they themselves then turn into a political group or some kind of leaders, then they fail in their purpose too."

My captor paused once more, allowing the weight of his discourse to penetrate my mind, my soul.

"Please don´t have false expectations about this army you´re looking for either, my friend. This army that you may think has just sprung up out of nowhere. It´s not some kind of trend or bandwagon to be jumped upon. It´s been around for longer than you realise, its essence that is. It – right now anyway – may be an indigenous army from a small part of Mexico that no one´s heard of, but its heart is in the fight for human dignity worldwide."

I heard the man stand up and walk over towards me. He stopped close by and the smell of tobacco became stronger.

"Standing on the shoulders of giants. I think it was a compatriot of yours that once said that. Well, that´s what the EZLN are doing. The people here were already organised, they had strength in their commitment to what they wanted to stand up for. But it´s been a silent revolution up until now. I repeat, my friend, they don´t want power, they´re not the real beneficiaries of this revolution, they just cultivate a hope that´s sorely needed right now."

I turned my head and looked in the direction where I thought the man was stood. "Please tell me what I can do?" I asked, more convinced than ever by the rhetoric I´d just heard that this was a cause worth fighting for, in spite of the short time I´d spent in this man´s company in my spartan cell.

"Just relax here, my friend. I´ll be back with something else for you to eat later." The man cleared away my empty plates.

"Aren´t you part of the army?" I dared to ask.

The man laughed. "Let´s just say, for now, I´m here to look after you, OK?" He walked towards the door.

"Do they have a leader? Someone I can talk to?" I called out.

The man stopped. "There is a chain of command, but it´s not that easy to speak to these people. It´s a real army you know, not just a group of *guerrillas*. I doubt any of them will have time at the moment anyway. However ..." he paused. I wish I could see his face, gauge what he was thinking. "... there is one man, a kind of interpreter. Quite charismatic, I believe. Marcos, his name is. He´s, how can I put it? An acquaintance of mine. Although I wouldn´t know him if I saw him, at least without his mask. I´ll see if I can have a word with him if I can find him. He might be willing to come and speak to you." He opened the door.

"Thank you," I replied. "I´m ... umm, Max, by the way."

"Of course you are," the man answered. "And I´m Rafa."

*

I was alone again. I took off the blindfold and looked around the room. The sheets and blanket on the mattress were creased where my visitor had just been sitting and at one end a toothbrush and a small tube of toothpaste had been placed. Next to the bed in one corner was the object that Rafa had brought with him and placed on the floor soon after entering. My backpack, abandoned and forgotten in my *cabaña* in Palenque. My thoughts turned to Pete. And then back to Lina.

I fought hard to block out the images that were violating and taking over my mind and turned my attention to my backpack. Everything was there. Packed more neatly inside than when I stepped into the arrivals hall in another life. I ran my hands down the outside, feeling the rectangular object that the front pocket concealed. I undid the zip and pulled out the dogeared guidebook of Mesoamerican archaeological sites. This damn book will follow me to the grave. Behind this was the brown envelope that contained the copy of *El Despertador*, the sole physical link I now had between myself and the only person I´d ever truly loved.

I spent the next few hours poring over the bulletin produced by the Ejército Zapatista de Liberación Nacional, re-reading the editorial – my call to arms when I was still a free man in San Miguel de Allende. I began to read in detail the other parts of the publication that I´d somehow ignored until now. The First Declaration of the Lacandon Jungle, which started on the front page, followed by the declaration of war against the Mexican government, orders to the military forces of the EZLN and a message to the downtrodden and marginalised people of Mexico. There were laws to abide by in this new revolution too, talked over and voted upon by the majority of the members of the revolutionary group. Laws that covered areas such as war taxes, the rights and obligations of both the revolutionary armed forces and the general public, agrarian issues, women´s rights, labour, industry and commerce and of course justice. Everything was thought out clearly with the greatest of detail and presented in such a way as there would be no doubt of the roles people would play during and after the impending conflict.

A knock on the door broke me away from the crumpled pages. I tied the blindfold around my head obligingly and was plunged into a darkness my sore eyes were grateful for.

"Come in. I´m ready." I have to admit, I was pleased by the thought of this man´s company again.

The food was placed in front of me as before and I could at once smell the starchy aroma of boiled rice.

"If you face the wall while you're eating, you can take the cloth from your face if you wish," Rafa said amiably. "On the condition that you don´t try to look in my direction."

I shuffled around until I was sure that Rafa would be out of my line of vision and uncovered my eyes. Sure enough, there was a plate of rice on the table, accompanied by stewed vegetables – some kind of pumpkin perhaps. The obligatory *tortillas* had made their appearance yet again too.

I began to eat quickly, eager to finish the food in anticipation of another round of conversation with my charming captor.

"I see you´ve been studying. Reading our laws." Rafa paused. "So you know you have to contribute to our cause, according to the War Tax Law, don´t you?" Rafa said gravely. "You must´ve read that it says anyone – including foreigners – that passes through our land has to pay a price one way or another."

I stopped chewing the food. What would I pay with?

Rafa laughed at my obvious surprise, despite only having a view of the back of my head. "I´m just kidding. Sorry." *Chisp, chisp, chisp.* He sucked on his pipe. "Judging by the contents of your backpack, you haven´t really got much to offer anyway."

"Thank you. For bringing it here, I mean. And ... umm, thanks for the toothbrush too. I appreciate it."

"As an errant knight from La Mancha once said, 'A tooth is much more to be prized than a diamond sometimes.' And here, in the jungle, this is especially true."

I carried on eating while Rafa sat on my bed, smoking his tobacco. I could feel his eyes boring into my back. I wanted to turn around and put a face to that soft voice and wise words.

"So, tell me a little about yourself, Max. Where are you from?" Rafa asked when he judged that I´d just about finished my dinner.

I wiped my mouth with the back of my hand. "Umm, from England. From a town not far from London. Not really a well-known place. Just, umm, kind of like … there." Very eloquent, indeed. Well done for making such a speech.

"What´s it like living there in this town not far from London?"

What a question. There´s nothing for it, I guess the truth will out once more. What would he care anyway? It´s just my opinion.

"It´s like, umm, … you know, people say it´s a good place to live. I mean, it´s close enough to London for people to commute there so, in general, quite a few people make quite a lot of money. People normally live in nice houses with gardens, have one, usually two children, who they take to clubs and activities after school, things like that. They go shopping at the weekends and have holidays two or three times a year. Their lives are comfortable and they don´t really have to worry about many serious things, just the usual. Death and taxes, things like that. What else? Umm … The schools are good, I guess. We learn enough to get us to university or start with a good job in the city. People go to the gym, the cinema, the pub, meet friends and do the same things as everyone else." I gave Rafa the milder version of the bile that was building up inside me.

"Are the people happy there?"

"They think they are. They´re told they are. I guess they don´t know anything different from what they´re used to."

"Were you happy there, Max?"

After all that I´d experienced in the last few days; the disappearance of the love of my life, my own kidnapping, that I was now held captive somewhere unknown in a jungle or up a mountain, I found the fact that my happiness being questioned by a potential terrorist, even my potential killer, to be bizarre to say the very least.

"No, I wasn´t," I answered all the same.

"So, what did you do about it?" The question rang hollow and echoed around my head.

"Nothing," I replied honestly.

"You came to Mexico. To see some ruins. Drink tequila."

I remained silent. The brutal reality of my meaningless life was laid bare. My futile existence summed up by a man whose eyes I´d still never had the chance to look into.

"And what do you think of Mexico? Do you like it? Do you think it´s a good place for a holiday or a road trip?" There was no sarcasm in Rafa´s voice, he was just testing me.

"I didn´t know what to expect to be honest. I mean, I knew where I was going, the places, but I didn´t have any idea about what life would be like. We started off as tourists but as we went on with our trip, things changed, we changed."

"We?" enquired Rafa.

"Daniel and I."

"And what´s happened with Daniel? Was he the tall man that the police took away in Palenque?"

"No. No. That was … that was nobody. I didn´t know him. He was just someone I met. Daniel, Dan was ..." What was he to me? "... a friend that I was travelling with."

"Where is Dan now, Max? Is he here?"

I tensed at the words. What does he mean, is he here? In Mexico? Chiapas? In the room with us right now? "I don´t know, he ... he met a girl and we ended up going our separate ways. I suppose he´s in Guatemala now, or Honduras or somewhere like that. I don´t know." I thought of the guidebook that must be somewhere near Rafa by the bed. How my former travelling companion must be missing it right now. I smiled to myself.

"Sorry, you were saying. Things changed, you changed, didn´t you?" prompted Rafa.

"Yes. Yes. I started to notice the different people here. You know, like, the people that really make up Mexico. The poor people mostly. The indigenous people. I know for me it´s hard to tell if they´re truly indigenous but I supposed they were. By how they looked, I mean. The people begging on the street, the old people selling just a few pieces of cactus. As we travelled further south and east, I saw more and more clearly the kind of problems they have and how they live. And then ... and then someone ..." Lina, Lina, Lina, Lina. Where are you? "… someone told me the full extent of what they were suffering. What people have done to make them suffer. And so ... and so I came here. To Chiapas. To, you know, find the EZLN."

Rafa didn´t say anything. He just sat there in silence digesting what I´d just told him. He sucked on his pipe and puffed out a cloud of smoke. I inhaled it deeply as it floated over my head seconds later. I felt united with this man in a way hard to explain.

"Let me tell you a little bit more about this Mexico that you´ve thankfully started to realise exists and the people that nobody here – or anywhere else – ever sees," Rafa said eventually. "Nobody has ever given them an opportunity throughout this great country´s history. The Spanish, the French, the North Americans, not even the revolutionaries and liberals. This great country, which has been proudly independent for over two hundred years, has done nothing to change their plight either. Here today, we live surrounded by mirrors. Mirrors of the past and mirrors of ourselves."

I thought of the pieces of broken glass in the jungle campsite. How the eyes looked back at me. How Dan had become a mirror of what I wanted to be and I, a reflection of a side of him that should remain hidden away.

"This new Mexico, this new era that we´re about to enter is only going to make things worse for the forgotten, unseen people. This system of neoliberalism is designed to remove borders and globalise the economy, but it does so at the expense of ethnic and different social groups. The indigenous population, homosexuals, lesbians, the young, women. Just some of the minority groups that they want to exterminate with neoliberalism." More smoke. I breathed him in.

"You know, my friend, this neoliberalism is the new fascism, it multiplies the number of the excluded, aiming to eliminate the people who are simply not productive. Millions of people are and will be sacrificed because of this system of governance. Of course, nobody´s going to invest in the indigenous people in this new world. They´re just seen as second or third-class citizens, or not even considered citizens at all. Nothing more than a plant or a rock to those in charge. Just part of a landscape to be trodden on."

Rafa´s voice remained steady but there was a passion and indignation that had slowly crept into his discourse.

"The government isn´t interested in the people but in what the land can produce and so the indigenous population are an obstacle to this. They aren´t seen as profitable. They´re only accepted if they renounce who they are and form part of the system. Become WASPS, isn´t it? White Anglo-Saxon, protestants, no?"

I nodded my approval at his use of the English term.

"The worth of a human in this new utopia is their purchase power and, therefore, they just want to convert them into another person who buys; a potential customer. If they resist, they vanish from the face of the Earth. But the government doesn´t understand that this will eventually lead to a civil war in Mexico. And further afield too. It will be a broken world if the big corporations don´t accept the dignity of the people and the more of the silent mass they eliminate, the less of them will be left to exploit anymore. Supply chains will break, the only ones who will survive will be the poor subsistence farmers. And these people, with a little assistance, will be the ones who´ll recuperate the place that the modern World wants to exclude them from."

I sat and listened intently, without adding anything. I didn´t need to, and Rafa didn´t need to hear anything that I had to say.

"The dirty war has already begun, years ago anyway. But they use different types of bombs now. Now, they use financial bombs to kill the people. Obliterate them with debt and poverty. So, you see, my friend, that neoliberalism and globalisation are nothing else but the Fourth World War."

"The fourth? What was the third then?" I asked, hoping that this didn´t sound like too much of a naive question.

"The Cold War," Rafa answered before pausing for a few seconds. "You know, this new attack, this attempt to make Mexico a top player on the world economy is just another way to stamp upon the marginalised and forgotten of this country."

"The Free Trade Agreement?" I asked, not wanting to misunderstand anything that Rafa was telling me.

"TLCAN. NAFTA. Yes. The United States wants to buy Mexico, that´s what´s behind all this. It´s already begun to turn it into a cheap production line with the *maquiladores*, the giant assembly plants on the border. But soon their reach will spread south too, destroying everything in its wake, taking advantage of the poverty, not freeing people from it as they claim. But these promises will not dilute the discontent that´s slowly festering beneath the surface."

I heard Rafa stand up behind me and pace heavily back and forth across the width of the small room.

"I´m not saying that capitalism doesn´t have some kind of place or shouldn´t exist, no, but that there should be limits. If foreign companies want to come here and use our cheap labour, then they should pay the workers the same as they do in their own countries. Create a fairer global economy for all."

"Capitalism is a hydra," I offered, hoping that my mutated second-hand analogy would be well received.

"It *is*, yes, indeed." Rafa seemed pleased at my comment. "But it *can* have a place in the World if done in a humane way. You know, the rich can exist if they work hard for themselves and don´t exploit others for their own benefit. Get there on their own merit and hard work. There needs to be a dignified place for everyone if this is the system that is going to prevail. A place for the indigenous people to be treated fairly, create their own market economy, away from the subsistence farming in which they have no current escape. But sadly, right now, the majority of Mexicans won´t move a finger until it affects them personally. They´re comfortable with, or nullified by, the current status quo. I´m sure they´d move if they suffered the same misery as most of the Chapanecas. Suffering is the engine of change after all."

"And that´s why the EZLN wants to march on Mexico City? Attack the large corporations. To stop the violence that capitalism is causing the indigenous, the poor?"

"No, not really Max. It´s more to do with political violence than the violence of capitalism. The crimes that the government has committed against its own people. You know, the Partido Revolucionario Institucional is a criminal organisation full of narcos and murderers. They hide their true intentions behind fake smiles and handshakes. They´re thieves using public money to sell their brand and product and while the people listen to their promises their land is destroyed, stolen and the innocent continue to be persecuted. They rob everything, the politicians do, from the top down – the governor, civil servants, local mayors. The money and funding that´s destined to be used here is in control of the regional governor but it doesn´t get down to the *ejidos* who know where it´s needed most. There´s nothing left for the communities once everyone above has taken their slice of the pie. It´s a governor´s duty to provide service for all its citizens, but you´d never know it."

Behind me I heard Rafa let out a short, sharp puff of air. No smoke followed the exasperation this time.

"We´ve listened to the rhetoric of cynicism enough. The agreements and promises that have been broken time and time again. They cannot decide our programmes, our legislation, how we should live. Here we can. The *ejidos* and communities. We can make our own decisions about our future and we´re not going to listen to a bunch of hypocrites who have used their power to deform the past and hide and eliminate a great part of this country´s history, its roots. You know, in Aztec mythology it´s not the vain and wealthy Tecuciztecatl but rather the humble, yet brave, Nanahuatzin who eventually becomes the Sun. And this is as relevant now as it has always been. It´s time for a change. The people will rule and the government will have to listen. They should, and will, govern by obeying the rightful owners of the land they claim to control.”

Rafa stopped pacing and sat down heavily on the bed. He sounded tired, which reminded me that it had been possibly the longest day of my life. My eyelids started to weigh my face down. I was glad I was facing in the opposite direction.

“There are some people trying to change things though. Colosio, for example,” I said, summoning the last of my own energy, eager to keep the conversation going, despite my exhaustion. Eager for this man´s company a little while longer. Rafa´s words the only thing soothing the pain of not knowing anything about Lina.

“He´s just a boy scout. He´s a lost little boy desperately out of his depth with his hands tied behind his back. He appears to mean well, yes, but don´t forget he´s a product of PRI, hand-picked by our dear Presidente Salinas, no less.”

“He´s popular, though, isn´t he? The people seem to like him,” I added, remembering the rallies I´d seen on television with Carlos and the hordes of supporters that mobbed and cheered the presidential candidate wherever he went.

“When a candidate for PRI makes a visit to a town on the campaign trail the people *have* to like him. They´ll lose wages from their jobs – if they have one – if they don´t show their full support by attending campaign events, even if they want to vote for another different party.”

Rafa paused to allow his words to penetrate into my mind. Of course he knew that although the politicians in the United Kingdom were also corrupt, this was on another level altogether and I needed to understand the true extent of this camouflaged dictatorship that they were plotting to fight against.

"With Colosio, there will be hope and then disappointment, as there always is. But, I don´t know, on a personal level maybe, and in spite of the party he represents, I could probably sit down and discuss our demands for the future of the country with him. It seems as if he would listen to us at least anyway and not try to flush us out of the jungle in a rain of bullets."

"People say that things are starting to improve here because of him. Things are getting better." I remembered Carlos again and our time spent watching the news together.

"Look, my friend, I´m sure there´s no need to tell you, but never trust a politician, even the ones that want to speak freely. It´s probably a publicity stunt, a photo opportunity for them to further their own careers and fill their pockets. You know, hospitals have been proudly inaugurated here but while the equipment was being delivered under the glare of the TV cameras at the main entrance, it was being taken directly out of the back door. Now these places stand empty. There´s no equipment or staff there. PRI´s wonderful healthcare plan for Chiapas in action."

"Aren´t there any other parties that you can work with? Apart from PRI?" I could already predict the answer as it left my lips.

"We respect those that respect us. And everyone´s points of view are considered. We´ll sit down and talk with them, sure. We´ll listen to them, of course, but at the end of the day, you can change the colours of the parties and their pretty little logos and flags but they´re the same beast. None of them take into account the people that live on the edge of society. In this country the common people are only seen when they commit a crime, appear in court or if there are images of them lying dead on TV. It´s a virtual world these days, my friend, and people live through the media and the screens in their homes. And everything that we see is a lie."

I was losing my battle now against my eyes but I didn´t want this day to end. "So, what can we do?" We? I said it. *We.* I was dying to belong to something.

"We can construct a different way. You know, the capacity to decide the fate of the World is in the hands of the media. In the end, what we really need to do is wage a war of words and not bullets and the independent media is the key. People need to see what´s really happening, not only in the biased traditional channels that the political parties control, but via international observers, the independent press, and more importantly for the future, the internet. These are more difficult for the government to control and manipulate. You know, journalists are murdered here incredibly frequently so that the truth is never told. However, if the entire planet is informed on multiple levels, things will be too hard to ignore." Rafa stood up again. "I´m sorry. I have to go now, it´s getting late. Would you mind?" he asked politely.

I tied the blindfold around my head obligingly and heard Rafa take the plates away from in front of me. I could smell the stale tobacco impregnated into his clothes, the damp vegetative odour of the jungle on his boots.

"Get some rest, my friend." With these words he slipped out of earshot and disappeared into the night before I could say anything.

On my own now, I was suddenly overcome with the tiredness I´d been fighting, hands were dragging me away from my chair, legs that didn´t belong to me took me over to the light switch by the door. I stumbled my way to the mattress in the perfect blackness. There was no light to be seen through the window, no traffic in the distance or music from neighbours. Just the sounds of the insects in the rain forest as I was sucked into the pit of a sleep that would pin my body down until the underwater light of the morning began to filter through the small window and the roosters announced a new day was beginning somewhere deep in the mountains of Chiapas.

*

The next morning, I woke from a profound, dreamless sleep unaware of the environment in which I´d slept. The blurred image of an unfamiliar ceiling started to filter through into my blank, confused mind. The faint smell of woodsmoke and the shrill buzz of insects did their best to try to remind me of where I´d awoken.

When I finally managed to focus on my surroundings and begin to recognise the austere furniture, bare walls and slop buckets of my enclosure, the previous day came flooding back to me and excitement surged through my veins.

Was I really now in the custody of the Ejército Zapatista de Liberación Nacional? How had I ended up in such a place? Why me? Who back in England would believe where I was right now? I quickly noticed that my breakfast was already waiting for me; eggs that were now stone cold, corn bread and a slice of papaya with a thin layer of fruit flies on it. I kicked myself for oversleeping and missing the visit from Rafa.

After breakfast I waited in anticipation for the knock on the door. It didn´t come. Disappointed to be alone I tried to distract myself by re-reading the twenty pages that made up *El Despertador* or flicking through Dan´s guidebook for the umpteenth time. I´d already filled both sides of the sheet of paper left for me, writing as small as I could in order to cram as much of what was in my head – and heart – down onto the limited space.

As morning turned into afternoon the knock finally came. I put on my blindfold and eagerly announced my readiness.

"I hope you rested well," Rafa said as he cleared my breakfast debris away and replaced it with my lunch. "You were sleeping very deeply this morning. I didn´t want to wake you up."

"I´m fine, thank you," I replied. I wanted him to sit down as quickly as possible so I could get on with, and finish, my lunch. Eventually, I heard him let out a sigh as he sat down on my unmade bed. He sounded tired again. It must´ve been another busy night doing whatever it was that a clandestine member of the EZLN did during the dark Chapanecan nights. My chair was already in position and I whipped off my face covering and started to devour the rice and beans. I listened as Rafa carefully prepared his pipe and soon the familiar smoke was floating my way. I left half of the food uneaten.

"So, what about you, Rafa?" Today was my turn to find out more about my captor. "Why are you fighting here?"

There was a long pause. I don´t know how but I knew that he was pleased with my unforeseen interrogation.

"That´s a good question," he replied finally. "What am I doing here? Well, firstly, let me tell you that I´m not indigenous. I´m *mestizo* – mixed race, caught between two worlds – like the vast majority of people in this country. Like Marcos too. But we´re not just middle-class white men doing as we wish among the indigenous, nor are we intellectuals that are telling them what to do either. Marcos, we, aren´t trying to lead them; we serve them. The indigenous leaders, the *comité* of the EZLN are the commanders. Marcos is just a sub-commander, that´s all, and he serves under them, serves all of them. And I, well, where Marcos goes, I go."

I pushed the remains of the rice and beans away from me, sorry for the waste but there was only one thing I was now interested in.

"We were not just filling the void in our own lives and trying to be heroes, no. We saw the injustices that the people were facing and the crimes that the government was committing, down here in Chiapas especially, and decided we had to act against the racism that was evident throughout the whole spectrum of society. But we also saw that racism exists, not just from the point of view of white people and *mestizos*, but from indigenous people too, many of whom hate themselves for who they are and are ashamed of their roots. We would be wrong to try to just speak to the wider world about our cause, we needed to realise that we too had to convince the very people themselves we´re trying to bring dignity to. These people, are people who are stuck in the middle in a kind of limbo. They feel that they are no longer connected to their past and their ancestors, but also feel that the present and the future is closed to them too."

"Isn´t there a lot of support from people in the cities? I mean people who are informed enough about things to know what´s happening here? People like you?" I asked, keen to see if Rafa would open up about who he was and where he came from.

"There are a few people, yes, but they´re still contributing to the current system, still voting for the same old political parties. They´re sympathetic and we appreciate their support no matter how small it may seem, but really, they can do very little unless they try to change the government and the system, and for them, alone and unarmed, they would end up like the students back in sixty-eight. The idea, my friend, is to fight to live, not end up as martyrs. Martyrs can do nothing if they´re dead."

It was clear Rafa wasn´t going to speak about himself personally. He was part of a bigger movement, a community trying to build a better future together, there was no place for Rafa the individual among the greater scheme of things.

"So, we came here." I could imagine him sweeping his arm in front of his body, gesturing to the jungle and mountains below him as he stood in a clearing in the forest or on a summit overlooking the land he protected. "We were completely alone here at first, just a handful of us, learning by ourselves to survive in the jungle. We needed to live the jungle, be accepted by it. We were cut off almost entirely from the rest of the World on this island, this desert, isolated in the middle of this sea of green, taken out of time itself."

I was alone too. But it was different. I didn´t have the escape of this beautiful solitude. Did Lina? Was she living her own desert in captivity, sheltering in the deep crevasses of the roots of the forest giants, marvelling at the bromeliads and orchids luring her to stay? Conversing with her own spirit walker, her own mysterious Rafa? Where was she?

"Ideologically and physically on our own, we were. We had practically no contact from the outside world, what little we knew filtered through when people brought us supplies occasionally or what we heard on the long-wave radio we had. At that time the EZLN was a ghost moving through the shadows of the mist and the darkness of the mountains. People didn´t know who we were, they thought we were thieves at first. But, little by little, we gained the trust of some of them with our honesty and sincerity, not like the politicians.

"We started to spend a lot of time around the indians, getting to know who they really are, their customs and beliefs. And the closer we became to the people, the more we saw the hate and death that had grown inside them. They had nothing but hopelessness, so we helped teach them self-defence, survival, how to fight against the ethnic cleansing, and the rape of women so common here. But we could only show them so much, and in the end, it was us that became the students. We were the teachers no more, learning from the men and women of the corn. People without a voice, without food, without hope."

I looked at the leftover rice and beans that had been brought to me so generously. I felt guilty about taking this away from someone who might need it more than me, a spoilt white kid here because he couldn´t stand being at home in his comfortable house, his comfortable life.

"More people gradually joined us and we became the men and women of the mountains who walk in the night, without a face, looking for a better way of life, a better way for them to govern themselves, better for all the people."

Chisp, chisp, chisp. Rafa inhaled deeply on his pipe.

"You know, my friend, they say that the indigenous people are not ready for democracy, but really they´re the most democratic people there are, making decisions based solely on the will of the majority. The majority decides what´s best for the community."

"But if the group imposes itself on the individual, isn´t this considered undemocratic?" Where had that come from? I´ve got no right to challenge this man´s philosophy. For heaven´s sake, I *agree* with it. With everything he´s telling me.

"You´re correct. I´m glad you pointed that out," Rafa replied, seemingly pleased that I was contributing something to the conversation at last. "For many things unanimity works and for others it doesn´t. But here, right now, we´re talking about survival and what´s in the best interests of the vast majority, so it has to be that way for now. Look, we know that we can´t provide a fool-proof answer to everything. We simply don´t have all the answers and we´re learning constantly about what´s the best thing for the largest number of people. That´s why we´re very receptive to all kinds of criticism and flexible to change. We´ll do whatever the people choose, what most of them want us to do."

He stood up slowly, he sounded like he was stifling a yawn.

"It´s been a challenge here. Most of the inherited lands of the cattle farmers have been in the same families since the seventeenth century. The land-owning *Caciques* use their corruption and violence with the help of their *guardias blancas*, their ruthless guns for hire. The indigenous leaders too, the p*rincipales*, can be a stumbling block. Although they´re not as easily manipulated by others as many people believe, the really traditional authorities in some communities are simply not so democratic. So, here we have another battle to be won; the fight against the traditional mindset of the communities to try to form a more modern, generic and open society that breaks away from traditional internal thinking. And to create something more global, away from the tribal leaders and shamans who control the people with primitive ceremonies and alcohol. We´ve tried to break these ancient ties, the ways of governing that are corrupt and controlled by the historic powerful families, *caciques,* land owners, large companies, corrupt local officials and tribal elders. You know, sometimes not all that´s traditional in the World is good my friend."

Rafa was now pacing slowly across the room as he´d done the previous evening.

"The willingness to start a new world for the marginalised grew from the bottom up and the path for them to govern themselves gradually opened. It was time for community democracy to break away from the traditional systems and corruption that have ruled these lands and others like them for so long.

"And so, the local system started to change. The inclusion of women was an incredibly important factor. Many joined our ranks; many more inspired their husbands to enlist. We helped organise the people to study, to fight, to resist. The indians became politicised and started to plot against the oppressors, the politicians and foreign companies." Rafa paused, seeming to read my mind once again. "I guess, Max, that you must be thinking that you don´t belong here, that you won´t be welcomed maybe. Well, I can tell you that from the communities there is no blame on the individual, no matter where you come from or who you are. There is no price to pay for someone else's past or other people´s greed. So please, don´t feel guilty about anything as they´re not going to treat you like a *conquistador*. They´ll be no rancour from them. If you commit, you´ll be welcomed."

I relaxed a little, only now noticing how tense I´d become.

"We don´t want the indigenous people to completely forget their past, we want them to learn from it and embrace it. However, we don´t want them to live like they´ve always done. Sure, it´s essential to take elements from their culture and traditions and keep them alive, learn from their ancestors, but they´ve got a right to TV, radio, electrical appliances, leisure facilities, and things like these. It *is* possible for different worlds to coexist in harmony."

Rafa was now standing close behind me. I could clearly hear his breathing just inches away from the back of my head.

"Many support us now on this new path. But many more don´t."

It was impossible to tell how he felt as he spoke these words. Anger, disappointment, regret? His calm delivery was a challenge for me, especially with my visual impediment. If only I could turn around and see his face, his expressions, his feelings.

"We need to open their eyes," Rafa added distantly.

"How?" I fired quickly.

There was a long pause. Rafa remained close to my back. I could smell him, feel him.

"Cover faces to be seen," he said finally. "And take up arms to be heard."

Night cast its heavy blanket over the Highlands, bringing with it a veil of mist and a chill that crept through the open window and under the large gaps at the bottom of the door. I´d killed as much time as I could while going over and over in my head the conversations I´d had with Rafa, at the same time looking forward to the next one that would hopefully begin shortly with a knock on the door and polite salutations.

Soon enough the sound of knuckles on wood preceded Rafa´s arrival. Facing the wall diligently, my eyes defiantly uncovered for the first time, my dinner of *tortillas* and beans was placed in front of me, along with the added bonus of a small tin of sardines. I remained steadfast with my stare ahead not wanting to risk the wrath of a man I still knew little about. He withdrew his arm and I thought I caught a glimpse of a gloved hand, a wristwatch maybe. I listened to Rafa´s footsteps behind me and waited for him to sit down on my bed. This time he didn´t. He stood somewhere on the other side of the room and I began to hear the rustle of paper as he presumably picked up *El Despertador*, which I´d forgotten was still on the mattress where I´d discarded it. I left the food guiltily untouched on the table.

"You know, you´re not going to find the answers to who we are in here, my friend." I heard the paper flop down again on the bed. "We may have written laws, given commands, declared war, but the EZLN is not the alternative. As I said before, we´re not looking for control, to take over, or worse still, to become politicians."

"Then what are you then?" I asked. I was looking for a definition; everything right now was still too vague. What were they going to do? If I was to be a part of this thing, if *we* were going to be involved, I needed to understand everything and all I was getting were philosophical soundbites.

"What are we?" asked Rafa, to me, himself, the room. "Democratic revolutionaries? Realistic dreamers? Patriots maybe? Whoever we are, it´s important to remember that we serve the indigenous people. We build clinics, organise vaccination campaigns, provide meeting places, sports facilities, schools, and many more things, but we´re also their armed branch. An army. It´s called the Ejército Zapatista de Liberación Nacional, but real Zapatism is undefinable, intangible. The indigenous people have their own reasons to join; others, like you Max, have their own personal motives. Everyone can take from it what they wish. What must be clear is that although it´s an indigenous movement, it aspires to not only be just that.”

“What does it asspire to be then?” I needed straight answers. I wasn´t intelligent enough to fathom out my own interpretation that I could take back home with me. I was here. And I was ready to fight. The walls of this room were closing in and getting too small for me now. I had to get out and release this rage somewhere and I needed to be fully convinced of the cause.

“Zapatism is an intuition for all the excluded people of the World. It´s not an ideology, as it won´t give every different person an answer to what each one of them is looking for. The principal ingredient you have to remember is that for us, ourselves, we want nothing. But for everybody; everything.”

I can do that. I have nothing anyway. I´ve lost the greatest thing I´ve ever had. I´ll give everything I have left.

“After the war, we´ll hand over to a civil movement where community democracy will open up the political system and restructure the whole nation. There will be a world into which fits many other worlds.”

I couldn´t help but feel like I was listening to a speech by Colosio, although instead of a crowd of cheering supporters, I was the sole lucky recipient of the words. Don´t just waste them here with me, Rafa. I know you don´t want to be a politician but your talents are wasted as a *guerrillero* – if that´s what you really are.

“We´ll graft a branch of us into society and the communities. Give collective control over the reigning authorities. Create a more participative democracy. Strengthen links with fellow Mexicans, *all*

Mexicans. Integration not separation is what should happen, and combine the community and the nation as one. This rebellion of the excluded that the World is going to be witness to should be the rebirth of the nation. All nations."

I was hanging on every word that Rafa was saying, transfixed.

"We just want to be on the minds of the political powers, affect the economy and leave a mark on society. If we survive, we'll disappear, into the dark of the night, to the mountains, the jungle again if we achieve our objectives. But we'll be watching and waiting to see if things change."

"But the government knows about the EZLN, doesn't it? The army has already destroyed a camp in the jungle, haven't they?"

"That's true, yes. The government knows we're here, knows we exist, but they don't want to do anything until NAFTA comes into effect. They wouldn't want to do anything to sully their glossy new image in the eyes of the watching world. A revolution shouldn't be part of a first-world country, no? Who would want to be in partnership with a nation in the middle of a civil war?" Rafa laughed quietly. "You could say that NAFTA is our sworn enemy, but right now, it's also our dearest friend."

He moved away from me and I could hear his boots shuffle across the floor, backwards and forwards again, mentally and physically on edge as he was.

"We want the eyes of the World to know what's happening here. And they will, believe me. You know, Salinas is an incredibly smart man, but he's underestimated what's coming." Rafa warned, his placid voice just starting to sound a little threatening.

"What is coming?" I asked, knowing full well the plans to march on Mexico City, defeat the army and liberate the people.

"A fight. But the conflict is just the first step," Rafa answered. "We're not looking for a revolution or a coup but recognition for the social classes that are suffering under this current government and system. We need to humanise the World so that everyone has the opportunity to have a dignified existence."

Rafa had moved back close behind me again as he'd done several times before. If I turned around, I'd be able to touch him easily.

"You know, my friend, the indigenous people are already condemned to a silent death. If they're going to die, they'll die this way. They were left without options and their only way now is to come out. To fight. With the problems of being stripped of their land, their squalid living conditions and the abuse of their rights, there's no other way than to take up arms. But these arms will only take us part of the way. You must know that the greatest weapons we really possess are reason and truth."

"But if they don't believe you? If they don't believe what you say the goal really is?"

"After we have their attention through force, it will be the turn of dialogue. Only dialogue will lead to peace in the end. The only real thing we have to offer is our word, and if you know anything about us now, my friend, you know we keep our word. However, if they don't believe us, we also have the sword and we will have no other choice but to convince them in another way."

"But if you're violent, you're just as bad, aren't you?"

"No," Rafa answered quickly. "The difference is that our violence is reactionary. An accumulation of the rage of injustice. Theirs is carefully measured, a well-thought-out plot against the marginalised. I said that we're an army, it's true, but an army fighting for a pacific option. War is peace."

"And freedom is slavery," I responded automatically.

There was a long pause as we recognised our mutual literary knowledge; a bond had been further forged between us. Rafa inhaled deeply behind me.

"We need determined, prepared, committed people. I want to know how far you're willing to go, Max?"

"How far should I go?" I asked.

Rafa placed his hands gently on my shoulders.

"To die if necessary."

As if sensing the tension that had taken control of my body Rafa released his hands slowly from me. He walked over towards the door and I heard it creak on its hinges as it was opened. Seconds passed as Rafa paused silently in the doorway.

"Death is not so terrible as it sounds, my friend," he said in his calm, composed voice before closing the door behind him, leaving me alone, his words crashing around inside my head.

To die, if necessary? It´s true. It doesn´t actually sound so bad.

Players would stand in the centre of the court and use a solid rubber ball that could bounce off the sloping stone walls on each side. Traditionally, in the pre-Hispanic ball game "pelota", the ball was not hit with the hands, but rather the hips, although in some sites in Mesoamerica, such as here in El Tajín, sticks and gloves have been found, suggesting that the game actually had several different variations.

The largest playing area at El Tajín, the South Ball Court, is notable for its bas-relief panels depicting scenes that allude to myths and rites associated with "pelota", such as the sacrifice by decapitation carried out after the game or–

I put the guidebook down and hurried over to the table, ready to hear what the next step in my fledging relationship with Rafa and the EZLN would be. The thought that he may be able to tell me something about Lina was there too, gnawing away at me, although I knew I wasn't about to ask. I wouldn't be able to bear the disappointment, hear Rafa's apologies. I buried the feelings, cauterized my wounds. I put on my blindfold, frowning as I did so.

Something wasn't right. I'd heard three knocks instead of the usual four, hadn't I? Softer too. The door opened and instead of the heavy boot-clad steps I'd become used to, I heard a light shuffle of feet across the concrete floor. As the food was put in front of me, I rebelliously uncovered my eyes ready to face the punishment for my blatant disobedience.

It was, of course, not Rafa, but an elderly indigenous woman who'd delivered my evening meal. She said nothing and just smiled a warm, toothless smile at me, nodded and gestured to the food before going about replacing my makeshift bathroom buckets. I watched her as she made herself busy, trying to avoid my curious stare, but inquisitive enough to glance up at me as she cleaned and tidied the room. Once her duties were complete, she shuffled out again in her dried palm leaf sandals without saying a word.

Why wasn't he here with me? Didn't he want to talk to me anymore? Did he have some awful news he couldn't tell me? Maybe he´s been tasked with something important. But isn´t he just someone who´s looking after me and not part of the actual army itself? All these thoughts overlapped one another as I chewed absently on my dinner, my mind distracting my tastebuds away from what was on my plate. I finished what I´d been given and paced around the room as Rafa had done, preaching to the converted as he told me about the philosophy of what the EZLN was trying to do. What *he* was going to do.

An eternity later, three soft knocks announced the arrival of the ancient woman again and, dodging eye-contact, she walked past me towards the table to retrieve my empty plate. She picked it up with a branch-like arm and exchanged it with something else she´d been carrying across her chest. She smiled again as she made her way to the door and I was left as alone as I could ever be, a pile of plain white sheets of paper left on the old wooden table; a reminder that Rafa was still present through the deeds of the elderly indigenous woman now tasked with my well-being.

*

The next three days I was in purgatory. Seventy-odd hours of fitful sleep and dreams of feathered snakes. Four hundred and something minutes of re-reading the familiar material that had been packed for me in the outside pocket of my backpack. Nearly two-hundred and sixty thousand seconds of filling the pages that my new housekeeper was constantly bringing me when she came to give me my food or clean the room.

Time passed slowly; time raced by at breakneck speed. I could see myself from above as I slept. I was an insect crawling on the ceiling, my body armoured with overlapping obsidian discs. I was missing a leg, smoke pouring from the stump where the limb had once been. I brought the food and placed it in front of me and then went to be with my family in a hut somewhere not too far from here. I ran through the jungle, picking off leeches, a gun in my hand, a jaguar clawing at my heels. I was the jaguar. I was a tree. I was *all* the trees, and plants and life on Earth. I was Mother Nature. Pachamama. I was the Big Bang, the creation, the creator, the destroyer. I could see everything and nothing at the same time.

I let my mind take control of my body as it seemed to be able to chalk off the hours of waiting much more effectively than I ever consciously could.

Am I?

Am I what?

I´m waiting, nothing more, nothing less.

And while I´m waiting?

*

I attempted conversation with the delicate Margarita, as I dubbed my only present link to the outside world.

"E´ch´uk abu´un, mu jna´li ak´opiké," she replied in a voice as creaky as the door through which she appeared thrice daily. A phrase that she repeated with a toothless smile whenever I spoke to her. *E´ch´uk abu´un, mu jna´li ak´opiké*, etched into my lexis forever, not knowing what it meant but in love with the exoticism of the words all the same and the kindness of their delivery.

Three days. It could have been three weeks for all I knew. I stared at the light bulb that attracted the various insects that were my constant companions, my allies. I got to know them all very well. The mosquitos, the impossibly delicate lacewings, the hard green beetles that flew in crazy circles and crashed into whatever was in their path with a loud smack. Some fed on me. I let them.

As I lay on my mattress and watched the familiar entomological air display, a new sound began to enter my ears. A rumbling, faint at first but rapidly growing louder outside. A landslide? No, it hadn´t rained that much for any risk of that. Horses. It was unmistakably the sound of horses. Two, maybe three, I don´t know, but they were loud, and getting closer every second. They stopped outside the building and I heard the clink of metal on bridles and then feet landing with a thud on the ground as they dismounted. Seconds later the door was flung open without a knock or the opportunity to creakily announce a guest´s arrival into my humble abode.

There were three of them. All wearing a uniform of coffee-coloured shirts, multi-pocketed combat trousers and high black boots. Strings of bullets and shotgun cartridges formed an X across their chests and rifles were slung over their shoulders, the barrels protruding vertically from behind their backs. Their faces were covered with black balaclavas – *Cover faces to be seen. Take up arms to be heard.* – and they wore faded green military style caps.

Two of the three were almost identical in stature but there was one obvious difference from the third that was impossible to ignore. The *guerillero* in the centre stood almost a foot taller than his two companions and despite the balaclava, I could see that around his eyes his skin was much paler than those of his more diminutive comrades. He fumbled with something in his pocket.

Chisp, chisp, chisp. Smoke flowed in my direction and the familiar smell soon washed over me once more, purifying me.

"Rafa?"

He took another puff of his elegant wooden pipe. Sherlock Holmes in battle fatigues.

"I´m much better looking," the tallest *guerrillero* replied, his seductive brown eyes full of humour. He undid the buttons of a bulging pocket in the military vest he was wearing and silently handed a piece of black material to me. I unfolded it. It was a balaclava. I was one of them. I was part of the EZLN.

All of my knowledge, everything that I´d ever known or learnt or done in my life was now useless. It was time to walk into the night, live and learn the jungle, be taught by it, embraced and punished by it, to learn how to survive. How to help others to survive. This was my time. The time when I knew what, at last, I had to do. The time when I finally met the real Subcomandante Marcos.

The visit was brief and I was left with too many unanswered questions swirling around my mind. I wanted to know everything; the past, the present and the future. *My* future. But Marcos left almost as quickly as he´d arrived and he – along with one of the two indigenous comandantes – was soon swallowed up by the jungle and out of reach.

The remaining soldier, Comandante Javi, was to look after me, take me to wherever it was that I was going. He said almost nothing as I quickly packed away my meagre possessions for the mystery journey but I could see through the narrow slit in his balaclava that he wasn´t impressed that I actually take along anything at all. From out of nowhere, he produced a pair of battered old boots, threw them down at my feet and gestured with a nod of his head for me to put them on. I didn´t hesitate for a second and quickly slipped off my equally worn trainers. Amazingly – or deliberately – they were the perfect size and despite their appearance, were far more comfortable than I could ever have dreamt of.

Outside, two slim chestnut-coloured horses were waiting for us. I attached my backpack to the saddle of the one allocated to me and then paused in order to observe where I´d been held captive for the last few endless days.

The building in which I´d been housed was nothing more than a simple concrete box located in a small clearing in the jungle. There were two other structures close by; wooden huts that passed as houses for the two families that presumedly lived there. The chickens I´d heard clucking and scrabbling in the earth through the small window in my room pecked around at the ground close by. Smoke was snaking out of a metal tube acting as a chimney from one of the shacks, my own private chef now preparing food solely for her family. I would no longer be a burden, no longer take food from their mouths.

I mounted my horse with difficulty, my equine experience nothing more than a couple of donkey rides at a holiday camp as a child, the stiffness of my body from six days confined to ten square metres not exactly helping with my agility.

Clicking to his horse but without uttering a word to me, Javi led us down the track that the 4x4 had brought me up, although we didn´t follow this for long and he veered off at a right angle and disappeared into the dense undergrowth that ran along its sides. My horse knew where it was going and tailed my silent guide without the need for me to manipulate the reins that were limp and useless in my hands. I turned my head quickly, nostalgically longing for one final glimpse at what was now a historic place in my life. Would there be a plaque attached to the facade one day celebrating my residence there?

Margarita was now standing in front of the shack with the smoking chimney, flanked on either side by at least two generations of women and children. There was a conspicuous absence of men. She raised a fragile hand and waved at me but before I could respond, the light of the day faded and I was embraced by the arms of the damp forest that would hide us as we prepared for the impending war and an uncertain future.

Comandante Javi led us deep into the jungle along a track, which although hardly wide enough for our underweight horses, looked as if it was well trodden. A secret supply route maybe, a link between army camps? There was no need for him to use the machete that hung from his saddle to clear branches or vines out of the way and we made what I considered to be relatively quick progress, although I doubted that I knew very much about these things.

The cool air of the Highlands gradually became warmer and despite the rough terrain which often obliged us to climb hills along the path, there was no doubt that we were, overall, descending. The jungle was thick on both sides and there was nothing left for me to do other than face Javi's back, complete with the rifle and bullets that weighed down his small frame. I, on the other hand, had nothing more on than the fresh set of clothes I'd changed into that morning that had begun to be soaked through as we went further down into the soupy air of the lower reaches of the rainforest. The balaclava I was now wearing, which at a higher altitude had been something of a comfort, now seemed like it was sucking energy directly out of my skull, every bead of sweat adding to the vice that was gripping my cranium and shrinking my throbbing head.

After what must've been at least two hours we found ourselves at the bottom of a steep slope beside a fast-flowing stream. Javi stopped, dismounted and gestured for me to do the same. Soon the horses were quenching their thirst and Javi was crouching down by the creek filling an olive-coloured canteen that had been swinging – like his machete – hypnotically from the saddle of his horse. He thrust it my way. Through his balaclava I was sure that he was glaring angrily at me and annoyed at the job that he'd either volunteered for, or more likely, been given. I took just a few small sips, not wanting to give fuel to his fire and handed him back the canteen, which he snatched roughly from my hand.

"There have been tourists here before," he said suddenly, taking me aback at what may well have been the first real words I´d heard him utter. He spoke a high-pitched, truncated Spanish and it was evident it wasn´t his native tongue.

"Oh. OK," was all I could answer, surprised and a little confused at what I´d just heard.

"They came here also looking for something. They asked too many questions about the people here. About us." He screwed the top back on the canteen without drinking and attached it again to the saddle of his horse. "We´ve had problems with them. They are not to be trusted."

I felt Javi´s jet-black eyes penetrate me for several long seconds. Was this the moment that I´d become insect food? Javi turned around and thankfully mounted his horse as smoothly as if he´d done it ten thousand times, then crossed the stream and began to climb the slope on the other side. I felt threatened, my stomach acidic and my legs weak, but I did the same as my guide – albeit a little more slowly – and we were off through the thick jungle again.

The canopy above us did its best to hide the hour of our journey but the diminishing subaqueous light told us secretly that the day was coming to an end. We plodded on, my sweat running down in rivers, merging with the glistening surface of my horse´s hide. The atmosphere was damp and I could imagine myself pulling leeches off my pale body, uncoagulated blood running down my skin, diluted on its course by my perspiration; condensation on a cold beer glass.

The light was grey and the intense green of the jungle had been drained from our surroundings. I looked at the passing vegetation and she was there. She was everywhere. Her hair the twisting vines that strangled their hosts. Her eyes, the sunken knots on the trunks of the giant trees. Her arms the pale branches reaching out for my embrace. Mist began to swirl around us and she was taken from my grasp. The jungle at my side merged into one indecipherable barrier, hiding her away and all I could see was the back of Comandante Javi and his horse as they parted the wispy air that blocked their path. The odour of burning wood began to invade our senses suggesting that a village – or at least a hut or two – wasn´t far away up ahead.

The track that had held us in its clutches soon widened out and we emerged into a clearing a little larger than the one we´d set off from several hours before. On the windless air smoke hung, penetrating our clothes, absorbed by the wetness of the material that clung to us. Chickens and dogs littered the ground in front of the huts, washing was draped from lines strung between trees. Upon hearing us arrive an elderly man appeared from one of the wooden huts, studying us suspiciously, distrust on his face. We dismounted and Javi quickly pulled me to one side as we tied our horses up.

"The people help us, give us food," he said. "But they do not speak Spanish here." I thought of Margarita and the beautiful language she responded to me in.

We were welcomed into the old man´s home, its sole room performing the function of kitchen, living space and sleeping quarters. Gaps – many themselves larger than the wooden boards used to construct the walls – let in the remains of the dying light, hungry insects and the heavy smoke from outside. Comandante Javi spoke to the old man who´d greeted us coldly, while his wife and daughter busily prepared something to eat through a mix of worried and inquisitive glances. Small children, as dark as the developing night, crawled around on the dirt floor of the hut at our feet, mingling with a litter of whimpering new-born puppies, their eyes still glued tightly shut.

Soon we were eating the simple meal that had been generously laid out for us, every mouthful taking me a step closer to a sleep that I feared would be littered with strange dreams and insect bites. But for now, with the smoke deterring the bugs and the hot food extinguishing the nerves in my stomach, I was more comfortable than I ever would´ve imagined.

As the women cleaned the dishes and began their endless daily ritual of preparing children to go to sleep and the food for the following day, we were ushered outside by the village elder. I followed Javi and our host at a short distance, keen to listen to the dialect they were using, albeit without being able to understand a word. Other families appeared at the entrance to their own huts, eager to see who the visitors were. After a short conversation full of polite noises from Javi and what looked like angry gesticulations from the elder, my guide led us back to where we´d eaten earlier; the rest of the family that had been there before now nowhere to be seen. By the light of the dying fire, I saw Javi lie down on a blanket on one side of the room.

"You should take your boots off every day," he told me stiffly. "The jungle does not forgive any weakness." I did as instructed, without the slightest hesitation.

We lay in silence for some time as the embers of the fire waned into the darkness; burning fireflies that guided me into a realm of blessed unconsciousness. Far above our heads gods and demons stirred and came alive and only the stars kept rocks from becoming beasts that stalk the deadly night.

*

I was awoken the next morning by the sound of activity in the kitchen just a metre or so from where I´d laid my head. The early morning light was starting to enter through the huge gaps in the walls and the fire had either been rekindled or made from scratch and was heating a large pot that was suspended above it.

The two women who´d prepared last night´s meal were busy getting together more food; *tortillas* and some thick liquid that was being stirred slowly in the pan that hovered above the fire. Javi was nowhere to be seen. I stretched, put my boots on and stood up. Seeing that I´d now started to join the land of the living, the younger of the women timidly offered me a plate of *tamales*, which I accepted gratefully, before she spooned a ladleful of the hot liquid that had been simmering above the fire into a wooden cup. After finishing the *tamales,* I sipped on the drink I´d been given; a thick, bittersweet mixture with a hint of cinnamon. My body was grateful for the calories and began to revive itself as Javi appeared at the entrance to the hut.

"We have to go now," he said to me robotically.

I finished my delicious breakfast as quickly as I could, thanked my hosts sincerely and followed Javi to the horses, which he´d already prepared for our departure. I looked around me at the oasis in the middle of the jungle. These people would probably die in this patch of earth; the act of living was nothing more than a habit they´d grown accustomed to. Their children would be born here but under what circumstances? Their fate was unknown. Would they stay here? Be moved away, their land reclaimed? What would happen to them? Would this revolution actually change anything?

I undid the straps on my backpack and took out the copy of *El Despertador,* Dan´s guidebook, my passport, the wad of pages I´d filled with heartfelt notes, and the toothbrush that Marcos had given to me and put them all into one of the smaller saddle bags on my horse. I held the camera I´d seldom used on my adventures with Dan, weighing up how useful it would be in my new life. Eventually, I opened up the back and tore out the cartridge inside, not caring about exposing the unused section of film attached. I placed the camera back among the majority of my possessions and slipped the roll of film into one of my trouser pockets. I then unfastened the backpack from the saddle and walked over with it to the elderly man who´d greeted us the previous evening and was now waiting impatiently to see us off. I put it down in front of him and bowed, hands together, in the most indigenous manner I could muster, hoping my gesture wouldn´t patronise him in any way. Here were my clothes and other possessions from a previous life that I´d no longer need, for what they´re worth. I pointed to the backpack and smiled. He looked down at it slowly and then back up at me, his expression didn´t change.

Satisfied with my little act of generosity, I mounted my horse next to Javi, who'd been waiting and watching the scene with interest. Unsurprisingly, he said nothing, dug his heels into the side of his animal and we were funnelled again into the mouth of the forest that awaited us.

*

I don't know if it was my imagination but there was something different about Comandante Javi today. I wasn't presented with only his back for company hour after hour; instead, he glanced backwards over his shoulder when we negotiated a tricky section of the path or if a low hanging branch made for a potentially hazardous obstacle. He offered me water at regular intervals and although he didn't utter a single word in my direction, he appeared either concerned about my well-being or there was a refound commitment to his remit of bringing me through the jungle unscathed.

After several hours of hot and sticky riding that had left me numb past the point of pain, I heard the sound of fast flowing water. We soon arrived at a shallow river, punctuated by rocks that formed swirling eddies fed by waters plunging down a small waterfall just a few metres upstream. It was idyllic, an unexpected nirvana complete with pool suitable for bathing at the foot of the waterfall.

Javi had already dismounted and was retrieving something from one of his saddle bags. I followed suit, almost losing my balance on my rubber legs as I hit the ground. Javi held my arm until I found my feet again and then handed me some *tamales* left over from breakfast before finding a flat rock next to the pool to eat lunch. I sat close by, willing him to speak to me, his silence a temptation hard to resist.

Above us, a flash of yellow and orange stole my attention as a toucan searched for fruit above. Near my feet a line of leafcutter ants shouldered huge chunks of foliage as they made their way back to their colony. By the side of the river, Javi was poking at what appeared to be excrement.

"Jaguars," he said, sensing my curiosity.

I looked around me. "Umm, is it dangerous?"

"No. Not with the horses here," he replied without looking my way. "And they only hunt at night."

At some other point of my life I would´ve been relieved not to be on the menu, but after being picked up by an outlawed army on the side of the road near Palenque and then having lived to tell the tale, I´d somehow lost most of my fear of dying. Besides, death by jaguar would have to be quite high up on the list of interesting ways to go.

I began to eat the food Javi had given me, although the searing heat of the day had sapped away my appetite. If only I could take this damn balaclava off, jump into the water and plunge my head into its cool depths. He´d already seen my face hadn´t he? But Javi still wore his and I wanted to follow his example and do nothing to jeopardise my involvement with the EZLN.

I cleared my throat. "Umm ... is it possible to tell me where we are?" I asked politely.

Javi paused for a moment before speaking, fixing me with eyes as dark as the pool that sat invitingly at our feet.

"We are on our way to La Graciosa," he replied, before falling into silence again.

Right. That really didn´t help me out that much. He picked up the jaguar faeces and held it close to his nose and then let it crumble through his fingers.

"The land is our mother. She looks after us, gives us life. We need to respect her, cherish her." He stared across to the other side of the river. "The mountain and the jungle is ours, the night is ours, and that is what they do not know." He looked my way and held me in his stare. "They want to take it away from us with their arrogance and greed. And they already have. We have been left without land, or the land that is left is impossible for us to use. First we were told that our gods are not true gods. Then the big companies come and destroy the forests. The government creates reserves, says it is protecting the environment, but we are told we cannot touch the trees, cut them down to plant what we need to eat. If we do, we have to pay or go to prison."

I thought of Lina and the first time I´d heard her explain this to me in her classroom in San Miguel. How I wanted to see her, be with her again and touch her soft skin with the back of my hand, tuck a curl behind one ear, kiss her. This, this moment being here now seemed so unreal, hearing things from the mouth of one of the very people she´d told me about just a few short weeks ago, *days* ago. And now, I was here in this forgotten, tainted paradise listening to Comandante Javi explain first-hand what was happening to him and his people. Lina had designed this, she´d planned this somehow and I was sure that she was watching and smiling a satisfied smile at what she´d done.

"What we need is not a big place. Not a small place either. We just need a place, nothing more. A dignified place among our nation, to be treated fairly, as equals, have rights as everyone deserves, to take us into account and treat us with respect. Not just be the ones who are exploited by others all the time."

Javi spoke slowly and clearly in his indigenous accent and I had no problem understanding him. I didn´t know if it was for my benefit, so I could comprehend exactly what he wanted to say, or if it was his way of speaking his second language.

"We do not just want to only eat *pozol, tortillas* and *frijoles*, we want the right to eat meat, feed the children properly so they are not sick. Make a better life for them. We need to protect them, nurture them. We are not going to hand down our desperation to our children. Our children will learn about their ancestors´ old customs, respect for elders, culture, nature. But also about the modern World too and how we can live together. The old and the new."

He stood up and washed his hands in the pool in front of our picnic spot. He cupped some water in one hand and then wet his face under his balaclava, his identity remaining a secret.

"We have divided some communities, but you must know that we have never confronted people who do not agree with our ideas. Some people in the towns and villages are against us because we ask for donations. Some people have left because of this. But we are looking after their properties and animals and will welcome them back if they decide to return," Javi explained facing the waterfall.

"Those people last night. Do they support you or are they just following the laws of the EZLN?" I asked.

Javi turned around slowly, menacingly, although it may have just been his calm and placid nature that was controlling his movements.

"Most indigenous people will not fight because they are dying anyway. They are fighting their own battles against disease and poverty. But we can."

He walked past me and began to prepare for our onward journey. I again did the same. As I was fiddling with some straps on the saddle he approached and stood close to me.

"We do not want war, but they do not see us like human beings, what we are, what is ours. If we do not fight, nobody will. If they do not respond to our demands, nobody will. Our gods prepare us to leave this life. So, death is not a problem for us. If necessary, we will give our lives. That is the way it is."

Comandante Javi didn´t speak passionately. He didn´t express himself melodramatically and there were no literary quotes highlighting a poetic discourse like Subcomandante Marcos. Marcos was fighting for the indigenous people, it´s true, but there was something in the steely delivery of Javi´s words and a quiet determination built on loss of life and destroyed hope that set him apart from the *mestizo* that had convinced me to fight a battle that on the surface wasn´t even mine.

"We are fighting to defeat war. We became soldiers so that one day soldiers are not needed. But the people will only listen to us if we have guns. If we invade their world. Come out of the jungle and into the city where they can see us. This is not revenge. We do not have hate inside. If someone attacks us, we will fight back."

Despite the sticky heat of the jungle, I was chilled at the cold words I was hearing. How can he not want revenge? I wanted it. I desired it for all that had been done to these people. All that had been done to me.

"When we come down from the mountains and out of the jungle people will see what is behind the masks. We will come out and fight them and tell them to look at us and see who we are. They will realise and then learn that our fight is the fight of everyone."

He mounted his horse with the agility of a gymnast. I struggled up into my own saddle, silently cursing the endless hours spent bouncing up and down over the last two days.

"You need to learn too," Javi said to me once I´d made myself as comfortable as possible, trying to hide a grimace as I did so.

"What? To fight?"

"No. That there is a lack of health, food, education, hygiene, freedom, democracy, independence and peace. And when peace comes you need to learn that the war is not finished. Peace means solving the problems for our comrades in the villages in other parts of the country, in all the country and for all Mexicans."

Javi was nowhere near as eloquent or captivating as Marcos, but I was left rattled by his speech and the precise delivery of each word. He squeezed his heels into his horse and set off towards the river. On the point of crossing, he tugged on the reins and stopped at the water´s edge. He turned his head around, somewhere above a howler monkey screamed, birds flapped in the uppermost branches and the constant crash of the waterfall played out its eternal soundtrack. Javi pinned me down with his eyes.

"All we can do is fight. To use arms so we can live. Then we will see what happens."

He released me from his stare before turning around and then guiding his horse across the rapids and towards the narrow track that would lead us, eventually, to La Graciosa.

A blackout. A pause in my consciousness when something else takes over. I´ve suffered them before and have woken up in places that are unfamiliar to me surrounded by people that I´ve never met. They speak to me as if they know me, know who I am, ask me questions that the look in their eyes tells me I should know the answer to. They talk of times we´ve shared together, things we´ve done, but I don´t know them, I´ve never seen them before and I try to leave as quickly as possible, asking the nearest passer-by I can find where I am and how to get home. Sometimes I wake up miles away from where I should be, way outside my familiar territory, an urge to just get to somewhere I recognise in order to stem the rising panic that I try to conceal from all those staring eyes. Objects appear too. Things I can´t remember ever acquiring or even liking just appear in my hands. I have no recollection of how they get there, where they come from.

And now I´m on a horse. I´m sweating and itching from the bites I have all over my body. I look at my hands, they´re filthy, red raw, not mine. I´m stifling hot, my head covered with something clinging to my face, although I can still somehow see. I can see the trees around me, hear the hum of insects. Fruit seeds are falling from the trees above, thrown down, discarded by monkeys. Higher still a shadow passes over, gliding and soaring in the sky, watching our every move.

I feel the heat take over me, pushing me down on this animal I´m sitting on. Flies are battered away by its eyelashes. It´s annoyed but carries on its steady rhythm. There´s someone in front of me. I can see him through the sting of sweat that runs into my eyes. A gun. Bullets. This can´t be happening, I must be somewhere else, in hospital again perhaps, waiting for a specialist to come and tell me there´s nothing else they can do for me, that they´ve done their best and now time will have to tell.

He´s wearing a ski mask. That must be what´s covering my head too, making me so hot. So unbearably hot. The daggers in my head are coming back, piercing my skull as the drill once did, twisting deeper into me. Someone doesn´t want me here, not now. I can feel hands pushing me away in all directions, folding me up until all that I am is the agony on the side of my head. I crawl into the wound, into myself, implode. The heat dies away. The horse is gone, the trees are gone.

I am alone.

We came to a road. The first sign of any kind of life since I left my backpack at the feet of the elderly man that had been our unenthusiastic host the previous evening. I´d lost track of the hours we´d spent riding through the dense jungle today. Was it possible that I´d fallen asleep on the back of my horse without falling off? A limp body slung over the back of a horse with no name? A corpse with no name. Anything´s possible now. We stopped at the intersection where our path crossed the rutted tracks of the road. I could see that the path continued into the jungle on the other side but Javi steered his horse to the right and we began to follow the wider dirt track up a gentle winding slope. After the confines of the claustrophobic forest the space afforded to us by our new route left me feeling exposed and vulnerable. However, as we rode at a trot, faster than we´d done on our journey so far, I appreciated the light breeze that was starting to cool my overheated body down.

Not far up from where our path had emerged, I saw that a roadblock made of black rocks and long branches was standing in our path. It was manned by a small group of people wearing similar uniforms to Javi, but instead of black balaclavas their faces were covered with red neckerchiefs, bandanas that indicated that they were still part of the EZLN. Javi greeted them with a few words in a language unfamiliar to me and we were let through. Suspicious eyes followed me as I passed.

Soon we arrived at the collection of buildings that made up the village where we were to stay the night. The majority were simple wooden houses arranged around the widest part of the road but in the centre of the village stood a large concrete structure adorned with graffiti and colourful murals where Emiliano Zapata and Che Guevara vied for pride of place. Slogans – *¡Tierra y Libertad! ¡Viva EZLN! ¡Por la Vida!* – were painted on any space not taken up by images of masked indigenous people tending to patches of crops, invariably corn.

We dismounted and tied our horses up near a trough half full of murky water, which they began to lap up eagerly. There were a surprising number of people on the streets and in front of the larger concrete building, the majority wearing the same red scarves that the men on the road block had sported. Some too had the black balaclava I´d grown used to tolerating during the heat of the day. Among them were a large proportion of children and women, their brightly-embroidered dresses and skirts in sharp contrast to the symbol of resistance that covered their faces and heads.

"We wear masks not only to protect our identity but as a sign of solidarity with the collective Zapatista movement," Javi explained to me noticing how I´d obviously been staring at the people around us and their attire.

There was a steady stream of villagers entering the settlement´s most important structure and we quickly joined them. Inside, chairs were laid out facing a makeshift stage, most of which had already been taken. Javi sat me down somewhere near the back of the hall and then took up a position at the table on the raised platform at the front where a small group of other men and women in masks and uniform were beginning to settle down. Soon the room was full of people, young, old, men, women, babies. I guessed around a quarter wore some kind of face covering in support of the EZLN, even some of the very youngest.

For the next hour or so, I sat and listened to the cascade of indigenous dialogue as the representatives of the Ejército Zapatista de Liberación Nacional spoke to the crowd. Occasionally, Javi read through some official document in Spanish, rattling it off as quickly as possible in order for it to be translated into the local languages of the area. Hands in the crowd rose in unison in the many pauses in the meeting as motions were voted on and unanimity was reached.

It was almost impossible for me to follow with any coherence what was being approved and so, with my attention wandering, I found myself increasingly staring around the room. It was without doubt used as a school – among its many other functions. Pictures by young children were pinned to the walls depicting more crudely the same elements of the murals that embellished the outside. Freedom, dignity, and the right to work their own land were the striking themes that were displayed for all to see. Brightly-painted images of *campesinos*, some bent over working the earth, others wearing masks and raising a fist, made for entertaining viewing until the meeting was brought to an end.

As people began to file silently out of the hall, Javi gestured for me to come over to where he´d participated in the meeting. He introduced me quickly to the other comandantes at the main table, who greeted me warmly in Spanish, asking me my name and where I was from with genuine interest. There was no need to ask me what I was doing here. The introductions over, Javi led me from the hall, seeming almost embarrassed about the babysitting duties he had to carry out and the burden he was lugging around the jungle with him.

Night was falling fast and groups of birds squawked and jostled for position in the trees around the village, filling the humid evening air with their violent shrieks. The jungle is never silent. The jungle can never be silenced. As long as these people live.

"It´s a school, no?" I felt I had to say something but why didn´t I ask about what they were voting on? Something important, not the obvious banal rubbish I usually come out with.

Javi nodded. "It should be, but the teachers who are supposed to work in the region do not come. Some, at best, only come once or twice a week. So, we try to teach the children as well as we can. Most do not know Spanish, so it is difficult for them to find a job if they want to leave the village. Those that have left for the big cities are ashamed of where they come from and will not come back. Many of them do not even help their families anymore."

I looked at the small children who were running around nearby, their bare feet kicking up dust that would be transformed into thick mud in the rainy season. Right now they seemed happy, excited by the amount of people that had come from nearby villages and hamlets to participate in the meeting. Nature or nurture? What would they become with a different opportunity to live their lives?

"What can be done to help with the education here?" I asked.

"We want real schools. Real promises. The government has until now pacified the people with promises, neutralised them with campaigns that are not real. But we have something that the government does not have. We have the participation of the community to make decisions. The people decide in the villages."

Javi faced me and his usual hard stare had been replaced by something more serene and unfamiliar to me.

"It is beautiful the way democracy works in the communities. It is probably the only healthy thing we have left in Mexico. The rest of the country could learn from this. It has changed the way that the *principales* think since the Zapatistas came here. Now they take more notice of the women and young people. They can vote now on what happens in the communities. The women also spoke in the meetings and then convinced their husbands to stop drinking alcohol and that there was something worth fighting for. It has not been easy for them and many faced abuse from their husbands. The companies often pay the indigenous people in alcohol and it takes a long time to change people. But we did it, the women did it, and that is how it is now."

The light had almost disappeared since we left the school and I knew that it would soon be time to eat something and then go to sleep straight after, wake up early and then take the path again to La Graciosa. Although I could – and wanted to – learn from these people, stay with them and observe their way of life and their customs, and then give back what I could, there was something else that I was destined for. Something Lina had set in motion and now something that Marcos wanted me to do. The reason why the reluctant Comandante Javi was leading me through the jungle.

"You will eat and sleep here tonight," Javi told me stopping outside a tiny hut without a door. He left me to make myself as comfortable as possible on the blankets that had been provided for me, which lay on a dry grass mat on the dirt floor. Several minutes later he came back with a plate of hot food and a large calabash gourd full of fresh water.

"I will wake you up in the morning," he said abruptly and made to leave. Something stopped him and he turned around again, as he had done in the jungle earlier that day, his face invisible in the shadows. "Sleep well," he added as if prompted by a voice inside his head. I knew whose voice that was.

*

I was glad to be alone. I ate in the darkness and sat listening to the sounds around me. I could hear the faint murmur of people talking; discussing education, supplies, military tactics perhaps? The eternal hum of the insects began to sing me into a weariness I couldn´t fight. I took off my balaclava and lay in the blackness. Take me away. Take me somewhere where there´s no need to fight. Take me to a place where there´s no need to kill. Guide me into her arms again.

I got up, left the hut and stood on the edge of the jungle, the village behind me was now bathed in silence. There was no path to take, but the silver leaves and branches parted as I approached. I blindly entered the pitch black of the awaiting trees but my senses told me where to go, where to place each careful step.

Everything was clear, the night air a carrier of all that moved in the shadows. I could smell her, she was close. I walked deeper into the forest and soon the branches and leaves that had bowed down to me were replaced by the trunks of ancient giant trees. They grew as I approached, reaching up to the sky, trying to fool me, overwhelm me. They were no match for me though, and I sank my sharp claws into the warm bark and climbed until I was above the canopy. I surveyed my kingdom, the moon turning the tree tops into clouds of platinum. She was there, on the horizon, waiting for me at the top of the mountain. I sprang from tree to tree in pursuit, below me the undergrowth moved as it was crushed under the weight of the chasing pack. The *cabaña* was in sight. I sprang into the air and soared towards it. I landed softly on its palm-leaf roof and then crawled down through a gap between the wooden boards that supported it.

She was there. I laid down beside her, I could hear her breathing deeply, shafts of moonlight bathed her in iridescent mercury, her chest moving up and down in sync with her breath. I ran my fingers along the velvet skin of her thigh, desperate to feel her shudder again under my touch. Her skin was cold and hard. She opened her eyes. Blackness. A blackness that suddenly burned brightly. She sank her fangs deep into my neck. I screamed and fought against her scaly grip but the sap was being sucked from my body, my trunk. I was sliced into small pieces, hauled away by rusty chains. My heart set on fire, my soul blackened. I was smoke. I drifted into the moonlit night. There was nothing above me but the stars waiting to do battle with the sun at dawn; below, nothing but a steaming void where the jungle once stood.

*

"Get up. We need to go."

I was awake but lay with my eyes closed hoping that my aching body would somehow bring itself to life, receive energy from the birds and insects that were screaming at the new day. The first rays of sunlight started to appear through the gaps in the hut´s walls, banishing forever the gods and beasts of the previous night and turning them into stone.

I sat up and took the coffee that Javi was holding out for me. I winced at its bitter taste but the hot liquid comforted me almost immediately. Nostalgia spread through my body. Another world, another life.

"Five minutes. We will eat on the way." With that, my guide, minder, or whatever Javi was, left me alone to finish my drink and ready myself for the journey ahead.

A little more than five minutes later we were heading down the dirt road that led us here, the murals at our backs bathed in the early orange morning light, sickles perpetually raised for eternity. Soon we were taking a sharp left at yesterday´s junction and were again on the path to La Graciosa.

Heat, bugs, sweat and pain were my companions once more on what I hoped would be the final leg of our hack through the Lacandon jungle. Our only respite came when we dismounted for a few minutes next to a stream or river so we could refresh ourselves and the horses and hastily stuff food into our mouths before continuing. I paid no attention to the wildlife; the colourful birds and the crash of the canopy as monkeys disturbed by our presence moved away from the track on which we were trapped.

It was clear that Javi was in a hurry to arrive quickly to our destination with some hours of daylight to spare and pushed his horse as hard as he could. Mine followed obligingly, my distinct lack of experience not a hinderance to its progress. Its impressive surefootedness alluding to a life spent ploughing through similar terrain, which it did with ease. We were ascending, there was no doubt about it and eventually we levelled off onto a forested plateau, the jungle much less dense than the previous miles we´d already traversed. The trees began to thin out and I could see through the increasingly sparse forest that there was a clearing not far up ahead. Javi brought his horse to a halt. Mine followed suit panting from the extra effort of dragging me behind the more skilful rider and his mount. Our horses´ hooves now silenced, I could hear voices and shouts coming from not far up ahead. Javi manoeuvred his horse with a twist of his body and turned to face me.

"Marcos is a good man. He has helped us get our message across to the people. We trust him."

The snap of several gunshots in quick succession made me jump. My horse moved from side to side before regaining its calm. Javi didn´t flinch or look behind him in the direction of the gunfire, his horse too remained unmoved.

"And he trusts you," Javi continued, looking at me gravely. "He has always told us to be small in front of the weak. Be great in front of the powerful." He paused, staring at me with his passive aggressive eyes. "Do not disappoint us." He continued to stare at me silently.

I won´t, don´t worry Javi. Don´t worry Marcos. I´ll channel my hate, the anger, the loss I have inside. I won´t let you down, or anyone, any more. I´ll prove that I´m not a tourist or some gap year student just here to take photos or build a school or hospital out of mud, looking at the poor people through rose-tinted glasses, oh so colourful, so ethnic, and then go back to their privileged lives. I am here to be trusted. I came here for love; but now I will bring down a regime. With you. With all of you.

I was sure that Javi could read my mind. But what did he *think*? I would never know. He turned his horse around again and led us towards the clearing up ahead and the sound of the rifles.

*

La Graciosa was a collection of wooden buildings located in a patch of land that had been cleared of trees and reclaimed from the grip of the avaricious vegetation that surrounded it. It probably wasn´t as high as where I´d been held until the EZLN – or at least Marcos – were satisfied that I was useful and committed enough to join their ranks, but higher and cooler than the part of the jungle we´d crossed to reach here. The structures looked temporary, hastily built out of whatever wooden planks and trunks could be found and nailed or bound together with twine. Some had plastic sheets to protect their contents from the rains that often fell heavily on these lands, others were much more exposed to the elements. The ground sloped down steeply to the south and although we were in the dry season, I could hear the sound of fast-flowing water. To the north, the site was protected by a wall of rock that was impossible to scale. It was the perfect place to train a clandestine army.

Javi ushered me towards one of the smaller buildings in the middle of the clearing, our horses having been taken away by a young man in military uniform with the now trademark red bandana covering the majority of his face. I looked around me as we walked across the camp, trying to take in the incredible sights I was seeing. Lines of indigenous soldiers, Russian dolls, carbon copies of one another, all in army clothing of some description with red scarves and green caps, were following commands from their superiors as they marched together in unison. Other groups on the opposite side of the camp were lunging forwards with wooden replica rifles at the orders of their sergeant or captain, or whatever rank was in charge of them. I could see that many of those in command were young women, a thick braid of black hair spilling down their backs and mingling with the bullets that they wore draped across themselves.

We stopped outside the hut we'd been walking towards. Javi could see that I was engrossed in what I was witness to.

"Nobody will find us here. Not the government, the landowners, the *guardias blancas*. There are no roads. The indigenous people in the area do not come here. We do not live here either. Not even God comes here," Javi said. I wasn't sure if his last comment was meant as a joke. "We are safe," he concluded and led me into the small wooden structure in front of us.

Inside it looked like some kind of office. In the middle of a table surrounded by papers and leaflets was a CB radio. Javi greeted its balaclava-wearing operator warmly, exchanging hugs in a rare display of emotion. The other comandante quickly went back to his task of steadily reading something from a piece of paper into the microphone of the radio. The walls were filled with maps with handwritten notes scrawled on them and I recognised some of the town and village names. On many of the charts arrows and sweeping arches were drawn in various directions. One side of the room was taken up by a wonky shelf holding a surprising array of books. Marx, Engels and Mao Tse-Tung shared the space with a collection of U.S. army training manuals and books on revolutionaries such as Villa, Zapata and Morales.

"You can see that we are a cheap army," Javi explained almost apologetically. "But we are independent. We are producers of what we eat, what we use. We have our own resources. They are modest, but they are ours. We do not have many guns, only the ones that the people bought from the money from stopping drinking alcohol. They sold what they had too. Food and animals to buy bullets. They bought them from the local police also."

I could envisage Marcos making some wise crack about how corruption works both ways but Javi's deadpan delivery remained as constant as the waters in the river below the secret camp.

"We do not have many radios," we both glanced in the direction of the dated equipment being used on the table, "nor cars or ammunition, but we have people, not just here but in the whole of the country and in the World too. We know we have."

"How many of us are there?" I asked.

Javi shrugged his shoulders in the trademark matter-of-fact way of his. "A lot."

*

I was assigned to a unit consisting of twenty others, and of course, I was the only non-indian among them. There was no chit-chat between us to speak of, although those that spoke a little Spanish did their best to politely enquire to how I was doing whenever it looked as if the exercises were getting too much for me. I wanted to speak to them all, to shout Lina's name at them, shake them by the shoulders and ask if they'd seen her. She was the reason I was here. The rest of this was just a game to play to bring me closer to her. A game – albeit noble in essence – that for now, I'd have to go along with if I were to survive and get the chance to see her again. I attempted conversation with some of my friendlier comrades, tried desperately to describe the woman I loved, but anything outside of our tasks was ignored and they shuffled off as quickly as possible in fear of retribution from a superior.

And so, the majority of the days were spent on drills, marches with our fake wooden weapons held uncomfortably above our heads, or practising dismantling and cleaning the few real rifles that were given to us specifically for the task. Shooting practice was strictly limited to just one or two shots per person owing to the scarcity of live ammunition.

Despite the heat, humidity and the blisters that wept in agony at the end of the day when I took my inherited boots off before sleeping, I did my best to integrate myself at La Graciosa. Major Maribel, the stocky young commander of our unit, barked orders at us in Tzeltal, the indigenous group to which the majority of my comrades belonged to. I began to recognise words that were shouted over and over again at us as Maribel marched up and down our lines making sure we were applying ourselves as best we could and I soon realised that this was also the language of Comandante Javi.

I tried hard not to fall behind with the activities and although the physical effort was taking its toll, I excelled in stripping down and reassembling rifles and was often asked to demonstrate how to do it in front of others. I also admired Maribel. Not just her but all of the women in charge of other groups – around half by my calculations – and what they must´ve gone through in order to be in such positions. For me, they were the real inspiration of the EZLN and hopefully a sign of what was to come after the war is over. I of course imagined Lina doing the same in another camp in another hidden place, in the Highlands maybe, or deeper still into the depths of the jungle. I exchanged Maribel´s straight black hair for Lina´s curls, escaping from under her green cap emblazoned with three red stars. The orders delivered to the group in the language of the Tzeltals were whispered in my ear in seductive Spanish accentuated English. I would obey and serve her until the bitter end.

*

At various times of the day the different units took it in turns to use the larger buildings which doubled up as our sleeping quarters at night and normally contained rows of tightly packed-in wooden bunkbeds on which we slept. However, during the daytime training sessions they were transformed entirely into classrooms and our night time furniture was miraculously transformed into lines of desks. Here we learnt from various high-ranking members of the EZLN about the tactics of warfare, the laws of the Geneva Convention and the locations and hardware of the Mexican army. Everything was meticulously explained to us in Spanish and in the dominant indigenous language of each unit.

Javi kept an eye on me when he wasn´t engaged in meetings in the small hut with the CB radio that acted as the camp´s headquarters, and even found himself waving at me from a distance. Taking advantage of his amiability, I pulled him aside one evening, asking if it was possible – begging him almost – to put out word on the radio about Lina. There was sympathy in his eyes, a feeling of a man who had somebody, somewhere, of his own he couldn´t hold in his arms.

"I know about her. But I am sorry. The radio can only be used for EZLN purposes," was his response. I knew these weren´t his words. I knew that if he could, he would´ve helped me. And I knew that he had once heard those very same words spoken to him too.

In spite of the heartbreak, loneliness and frustration I was feeling, I did feel something else. Pride. I felt proud of myself, what I was trying to do. Proud that Javi was starting to see what I was made of. Proud to think that in his eyes I was no longer a tourist. Proud to learn to fight, defend, kill and die.

On several occasions Subcomandante Marcos made a guest appearance, rallying the troops with tales of injustice, making sure that everyone knew about Article Twenty-seven of the nineteen ninety-two constitutional reforms and generally underlining the EZLN´s main principles of justice, freedom and dignity. He always made a point to enquire about my progress and embrace me with an enormous hug. I always waited for news that never came. He didn´t hang around very long after his work had been done though, and disappeared into the mists of the mountains as quickly as he´d surfaced, a cloud of smoke from his pipe in his wake. He was a wanted man; in many ways.

Christmas day came and went without fanfare. I thought of all the people back in the U.K. sitting around a table obligingly pulling a limp cracker and pretending to be happy with their family. Maybe they were, who knows? They´d be eating a fat turkey with all the trimmings, drinking port, eating cheese, falling asleep in a comfortable sofa and listening to their beloved monarch tell them about her *annus horribilis*, the poor dear. The righteous would be attending mass and singing carols. Here, although there were a large number of Christians among the indigenous members of the EZLN, the day passed by unnoticed. There were no decorations, only moss hanging from the branches of the ancient trees. The only singing came from the birds and insects. Nobody ate turkey, meat only being consumed once or twice a month in these parts if the family is lucky. No drunken naps were taken and nobody wished it could be Christmas everyday.

I was five and a half thousand miles away from my family but here, among the near silent group of strangers, whose language I didn´t speak, I felt at home. Not in the way I did with Carlos and Emilia in the Caracol neighbourhood, and light years away from what Lina and I shared. But amongst the pain, I was growing more and more comfortable all the same. I felt an energy that grew with every passing day, with every long march with a sack of rocks on my back and my replica wooden gun held aloft, with every river I crossed and every fire I lit, with every plunge of my knife deep into the soft abdomen of a dummy stuffed with dry grass. With every step closer to her. My body, which had never been what could be described as muscular, was now tight, sinewy and with a suppleness I´d never known could exist. The near fat-free diet had made me a lean, mean, soon-to-be fighting machine. The frequent headaches that had often struck me like a bolt of lightning were now few and far between and I honestly felt physically great.

A couple of days after Christmas passed the mood began to change at La Graciosa. Marcos made more regular appearances and didn´t just motivate the troops in the temporary classrooms but brought in maps and gave direct orders to the other officials. Different municipalities were named and on the large blackboards that dominated one side of the room, plans drawn up for a rapid advance on each one. The directions of the retaliatory government forces and their predicted manoeuvres were also marked with bold chalk arrows. The towns of San Cristóbal de las Casas, Altamirano, Las Margaritas, Huiztán and Ocosingo were assigned to different units, with every member of each group tasked with studying in minute detail what was to be asked of them. Nothing was left to chance. Details of on which corner and at what time and the exact role of each person in the advance were thoroughly revised again and again.

When it was our turn to enter the classroom, I noticed at once that there was a large map of Ocosingo with various points marked and circled both in the city centre and on the outskirts. I sat down, eager to know what part I was to play in the upcoming battle.

One of the comandantes that I´d seen coming and going at the H.Q. hut waited for everyone in the room to settle, but before he could begin his briefing and I could get the chance to listen to his instructions, I felt a hand touch me softly on my shoulder.

"Come with me," Javi whispered to me quietly. "There is something we need to do. Do you know how to drive?"

*

Javi had already prepared our horses and he soon sprang up on his saddle and waited impatiently, but politely, for me to follow suit. I did as he wished, so many questions burning fiercely into my mind. What's so important that I can't be involved in the plans to descend on Ocosingo? Where are we going now in such a hurry? Why did he ask me if I could drive?

We set off, leaving the clearing behind and soon entered the forest that had brought us here secretly under the cover of its thick canopy. I hadn't noticed at first but in addition to his usual rifle that was slung over his back, two more firearms were attached to the saddle behind his riding position. Could one be for me? I'd only fired a gun twice in my life and wasn't exactly the best marksman in the World, despite my dexterity at stripping and cleaning the arms that were given to us to practise with.

We descended quickly on a track that dived downhill in a different direction to the one we'd arrived via. We rode quickly, the horses stumbling occasionally with the speed of our descent, the afternoon light would be gone in an hour or so forcing Javi to keep up a fast pace. I tried to find the horizon below the sun to measure how much daylight we had left but the slope and the trees made it impossible for me to do so. All I knew was that it would soon be dark and we would probably still be somewhere deep in the throes of the jungle.

With each lurch forward of my horse my fears were being steadily realised and we were soon enveloped in a murky twilight that made it difficult to see the track ahead, not helped by the evening mists that had started to blanket the area as the temperature dropped. Can horses see in the dark? Jaguars can, for sure, I know that much. Javi stopped suddenly in front of me and my horse – the white vapour of its breath spewing out of its flared nostrils – answered my doubt about its night vision by grinding to a halt a safe distance behind. Javi dismounted and I could just about make him out ahead gesturing for me to do the same. Something moved in the undergrowth close to us, sending my heart up into my throat. Thankfully, no claws sank into my flesh and there was just enough light for me to see that the rustling had been caused by someone who'd parted the dense bush and appeared suddenly by our side. He was wearing a blood-red scarf over his face and he soon took our horses' reins, leading them off into the clutches of the night.

We began to make our way down the slope on foot and I could see in the light of the moon that fought its way through the mist that Javi was carrying the other two rifles he'd brought with him across his back. We walked for more than ten or fifteen minutes until the dense company of trees around us suddenly abandoned our side. Javi crouched and pulled me down with him. In front of us was a road, a paved road. The first I'd seen since I had a sack thrown over my head and I was invited along for a scenic drive through the Mexican countryside. We waited for several more minutes until I heard a vehicle approach. We ducked down into the long grass, although with our balaclavas and dark clothes it would've been almost impossible to notice us lurking by the side of the road anyway.

An army truck rumbled by. I could see in the faint light that a machine gun was mounted on the roof of the cab and there were several soldiers in the back. It gradually moved out of sight and then out of earshot.

"The army is more powerful than us," Javi said quietly, making me jump. I was nervous about what was developing and there was no avoiding whatever was going to happen here tonight. Ocosingo would have to wait for now. I was very much involved in the evening's alternative plan, whether I liked it or not.

"They have guns and trucks and heavy weapons, but they do not know what they are fighting for. They are not fighting for dignity. They are fighting only for money. Do you think they will give their lives for money?"

I didn't answer. I was terrified by now. The soldiers, the machine gun. It was all getting a little too real.

"They have no objective or reason to fight, they just want to get out as quickly as possible. Take their salary and run." Javi paused.

Insects, mist, fear. I wasn´t sure if I wanted to be a part of this.

"The soldiers are mostly indigenous, like us," he continued. "Tzotzils, Tzeltals, Ch´ols, Tojolabals. Many have family here in Chiapas too."

"Have ... have you tried speaking to them?" I asked hoarsely.

"Yes. They need to know what we are fighting for and that we are fighting for them too. All of them."

Silence fell between us for several minutes before another vehicle could be heard in the distance. I ducked down into the long grass again, praying that we wouldn´t been seen. It approached more slowly than the army truck and when it was not far from our location it flashed its headlights twice in quick succession before pulling up almost level to where we were hiding.

"Come on," Javi whispered, and before I knew it my rubber legs had obeyed his orders and were taking me towards the battered pickup truck that was waiting for us.

Soon we were driving along in predictable silence, swimming in the fog of the Chapanecan night, the dark road leading us in the direction that the Mexican army had followed no more than a few minutes before. The driver was an anonymous copy of Comandante Javi, of Aurelio, of Tomás, Alessandro, Guillermo, Maribel. I too, with my coffee-coloured shirt, combat trousers, high boots and balaclava had now blended seamlessly into the movement.

Eventually, the pickup slowed to a halt alongside a chain-link fence topped with circular curls of razor wire. On the other side there was a large metal barn or warehouse; our objective for the evening. Close to the bulky structure was a smaller one. There were lights on inside. We would not be alone. Javi and the driver jumped out of the vehicle and started to rummage around in the back of the pickup. Between them they then began to place thick wooden planks over the shallow ditch that acted as a barrier between the fence and the road, forming a bridge that I´d surely have to drive across.

Javi appeared at my window, opened my door and handed me one of the three rifles he´d been carrying down the mountain on his back. He said nothing. I could see that he was holding a large pair of bolt croppers that matched the ones the driver was now using to cut a vehicle-sized hole in the fence. Javi went to join him in his task. I stayed where I was, waiting for my orders. Very soon, Javi returned again at my open door.

"When I give a signal," he said, waving a torch in front of me, "you go in backwards and stop at the left of the building, OK?"

I nodded enthusiastically and Javi and the driver, armed with their rifles, slipped inside the compound. I changed seats and placed myself behind the large steering wheel of the 4x4, my fingers on the ignition key ready to pounce when I got the signal from the flashlight.

Each second, each minute was an epoch, an archaeological period, continents separated, Gondwanaland split and drifted across the southern oceans. No cars or trucks passed. There must be other cogs in this well-oiled machine, other letter X´s on maps that were thankfully making our job less risky.

An arc of light, sweeping up and down. My signal, I almost missed it thinking of plate tectonics. I started the engine, it sounded loud, so loud, surely someone will come running over to us, spraying us with bullets from automatic weapons. I reversed as instructed. A few inches either side and the whole plan would be ruined, I´d be responsible for the death of these two revolutionaries. But the planks were wide enough, my nerve strong enough and in seconds I was outside the open door of the warehouse, the ear-splitting diesel engine running. Javi beckoned me to help him and together we lifted the three heavy wooden crates into the back of the pickup. The driver was nowhere to be seen, the lights in the smaller building were still burning brightly. We jumped back into the cab and left the compound, greedily eating up the tarmac of one of the only paved roads in the area as we headed back towards the spot where we´d crouched down earlier in the exercise. As one comrade vanished, another appeared and we were met by the man who´d taken our horses at the bottom of our descent. He handed us four large bags, which we filled with as much dynamite as we could drag away from the car and our horses could manage on our steep ascent back to camp. We barely made a dent in one of the boxes. There must be enough here to blow up a hell of a lot of whatever it was we were going to blow up. The horse-minder helped us load the heavy bags onto our horses´ backs and then jumped into the pickup, driving away at speed in the direction in which it had originally appeared. Everything was done in silence, as if there was a group telepathy between the indigenous fighters. I just copied what Javi was doing or followed his simple instructions to the letter, praying I wouldn´t make á mistake that would cost us dearly.

We mounted our horses, their backs sagging under the combined weight of rider and deadly load, and began our long journey back up the hill towards La Graciosa. So, this was my big test; this was what Marcos had planned to get me fully assimilated into the ranks of the EZLN. I was now an active part of their group. They trusted me and although he said nothing the entire slow drag back towards camp, I knew now that Comandante Javi trusted me too.

As Mexicans rang in the new year with fireworks, music and dancing, and as the country officially entered a new era in the First World, something was stirring in the jungle. Something was moving silently through the trees, snaking its way down towards civilization. A creeping mass, seeping out of the darkness like the crude oil stolen from the land around. They rode horses, flanked by lines of those on foot, stepping over twisting roots of ancient trees, gliding down the slopes that led to wider tracks and then onto roads that linked towns and villages. There they were joined by others brought in on buses and piled into the back of trucks, some holding torches; a lynch mob ready to hunt down their oppressors. The flames in their hands revealing the men and women of the night, some with balaclavas and scarves, others with their faces uncovered and unafraid of the consequences of being identified. They marched with a purpose, making up for the lack of proper weapons by the sheer weight of their numbers. The element of surprise and their deep knowledge of the damp hills from which they came as valuable as the training of any well-armed battalion they would come up against.

There were thousands of them, descending in unison on Altamiro, Las Margaritas, Chanal, Oxchuc, Huixtán, Ocosingo and San Cristóbal de las Casas, ready to begin the war that they hoped – that *we* hoped – would usher in a new tomorrow.

I sat in the same vehicle used to steal the dynamite two nights before, some of which had already been spent to blow a bridge that would prevent additional government forces coming in from the west of the city of San Cristóbal – to where I was now heading.

Javi sat next to me in calm silence, confident of his part in the plan. His ice-cool manner had rubbed off on me and although my heart was beating faster than usual, I was relaxed in the knowledge that, for now, he would be by my side. I gripped the rifle I´d been given by Javi outside the explosives warehouse, feeling lucky that I had possession of such a weapon – the majority of the indigenous troops armed only with pitchforks, sticks, machetes and if they were lucky, an unreliable old shotgun.

We entered the centre of San Cristóbal shortly after midnight and our large group fanned out and took up their previously studied positions. Javi and I stayed with the majority of the force and made our way towards the Palacio Municipal local government buildings in the heart of the city. We were gracefully met with virtually no resistance; the majority of the Mexican army in the area believing that the threat of greater insurgence lay in Ocosingo, ninety kilometres away – a manoeuvre inspired by Villa tricking the Federal army into thinking that he was going to attack Chihuahua. The books on the Revolution that lined the slanting shelves of the tiny headquarters in La Graciosa were apparently not just for decoration purposes.

Everyone knew where they had to be and what they had to do and while orders were given for various sections to storm the dormant government building in the city´s main square, I realised that we were not just *guerrilleros* but a fully-fledged revolutionary army, ready and trained to attack our specific targets.

The Palacio Municipal was ransacked, doors were kicked down, offices broken into and papers and files thrown out onto the street. The city hall´s furniture, at which bored civil servants had sat undertaking the administrative work that made up their day just hours before, was now smashed into pieces that would be utilised to form barricades on the city´s streets. As members of the EZLN took over the building, several insurgents appeared on the balcony overlooking the square and the multitude of revolutionaries that occupied it below.

By now, many startled local people had come out of their houses to see what was happening in their town and were mingling with the young uniformed indians outside the Palacio Municipal. I had no specific orders to speak of and so shadowed Javi wherever he went, which I suppose was what Marcos would´ve wanted when he assigned the comandante to me in the first place. Shortly after entering the building we ascended the ornate marble staircase inside and we too were soon overlooking the crowds below. A microphone was produced and taken by an unmasked comrade and the static hum of the building´s public address system announced his imminent speech.

"Today we say enough is enough." He spoke into the microphone reading from the pages he held in his hand. "To the people of Mexico. Mexican brothers and sisters…" I knew the words almost by heart. I´d read them a hundred times since opening the envelope Lina had left on her bed.

"We are a product of five hundred years of struggle; first against slavery, then during the War of Independence against a Spain led by insurgents, then to avoid being absorbed by North American imperialism, then to promulgate our constitution and expel the French empire from our soil, and later the dictatorship of Porfirio Diaz, which denied us the just application of the Reform Laws. The people rebelled and leaders like Villa and Zapata emerged, poor men just like us…"

That envelope. That bed. The circumstances that had brought me here. History and words repeating. Strands of time cut, waiting to be fused together again.

"… they don't care that we have nothing, absolutely nothing, not even a roof over our heads, no land, no work, no health care, no food nor education. Nor are we able to freely and democratically elect our political representatives, nor is there independence from foreigners, nor is there peace nor justice for ourselves and our children."

I closed my eyes, visualising every word as it had been printed on the first three pages of *El Despertador*. I blocked out the voice that was reading steadily and replaced in it my head with the soft, passionate, theatrical tones of Subcomandante Marcos.

"But today, we say enough is enough. We are the inheritors of the true builders of our nation." I imagined him pacing behind me, using his dramatic pauses to great effect. "The dispossessed, we are millions and we thereby call upon our brothers and sisters to join this struggle as the only path, so that we will not die of hunger due to the insatiable ambition of a seventy-year dictatorship led by a clique of traitors that represent the most conservative and sell-out groups in this country."

As I was privately serenaded by Marcos, through the radio around the nation others listened to the tinny voice of another EZLN representative fighting against the crackle of static as he continued to read aloud the same declaration of war.

"… according to our Constitution, we declare the following to the Mexican federal army, the pillar of the Mexican dictatorship that we suffer from, monopolized by a one-party system and led by Carlos Salinas de Gortari, the maximum and illegitimate federal executive that today holds power."

In municipalities around Chiapas, photocopied and faxed pages were held by indigenous soldiers of the Ejército Zapatista de Liberación, young and old, men and women as the call to arms was dictated to as many people as humanly possible.

"According to this Declaration of War, we ask that other powers of the nation advocate to restore the legitimacy and the stability of the nation by overthrowing the dictator. We also ask that international organizations and the International Red Cross watch over and regulate our battles, so that our efforts are carried out while still protecting our civilian population. We declare now and always that we are subject to the Geneva Accord, forming the EZLN as our fighting arm of our liberation struggle. We have the Mexican people on our side, we have the beloved tri-coloured flag highly respected by our insurgent fighters. We use black and red in our uniform as our symbol of our working people on strike. Our flag carries the following letters, E.Z.L.N. – Ejército Zapatista de Liberación Nacional – and we always carry our flag into combat."

On the streets of San Cristóbal de las Casas people could not only hear the unmasked insurgent with whom I was sharing the balcony reading aloud the First Declaration of the Lacandon Jungle, they could read it posted around on walls and lampposts of the city´s streets.

People strained their necks and stood on tiptoes behind the throngs of people in front of them as they tried to read a snippet of the declaration. Those close enough to the propaganda, and fortunate to have received an education that allowed them to understand what they were reading, passed on the message to those around them.

As we stood on the balcony of the Palacio Municipal, in the footsteps of the corrupt mayors and dignitaries that we hoped would soon be ousted from their positions, it started to snow. Pages and pages of paper were floating down on the light early morning breeze and the expectant crowd below. A bizarre ticker-tape parade, where people reached up and grabbed the white pages as they were tossed from the open windows above us. I plucked one out of the air as it fluttered past me. I recognised the words once more. Words that had been photocopied in haste from *El Despertador*. Words that were slowly embedding themselves into the consciousness of the people witness to the startling events of the early hours of the first day of the year.

I read to myself, blocking out all that was going on around me.

Therefore, according to this declaration of war, we give our military forces, the EZLN, the following orders:

• First: Advance to the capital of the country, overcoming the Mexican federal army, protecting in our advance the civilian population and permitting the people in the liberated area the right to freely and democratically elect their own administrative authorities.

• Second: Respect the lives of our prisoners and turn over all wounded to the International Red Cross.

• Third: Initiate summary judgements against all soldiers of the Mexican federal army and the political police that have received training or have been paid by foreigners, accused of being traitors to our country, and against all those that have repressed and treated badly the civil population and robbed or stolen from or attempted crimes against the good of the people.

• Fourth: Form new troops with all those Mexicans that show their interest in joining our struggle, including those that, being enemy soldiers, turn themselves in

without having fought against us, and promise to take orders from the General Command of the Ejército Zapatista de Liberación Nacional.

• Fifth: We ask for the unconditional surrender of the enemy's headquarters before we begin any combat to avoid any loss of lives.

• Sixth: Suspend the robbery of our natural resources in the areas controlled by the EZLN.

And now, it was Lina´s turn to be inside me. She read to me; I stared at her soft lips as she spoke.

"To the People of Mexico: We, the men and women, full and free, are conscious that the war that we have declared is our last resort, but also a just one. The dictators have been applying an undeclared genocidal war against our people for many years.

"Therefore, we ask for your participation, your decision to support this plan that struggles for work, land, housing, food, health care, education, independence, freedom, democracy, justice and peace. We declare that we will not stop fighting until the basic demands of our people have been met by forming a government of our country that is free and democratic."

She gazed into my closed eyes as she finished, staring intently at me, through me. She smiled. But it wasn´t me that she was looking and smiling at lovingly. It was Dan. He was here, bringing balance, harmony and life where I could only exact revenge, punishment, death. I opened my eyes, I couldn´t afford to do this now, I needed to push him away, sacrifice him, wear his skin and control his movement. And I needed to push *her* to the back of my consciousness too. Lock her away where she wouldn´t interfere with what I had to do in the cold air of Chiapas right now with my comrades. She was part of something else. Doing what she needed to do. She was gone, not part of the here and now. Please set me free. Just for tonight. Just for a few hours.

But no. It was impossible, they dominated me. Owned me. An occupying force that dug trenches deep into my burning mind. A scar that seared with blinding pain. Throbbing, bleeding. Time running out.

Running away. Running. Stealing her flowers. Their bright feathers becoming one. The moon goddess; the Creator.

Lina and Dan together forever.

Lina and Dan together forever.

Lina and Dan together forever.

A surreal dawn in San Cristóbal de las Casas slowly emerged out of the cold night before. The main square, where indigenous women normally unfurled colourful blankets on which they presented their knitted handicrafts and other objects for sale, was now packed with over a thousand insurgents of a revolutionary army. Among them, curious locals and bewildered tourists mingled and by now the area in front of the Palacio Municipal was awash with camera crews and reporters filming the events. This revolution *will* be televised.

I looked at the members of the EZLN, weary from a sleepless night of tension, waiting nervously for the impending retaliation from the Federal army that was still yet to materialise. They sipped on steaming coffee brought to them by residents of the city, ate the food that was kindly donated to their cause. A pair of female indian soldiers, no more than children, smiled timidly at the camera that was filming them as they stood guard on the steps of the town hall. Piles of folders and papers stripped from the building that occupied one side of the plaza and boxes of medicines sacked from city-centre pharmacies lay around for anybody to take.

I brought a sweet, lukewarm coffee to my lips as I sat on the steps of the local government building, surveying the scene in front of me. Everywhere there was something fascinating to see as the different groups of people merged into one landscape. And then there he was, surrounded by journalists, multiple microphones and cameras thrust into his face. Using the word as his weapon, the enigma that was soon to become an embodiment of hope was revealed, eloquently laying out the aims of the movement that he now seemed to spearhead, providing the media with a name for the *mestizo* in the black balaclava. This was the moment Subcomandante Marcos was introduced to the World.

At around six p.m. on the second of January the Federal army rumbled into San Cristóbal, part of a force of seventeen thousand soldiers deployed in the area to crush the indigenous rebellion. The heavily-armed troops smashed their way through the flimsy barricades set up throughout the city and headed towards the Palacio Municipal, which had been stormed by the EZLN the previous evening while the North American Free Trade Agreement had come into effect.

As the government forces arrived in front of the white colonial building on whose balcony I´d stood the previous day, the only traces of resistance they were met with were papers floating around on the breeze and graffiti supporting the Zapatista uprising. They went about diligently searching the Palacio Municipal room by room but the men and women of the night had vanished back into the jungle and up the mountains as quickly and stealthily as they´d arrived. They´d won the first round; had completed their mission. The EZLN had been presented publicly to the World, their programme had been spread in ink and on air and they´d achieved their initial objective of attracting attention to the miserable conditions in which the indigenous population normally live. The country had been shaken and people, finally, were beginning to open their eyes.

While the army was desperately kicking down doors looking for the insurgents who´d long since abandoned San Cristóbal, Javi and I were driving as fast as our old pickup could take us on the road to Ocosingo. By dusk, we reached our destination on the outskirts of the town, the antenna on top of the small building we were approaching hinted at the structure´s probable use as a radio station. Posted outside were two EZLN soldiers, faces uncovered, who greeted us with unusually friendly smiles and appeared far more relaxed than the majority of their comrades back in San Cristóbal. We entered the simple building and sure enough my assumption was confirmed by the equipment inside. We´d just arrived at the premises of XEOCH radio, the local station for the area. At the microphone sat another rebel, this time with balaclava and a smarter, newer uniform, suggesting he had a superior rank to the two surprisingly amiable guards outside.

If I could just get the radio operator on his own, away from Javi, convince him to give me the microphone just for a few seconds so that

I could call for Lina, send her pale skin and curly hair floating over the jungles and mountains as I´d desperately wanted to do back at La Graciosa. Surely someone would´ve seen her. But no. Javi exchanged a few words in Spanish that I didn´t catch and the operator left abruptly. Several seconds later, I heard the pickup drive away and the two of us were left alone on the top of the hill that overlooked the city, fog rolling in from the valley below, slowly being cut off from the rest of the World.

From the backpack he´d been carrying Javi took out various pages that he began to organise on the table that supported the microphone. When it appeared that he was ready to broadcast whatever it was that Marcos had given him back in San Cristóbal, he then turned his attention towards me.

"The other guards have gone. Can you watch the door outside?" he asked politely, although it was clear this was a direct order to a subordinate. I had no choice other than to obey.

As Javi got on with his task, I positioned myself outside, making sure I had a perfect view of the road we´d come up earlier in the afternoon. From my vantage point I could just about make out the city below fading away into the night, disappearing with every second. I quickly realised there was no electricity in the town, but it certainly wasn´t sleeping. Every so often a crackle of gunfire erupted, punctuated by the boom of heavy artillery as battles raged somewhere beneath us. I felt sick. I´d been lulled into a false sense of security in San Cristóbal among the tourists, television vans, slogans and romantic images of revolution. But now this was frighteningly real. I gripped the gun more tightly, my hands beginning to feel numb against the freezing metal. I´d been waiting for a war my whole life. We all have. Since we were handed toy guns to play with as children, action figures, tanks. We were being prepared to be what we truly are and have always been. No matter how noble the cause, what it all boiled down to was kill or be killed, and I simply couldn´t say if I was really going to shoot anyone that came up the hill that wasn´t part of the EZLN? Could I do it? There was no doubt I was always a sworn pacifist. I wouldn´t hurt a fly; any insect I found was evicted from my house with a glass and a sheet of paper and given a fond farewell. How would I be capable of killing another human being? I hadn´t become a Zapatista to kill and die. I had been thrust into their grasp in search of the woman I loved and I never wanted to be part of this war.

However, here I was, listening to the distant sounds of conflict that carried up the slopes on the cold evening air, prepared to do whatever I´d have to do not only to survive myself, but to assist in the survival of others.

During the night we took it in turns to do sentry duty outside the radio station, sharing the one warm jacket we´d salvaged from somewhere in San Cristóbal – a place and events that now all seemed like a blur. We slept little, changing positions every two hours and eventually the glow of the morning appeared through the thick fog that had taken control of the area throughout the night.

As birds and diurnal insects woke and welcomed in the new dawn, our hill became an island from which we could contemplate the sea of white that surrounded us. The morning also brought in new sounds, buzzing, which began quietly at first and then grew louder and louder as army helicopters started to fly over the wakening town.

We breakfasted on tins of sardines Javi produced from his backpack and as he broadcast a recording he must´ve made while I was on guard duty last night, I searched the rest of the building for anything that might be of use to us.

There was a small kitchen and I began to rummage through the cupboards there but the soldiers we´d relieved of their duty here the day before must´ve beaten us to it and the shelves were bare.
Suddenly Javi was beside me, moving as silently as a cat as he always did, which invariably left me startled when his voice spoke to me out of thin air.

"We need to go. The army is coming," he informed me calmly.

While I´d been searching for something to eat, Javi had received a call on the CB radio at the station. Having taken control of most of Ocosingo after fierce fighting at various points in the town, including the cemetery and a school, most of the Zapatistas had left in order to protect the villages nearby, which would surely face retaliation for supporting the uprising. But something, somehow had gone wrong.

Despite the detailed planning beforehand, a unit of the EZLN hadn´t protected the route into town from the north, hadn´t used the rest of the dynamite we´d stolen days before to blow up a bridge that would´ve prevented easy access to Ocosingo. And now, numerous battalions of professional Federal soldiers were flooding in from the north, blocking any escape in that direction and threatening to overwhelm the scant amount of Zapatistas that had remained in the town and who were still in conflict with government forces stationed in the area. Word was that the main body of what was left of the EZLN fighters had gathered in the central market and from there vehicles would complete the evacuation to safer, EZLN controlled areas or take us into the mountains and away from direct conflict with the thousands of soldiers streaming in from their garrisons northwards.

Up here, on our island in the sky, we knew that we were vulnerable to attack and the radio station would be an obvious target for the army to take out any time soon.

With little option left, we began our speedy descent on foot down into town, Javi negotiating the terrain – as he had done on his horse – with an enviable agility that I clumsily failed to match. The helicopters had multiplied in number and were buzzing over the town, circling like hungry vultures. I could hear planes too in the distance and the occasional booming thud of rockets as they pounded their poorly-armed targets. Surely one would soon destroy the place where we´d just spent the night.

A dream. I wasn´t here and this wasn´t real. The fog was stained pink as the sun bathed it with early morning light and I floated high above the scene. I could see for miles around, the distant mountains that held up the sky teasing us with their promise of sanctuary. I flew with the helicopters and the scavenging birds of prey, parting the mist as I glided over Ocosingo. The dulcet sound of munitions whispering sweet nothings in my ears.

*

We entered the outer suburbs of the town and took cover, assessing our options of how to best arrive at the market undetected. After our rapid descent, my legs were shaking hysterically, lactic acid and fear fighting their own battle in my weak thighs. The rest of my body mimicked my legs and I was soon shivering uncontrollably all over. This must be what shock is like. How strange. Fight it, Max. Not now.

Noticing the state I was in, Javi took off the jacket he was still wearing from the last shift he´d undertaken when guarding the radio station. He placed it over my shoulders, rubbing them furiously, bringing heat and sense back into my body. Whatever was going to happen that day, I was glad I would be close to Javi.

Sporadic gunfire echoed around the deserted streets as we crept closer to the small market that normally attracted villagers from the surrounding areas to come and sell their products each morning. Today it was a magnet for a different kind of clientele.

As we got closer to our goal, we saw that the town centre was littered with debris, clothes, odd shoes, bottles, spent shells and shotgun cartridges. Dark-red stains skidding across the street indicated where the wounded or the dead had been dragged to safety or mercifully moved out of sight of the town´s terrified residents, who timidly peered out of their windows while sheltering in what they prayed was the refuge of their homes.

The roads directly surrounding the market were still controlled by fighters of the EZLN, many of whom had positioned themselves on the roofs of the one-story houses that led to what was once the lively hub of the town. We dashed across the final stretch of open ground, helicopters juddering overhead, the doors on their sides open wide and nervous soldiers firing their machine guns at anything that moved beneath them. Somehow, they didn´t spot us.

Where once there were stalls selling avocadoes, mangoes, coriander and fresh meat, there was now carnage. At the main entrance to the market bodies lay, their blood spilling out onto the concrete that would usually be hosed down at the end of the day as the market closed. One young indigenous fighter lay on his back with his legs splayed, various objects surrounding him; a small green backpack, his cap and most strikingly of all, one of the fake wooden rifles similar to the props that I´d used while combat training in La Graciosa. I stared at the scene, trying to comprehend the desperation to fight while wearing oversized wellington boots and armed only with a piece of wood. A toy gun.

Two other bodies were nearby, neither one in uniform or with a scarf or balaclava covering their face. Stalls had been overturned and used as barricades; practically useless against the heavy fire that was aimed at them. We made our way inside and met what was left of the resistance.

Nine or ten EZLN members were there with around half the number of guns between them. I recognised a few of them as members of my unit – Maribel´s unit. A handful of residents trapped in the crossfire were also sheltering inside, wide-eyed and shocked, unsure of what was going on. Some of them sat propped up against walls, whimpering, wounded, bleeding and dying. A young girl – no more than five or six years old – hugged her knees close to her chest, hiding herself away from danger in her shell, a delicate broken sea snail. In one of her hands she gripped a soft toy, a rabbit or bear or something like that, the blood that it was soaked in disguising its original colour.

Over the course of the next few hours, some – but not all – of the snipers that had protected our path here managed to seek refuge in the market alongside our small band of survivors. They brought news that at least three battalions of the Federal army were now fanning out in an attempt to surround us. The artillery fire intensified and soon we found it difficult to hear ourselves think inside our concrete tomb. Through a small slit between the boards placed over one of the windows at the front of the building, I peered out nervously into the impending danger.

At the end of one street that sloped up and away from our position I could see troops kicking down the doors of each house and every small shop they passed as they made their way towards us. Through every doorway they darkened they released a barrage of bullets, unaware or uncaring about who or what was on the other side, intent on utter annihilation. Several of our comrades in response fired in their direction, forcing the soldiers to retreat to safer positions and observe the temporary stronghold in which we were hiding.

From their now more secure vantage points, the army began to probe the market occasionally with munitions to find out our defensive capabilities and to try to slowly wear us down, sapping our morale. For our part, during the afternoon, our sorry band of survivors fired as tactically as possible in order to keep the soldiers outside at bay, while at the same time using as few bullets as we could spare.

Night fell and we knew what was going to be thrown at us once the army could move in the shadow of darkness. But we were the ones that really owned the night, knew the streets and the surrounding area. With this knowledge there was still hope, although like our bullets, this was fast running out too.

The army continued to test our defences, firing rounds in the direction of the market every so often. We fired back, keeping them at arm's length for as long as we could. I gave my weapon to one of my comrades, who would undoubtedly know better how to take advantage of it and I went to tend to some of the wounded with what little materials I could find. I took off my balaclava, using it to soak up the blood pouring from a teenage girl's leg, desperately trying to stem the flow that had already stained much of the floor around her. There was little light inside the market but the half-moon provided just enough to see the girl's face. Her black eyes stared at me, a mix of curiosity, pain and resignation somehow transmitted itself through her stare. She didn't say a word, she was accustomed to death in Chiapas. Her beautiful eyes continued to stare at me as I released the pressure from her wound. I moved away from her, leaving her there in the market where she'd bought or sold *tortillas* or *nopales*, or whatever her family's land could grow, her white blouse with intricately woven colourful flowers pristine and free from the litres of blood that had flowed out of her. I moved on to the next casualty.

I was ready to die. I didn't want to of course, but the fact was I knew what the chances of survival were here and it was something that now wouldn't come as a surprise given the overwhelming odds we faced. I was ready to die because those silent fighters around me, my fellow EZLN comrades, had been ready to die from the very beginning.

The small band of brothers and sisters before me had broken their silence and were discussing something with each other, Javi looking like he was in charge, giving orders and directions. Once done with his instructions to the others, he came over to where I was trying to comfort an elderly man who'd been left blinded by a shell that had exploded close to him on the street as he was trying to get to the safety of his home.

"You need to go now," he said in his calm manner. "There is a bus ready to go. You need to help these people to get to Valladolid up in the hills. The road is protected by us for now but you need to hurry. From there you can get to the mountains." He was looking at me in the dim light, studying my face, properly observing my features as best as he could for the first time. "Go. Now."

"I´m staying here with you," I answered trying to sound as defiant as possible with my broken voice.

"No. You need to help them and then join the others. You need to protect the communities. Do not let the army do what it did in Guatemala to the people here."

I didn´t ask. I could imagine what the governmental forces here and in neighbouring countries were capable of. I´d seen the Guatemaltecas here in Chiapas, empty vessels of a people, living ghosts that had escaped the genocide that had killed thousands in another part of what was Mesoamerica. They didn´t exist anymore.

"Out the back, now. The snipers will cover you." He turned and with the other remaining rebels began to take up positions at the gaps in the blocked-up windows.

"Javi …" I murmured, almost inaudibly.

He turned to face me. "Tell the World. Tell your people," he said.

I wanted to tell him that I was already with my people, that I was part of them now, but he´d quickly taken his position and he and the rest of what was left of the Ejército Zapatista de Liberación Nacional in Ocosingo began to direct the full force of what little they had left at the Federal army so that the civilians, the wounded and myself could escape.

The bus rattled out of the centre of town under the protection of the few remaining snipers. A young EZLN soldier – along with me and one other wounded fighter the only uniformed people on the bus – crunched through the gears, clearly not used to driving such a vehicle. With white knuckles, he gripped the steering wheel as if riding a roller-coaster, leaning forward, red bandana discarded long ago, terror and concentration guiding his jerky movements. I guessed he was sixteen years old at most.

The rest of the passengers occupied around half the thirty-odd places that the old *colectivo* microbus boasted. We slid uncontrollably from side to side on the hard plastic seats as we leaned into corners; the blood from the wounded not helping us in our struggle to stay anchored in one place.

After several tense minutes of our escape a strange calm descended on us. The sound of gunfire faded away and the road straightened out and began to incline slightly as we made our way towards the sanctuary of the mountains. Our driver shifted down a gear as the bus slowed on the gradient. He was beginning to get the hang of things, his gear changes becoming smoother and less abrasive. Rosary beads and a crucifix swung from the rear-view mirror. On a panel above the driver's head large painted letters proclaimed that somebody was *Un Loco Soñador* – a crazy dreamer. Who was? The normal driver of this bus that usually made its way from some outlying village into the centre of Ocosingo, full of people on their way to the market where we'd left Javi and his merry band of condemned men giving up their lives for us? Who was the crazy dreamer? The person that had drawn these words? Javi? Marcos? Me? I looked around at my fellow passengers. Women, children, the elderly, the dying, the recent dead. What dreams did they have? Would they ever be able to fulfil them? I'd try to help them. I owed them. I owed Javi and the others that had sacrificed themselves so that this collection of people driving in the night towards the mountains could survive. What would I protect them with? I had no rifle, there were no weapons on the bus, not even a replica wooden gun. Reason and truth were useless on this dark road.

It didn´t matter, soon we´d be hiding in the jungle, safely in the arms of the rest of the EZLN that had already fled into the trees, into the embrace of their night. They would protect us. We would protect them. We would return.

The bus slowed to a virtual stop. The headlights, which the young chauffer had only just turned on when finally feeling far enough away from the town and the fighting we left behind, were switched off. I joined him at the front of the bus and we looked together at the path to freedom stretching out in front of us through the cracked window. *Un Loco Soñador* above our heads.

The predictable fog had already sunk down onto the surface of the road but it wasn´t thick enough yet to hide the lights and vehicles that blocked our path about two hundred metres further ahead. The light from the half-moon illuminated the misty air; a glow that made the obstacles in our way more visible. The fog that can hide your hand as you hold it in front of your body can also sometimes betray.

There were two vehicles; small army trucks that had parked perpendicular to the direction of the road, cutting it off completely. I could see movement, soldiers, fully aware of our presence, readying themselves for action.

The indian teenager that had driven us this far along our route to a freedom that we could almost taste stared up at me, his eyes pleading for me to tell him what to do. A few kilometres down the road to our backs Ocosingo was now occupied by more than three thousand heavily-armed Federal soldiers. Ahead of us, two parked trucks and a handful of men, undoubtedly almost as scared as we were, was all that blocked our escape to liberty. I looked ahead at the road and then back down at the fighter who was gripping the steering wheel tightly. The bus had now stopped and the engine was idling, waiting for instructions. I smiled warmly at the driver and squeezed his shoulder.

There was no need for telepathy, he knew what it was we had to do. As I returned to my seat, I gestured for the other passengers to hold on, the smile that I had given the young driver still carved onto my face. A crazy dreamer.

I held the hand of the fatally wounded EZLN fighter, the rest of the group of people having already automatically paired up and were embracing their partner or holding hands as we now were. Maybe they didn´t understand my instructions to hold on tightly to something solid. Or maybe they just didn´t want to die alone.

The gears crunched and the bus spluttered and crawled into life, gradually picking up speed. Not enough. We were no more than a hundred metres from the road block and going at barely thirty or forty kilometres an hour, which I prayed would be fast enough to smash the army vehicles out of the way. Or would it? We gathered a little more speed and headed for the small gap between the two parked trucks. I visualised them being parted by our beast, the soldiers diving for cover into the ditches that carried the torrential summer rains away and down into the reservoir that provided the town with water.

The first bullets smashed through the windscreen and our driver was thrown backwards immediately by the impact, his head burst open by the high-calibre munition that spread his brain over the plastic panel behind his seat. The bus swerved on the road and stopped sideways to the roadblock. Its engine stalled. A machine gun that was mounted on the back of one of the trucks emptied itself into the side of the bus, punching holes in the thin metal chassis that provided no protection to those sitting on its left side.

Bloodied bodies fell onto the floor, under seats and into the aisle, faces missing, torsos open. The discoloured rabbit, or bear, flopped noiselessly out of a limp hand onto the cold metal below.

Now the other side was shredded by the soldiers that had run towards us and who were now peppering the right side of the bus with everything they had. A thump in my leg, and into my side, my ribs, my hip. I fell onto the floor, slipping into the blood that was covering its entire surface.

Floating. I was floating again above the clouds with the helicopters, looking down at the valley below. I flew over cedar and mahogany trees and monkeys scattered in all directions. Birds took flight at my presence. Everything was running from me, scared at my power, what I could do. The plumed serpent recoiled from my maw of daggers.

I crashed down to Earth again. I am on the bus, on the floor sharing this small space with Gael, who'd gone to buy medicine for his sick father ... with Juana and her daughter, Valeria, who were trying to get home after buying dough for *tortillas* ... with Guadalupe, whose husband lay cold and dead in the street outside the market ... with Santiago, who was looking for a phone that worked so he could find out what had happened to his family in Tuxtla Gutiérrez ... with Miguel Ángel, whose hand I still held in mine and who had fought for a better life for his family, his people, for everyone.

My eyes wanted to close. I let them. I had finally escaped.

Hands pulling on me, dragging me through the life that has seeped out of those around me, dripping like the thick juice of recently cut *nopales* through the gaps in the metal onto the road below. Steps. It must be the steps, *thud, thud, thud,* on the back of my head. I feel cooler, a relief from the burning I was feeling before. Now warm again. Sickly, humid warmth. No, I don´t want to feel this. I don´t want to suffocate, breathe in the death of the others. Which way is up? I try to spit, to see where gravity takes my saliva but I´m paralysed. I have no control of anything, not even my lips, my eyelids. I tumble down a slope, forever climbing and ascending in this damp land. Javi. Javi? Where are you? He must´ve gone on ahead. Something heavy falls on top of me, pushing me down into the glistening grass, I´m pressed ever deeper into the earthy smell of fertile soil. More weight on top of me, crushing me. I´m pinned down. I´m Gulliver. I´m a *conquistador* enslaved by the dead weight of Tzeltals, Tzotzils, Ch´ols, Tojolabals ... *campesinos, rebeldes, inocentes.*

The smell, *that* smell.

I can´t breathe.

In the central market of Ocosingo five bodies lay face down with their hands tied behind them, holes in the back of their heads where they'd been executed, red scarves around their necks, coffee-coloured shirts and green combat trousers covering their slim frames. Large birds of prey circled above the town centre, attracted by the bodies left to bloat in the sun on streets strewn with the debris of tragedy. Hungry dogs sniffed an air laced with the decaying scent of war. Throughout the town, soldiers aggressively pushed people at gunpoint, taking them away as collaborators, their fate in the hands of a lawless military that would be responsible for the disappearance and execution of anyone that they believed was involved in the uprising.

Helicopters and planes continued humming and circling overhead, indiscriminately bombing and firing upon village after village, murdering innocent people, displacing thousands more.

The fighting continued. Pockets of EZLN soldiers fired up through the trees at the aircraft that were hunting them down. Natives firing arrows at the giant metal war machines. The army responded by shredding the jungle to pieces; anything and anyone in its way a valid target. Red Cross vehicles were left with holes in their sides, journalists shot at and killed, despite the white flag and clear identification on their cars that they were part of the large press contingent that had already made its way into the area.

As my broken body painstakingly knitted itself together, the war raged on. As Subcomandante Marcos became a household name wooing the media with his flowery words, Presidente Salinas de Gotari blamed foreign agitators and terrorists from El Salvador and Guatemala for the conflict. As I lay unconscious, patched up and sewn together in a room without windows, Mexico, at last, moved. It woke up, surprising both the government and the Ejército Zapatista de Liberación Nacional alike with demands for an end to the fighting. Millions of people spoke as one and could not be ignored. Finally, after five hundred years, the indigenous people had been seen and heard.

A tense calm followed the twelve-day war. A delicate ceasefire brokered by the bishop of San Cristóbal, who brought the opposing factions together, temporarily saving face for the beleaguered Presidente Salinas, while at the same time prompting further the Zapatistas´ cause. A media circus followed the peace negotiations, training a thousand cameras on the proceedings, hanging on every word as millions watched on television or read about it in the newspapers. But in my windowless hospital cell I was blind, my world nothing more than four white walls and a selection of medical equipment that was keeping me alive.

My wreck of a body recovered gradually from the bullets that had shattered my femur and most of my ribs and allowed more than two pints of blood to flow into the Chapanecan soil and soon the machines that had denied me my final escape were wheeled out of my plain, sterile room. I had no idea how much time had passed or what was happening in Chiapas, who was still alive or who was dead. The coma that had been induced in order to save my life had wasted away the little muscle I´d acquired at La Graciosa and even if I wasn´t handcuffed to the bed rail, I probably wouldn´t be able to make it to the door if my life depended on it.

Various doctors and nurses paid regular visits to check on my condition and progress, change dressings and administer drugs of some description. They didn´t look me in the eye and I didn´t speak to them. There was no point, I knew what stonewall reaction I´d be faced with. I counted the days since I woke up, or at least I calculated the hours based on the change of shifts of the hospital personnel, judging that at the most they wouldn´t work for more than twelve hours consecutively. No dawn glow welcomed in the new day, no dusk beckoned the gods and beasts of the night to awaken. Three weeks, more or less, passed by in silence and artificial light.

The only sounds that accompanied me were the whirring of the equipment that had me surrounded and the thoughts that rang around my aching head, stealing away the precious sleep I needed. As I lay in my bed, I became Pedro Páramo, Lina my Susana. She, the reason I do everything. I will always love her but maybe never have her and I could feel some part of me withering and dying every day without her near. She had been taken from me and I, like Pedro Páramo, will seek my vengeance. Not on Comala, turning it into a desolate purgatory as he had done, but on those that oppose us and the world to which I had been introduced by my one and only love.

I began to speak to myself, worried that by the time I eventually spoke to someone my vocal cords would have deteriorated and ceased working. But then, came the merciful breakthrough I craved.

I was moved to a wheelchair halfway through what I supposed was the end of the third week *a.w. – after waking,* my ground zero – and I finally got a taste of relative freedom when I was wheeled into a deserted corridor and taken to another room nearby for some x-rays. Then, during the fourth week, with the aid of a pair of crutches and the assistance of the nurse I´d seen the most, Nervous Nerris – my faithful Florence Nightingale – who seemed to be scared of my every shaking movement, I took my first unstable steps. And at the end of week four, *a.w.,* I received my first non-medical visit.

They stood by the side of my bed, both wearing baggy leather jackets and beige chinos, both sporting thick moustaches and stern expressions. Let the interrogation begin. Truth or dare time. I opted for a mix between the two and braced myself for what was to come. In my current position I had nothing else left to lose.

"What´s your name?" asked the detective on the left. At his side, his colleague was ready with a notebook.

"Max, Max Archer," I answered weakly. Too weakly. Come on, you can do better than that. I coughed to clear my dry throat. "Max Archer," I repeated with more authority.

"Where are you from?"

"England."

"What are you doing in Mexico?"

"I´m a tourist. I was on holiday."

There was a pause as something was scribbled quickly in the notebook and a new line of questioning was taken.

"Then what were you doing dressed like a Zapatista terrorist?" the detective asked sarcastically, spitting out the question.

"To escape. To escape to the mountains. I´m a tourist."

"Tourists don´t wear those clothes. Who sent you there?"

"Nobody. I dressed like them so I could escape," I repeated.

The two moustached detectives, or plain-clothed army, or whatever they were, exchanged angry glances at each other at my insistence that I was not a part of the EZLN.

"Listen *pendejo*, we know what you were doing there," said the one on the right now, sitting down on the end of my bed crushing my right foot under his weight. A bolt of pain shot up through my thigh, deep inside the soft bone cried out. I stiffened but tried not to show any emotion on my gaunt, face. He smiled, happy that he had got my full attention.

"Where are the camps?" he asked, shifting his weight roughly, the agony intensifying.

"I don´t know what you´re talking about," I said, gritting my teeth against the pain, trying with all my might not to let it show on my face. Maybe this wasn´t the right tactic, maybe I should tell them the truth, tell them what they wanted to know, avoid whatever it was that they could do to me to try to make me talk. I thought of Marcos and his doe eyes, his passion, his fluid motivation that stimulated the EZLN to great things. No. I wouldn´t give him up, any of them up, ever, even if I did know where they were. Where were they? Where was *she*?

"Tell us where they´re hiding, *cabrón*," my original inquisitor said, raising his voice up a notch or two, clearly annoyed by my defiance in the face of their questioning and the sharp pain I was silently enduring.

I was filled with joy, eliminating my agony temporarily. If they'd defeated the EZLN, discovered where they were, they wouldn't be asking me this. I'd take whatever they could do to me. I wasn't scared. I'd died before. I smiled erratically and said absolutely nothing.

They were no doubt experienced at this kind of thing. How many people had they interrogated during the course of their careers? How many poor souls had been tortured? Jubilation burst through my weak body as I realised that there was a look of tired resignation in their eyes and their body language screamed at me a lack of interest in what they were doing. Perhaps they'd already pulled too many legs off insects today and had satisfied their hunger for cruelty. I stared at them defiantly, summoning up the wildest expression I could muster. I could do crazy. I'll outdo anything that you can do. And I won't scream, that's for sure. I wouldn't give them the satisfaction of that. They had me in a trap, under a glass, but I was in control and they knew the look of someone willing to take the pain, someone who would fly above the jungle while they hammered needles under finger nails, poured acid into nostrils and inserted broken bottles into the most delicate areas. They knew who would be willing to die. No amount of barbaric torture would make me say anything and they knew it. No camp would be discovered because of me. Come on. Fucking do it to me. We're all born shocked and in pain anyway, fighting for breath, for life, as soon as our umbilical cord is cut. As soon as we inhale in the alien air around us. Connect me to that time again. Give me the original pain. I *need* it. Do your worst and I'll drink it all in, your hatred will quench my raging thirst. My war paint is on and I am more than fucking ready.

The detective sitting on my foot stood up, pushing his hand firmly into my leg as he rose. Oh, yes, I like it. More please. I smiled at them, I'd defeated them. They had no other option; they would have to kill me or give up. They could torture me all they liked. But I knew they wouldn't. There would be no point in them doing this. I'd been patched up as someone wanted me kept alive for some reason and if these brutes left me dead or like a useless lump of tenderised meat with nothing to show for it, then they would´ve failed in their duty. They had a superior and I was sure whoever it was wouldn´t want to have wasted all the effort put into my recovery and then have nothing to gain from it. So, they just left me alone in my bed, my leg aching with the aftereffects of the farewell I´d just been given and the black smoke of my defiance lingering in the air.

Week four *a.w.* ended without any more unexpected visits and I was left alone, apart from Nervous Nerris, who scurried in and out to check on me occasionally, and thankfully I never saw the menacing Thompson Twins again.

*

As time crawled by, I gradually became stronger and managed to begin to walk unaided down the length of the corridor outside my room with the help of just one crutch. I´d started to lose count of the days, each of them merging into one long painkiller-induced haze where night became day and day became a long stretch of boredom and self-provoked hallucinations to ironically try to keep myself sane. I summoned Dan to me first, putting him on trial, and he told me the tale of how after travelling through Guatemala and Honduras with Maggie they´d got engaged and were planning their wedding in Seattle this summer. I resisted the temptation to lunge at him, attack the traitor, to strangle him there and then and instead just let him ramble on about how much he was in love with his long-legged fiancée and how that everything that archaeologists have told us about the past is false. That farmers and hunter-gatherers didn´t suddenly just wake up one day with the skills and plans to build giant temples with huge monolithic rocks. It was giants. Giants from an advanced ancient culture, present in all cultures, all at the same time, all over the World. I listened. I planned.

Next came Javi, the upper half of his body in uniform as always but his legs were painted with the coat of a spotted jaguar, like some strange jungle minotaur. He wasn´t wearing his balaclava but his head was heavily bandaged and his face remained a constant mystery. In his arms he was holding a young indigenous baby who he´d rescued and was going to adopt. He told me he´d been promoted to the head of the EZLN and was in charge of restructuring the new society that had emerged in Chiapas. I asked him what had happened to Marcos and suddenly the room was filled with the familiar smoke I´d longed to inhale once again and the subcomandante was standing there in front of me in place of Javi.

Marcos told me how he and a group of soldiers under his command had marched on the capital, millions of civilians joining his caravan on the way as the tide of his followers grew bigger and bigger with each step closer to Mexico City. There, in a bloodless coup, the indigenous soldiers in the Federal army backed the uprising and the government was overthrown and replaced by a different system of democratic governance that was built from the bottom up with a network of community groups responsible for organising how the country would be run. He faded away and I was plunged into a loneliness I hadn´t felt since I was a guest in my jungle retreat and Margarita spoke to me in her beautiful language.

And then Lina appeared. I´d tried to prevent her from coming, tried to protect myself from thinking about what I´d lost. But she was there standing in front of me all the same, her sweet smile, pale skin and bouncy curls filling me with painful desire. She told me that she´d left *El Despertador* for me, that it was her wish for me to fight with her in Chiapas, but the authorities in San Miguel had got wind of her plan and she had to escape as quickly as possible into the Lacandon jungle. There, she´d become a comandante of the EZLN, running a training camp, instructing the indigenous people how to fight, teaching them how to achieve a better life through a beautiful blend of education and military tactics. She promised she would be waiting for me on the outside.

Interspersed between my frequent visits from Dan, Javi, Marcos and Lina, I was examined by a doctor I´d never seen before. He was a faceless man, hiding behind huge glasses and a bushy beard asking me a cascade of endless questions about how I was feeling, what I was thinking and if I could see or hear anyone else in the room when I was alone. I answered his questions adopting the same tactic as when the singing detectives sat on my bed and read me my bedtime story.

Truth or dare?

The bearded psychologist became the embodiment of the enemy, the *gestapo,* blinding me with the pen torch he used every time he wanted to know something. I had the urge to grab it out of his hand and thrust it deep into his eye and make my escape from wherever I was, but the pills he´d given me since the first day I saw him made my arms and legs feel like lead and the thought of violence somehow incredibly amusing. I floated with the helicopters again. Up and out and then back inside myself. Exploring. Was this enlightenment at last? Is this what I had to do? Talk to this shrink and allow him to slice me open so I could look inside? Enticing the dark side of me out into the open. Shed light on the evil that lies there. Eradicate it once and for all. But what if I were the dark side of me? I am what is needed to be eliminated. Would I still exist? Can I exist? Should I? Am I just the voice in my head or the being that hosts it? Fuck, these drugs are good.

*

One afternoon, or morning, or evening, Nerris came in accompanied by a huge man wearing a tight white polo shirt, black trousers and a nightstick dangling from a utility belt fastened with the very last self-made hole around his enormous waist. Nerris, with a worryingly trembling hand, began to hack chunks of my beard away with round-tipped scissors, before beginning to shave off the rest of the facial hair that had made me look like an emaciated Che Guevara. The whole time, the eagle-eyed guard was watching closely in case I was able to uncuff myself from the bed rail, shake off the effects of the sedatives and hold my nurse hostage with the safety razor while I made a bid for freedom.

Under the watchful gaze of the prison guard, who unlocked the handcuff that had attached me to my bed for the vast majority of the last month or so, Nerris helped me out of my hospital gown and into the stiff beige uniform that she´d brought for me to change into. I was now officially a number and not a name, absorbed into the endless ranks of the Mexican penal system.

The door to my room was opened from the outside and the guard led me down the long corridor, squeezing my arm agonisingly tightly as we went, enjoying the little perks that came with his job. I was flanked on the other side by a slightly less obese warden and marched towards a set of barred doors, where I was then handed over to another pair of escorts. Through another set of doors, which were unlocked after strict security controls we went, and then another, and another until we came to an armoured reception area. From there, after more rigorous security checks with the woman stationed behind the metal grill, I found myself on a brightly-lit corridor.

Daylight. The first I´d seen for God knows how long was streaming in through the reinforced windows along the link between two buildings. I strained my stiff neck to see through glass crisscrossed with thin wire and caught a glimpse of a desolate, soulless sight.

Line after line of high fences stretched as far as I could see, each one topped with roll upon roll of razor-sharp wire ready to shred to pieces anyone foolish enough to try to scale the boundary. Scattered all around were lights, high up on thin posts; sinister, leafless trees after a forest fire. Watchtowers, as large as any that would normally host air traffic controllers were set at strategic points. The only thing that wasn´t there to complete the grim picture were shower blocks and train tracks leading to nowhere.

It was a colourless scene, the surrounding buildings as grey as the cold metal that ringed the prison. I could see some people outside on duty. Police, soldiers or machine-gun toting special forces, patrolling each section between the fences, their heads covered with the black balaclavas that had become a symbol of hope and the fight against repression. Marcos was right. Mexico is full of mirrors.

I was jerked violently along the corridor, that fleeting glance of the world outside rudely torn away from me. Through more sets of doors and bars I was shoved. I lost count, it could´ve been ten, might be twenty. There were no doors in the jungle. No locks or bars. I was led down a flight of stairs, turning corners as the stairwell drilled down further underground, my right leg complaining bitterly about being bent and tested by such unexpected force. I remained poker-faced throughout. I wasn´t going to give them anything, even the slightest hint of my discomfort. More doors, security cameras, more checks and then I was finally pushed into a small cell and the door locked firmly behind me.

I was back on the Altiplano, although I knew little about this. I was back, just eighty-five-odd kilometres from where my journey had begun. Centro Federal de Readaptación Social Número Uno, Almoloya de Juárez – or simply *Almoloya* for short. The brainchild of Presidente Salinas, designed to do away with the privileges cartel bosses enjoyed in other prisons throughout the country.

With its metre-thick walls, cells located deep within the bowels of the Earth and ten-kilometre exclusion and no-fly zones, it was famously the most high-security, unescapable prison Mexico had ever seen. Hosting influential drug lords, heads of kidnapping gangs, sadistic mass murderers, corrupt politicians and ex-governors guilty of committing nearly every crime you could imagine, *Almoloya* was now my home for the foreseeable future.

My cell measured no more than four metres by two. There was a bed with a filthy mattress with an equally disgusting blanket, a small sink, a table and stool fixed to the wall, a tiny shelf, and a lamp. To complete the minimalist Scandinavian design was a squat toilet, no more than just a hole in the floor, which is apparently great for bowel movements, but agony for recuperating bones that were trying their best to heal themselves. The door was simple and made of solid steel, the only detail on my side being the small slot through which food, drinks and other objects could be passed and my ongoing miserable existence could be checked.

During the course of my first day in my new accommodation I figured out quite quickly that I was segregated from the other inmates, the only contact I had was the opening and closing of the slot on the door and the distant distorted sound of a television or radio that floated down the corridor from some other lucky soul who found himself hidden away from the rest of the prisoners. Occasionally, I could hear a gravelly voice singing something unrecognisable far away and defiant shouts drifting towards me from another part of the complex. Apart from these distractions, I was in total isolation. Splendid isolation. Why though? I wasn´t exactly a dangerous narco or anything like that. I was just some gringo caught up in something. Something admittedly highly illegal, but not something that warranted me to be cooped up alone. Perhaps the bushy bearded psychologist thought I could be a risk to myself – or to others. Whatever the reason was, I have to say, I was extremely grateful not to have to run the gauntlet of being a skinny, limping foreigner in a crowded maximum security Mexican jail.

I made myself as comfortable as I could and assuming I´d be here for a while yet, tried to adjust to my new routine. The small hatch in the door was opened at six a.m. every morning and then a further five times more until lights-out at nine o´clock at night. I was given three small meals per day with breakfast consisting of fruit, a glass of sour milk and every few days or so some bland, cardboard cereal or other. Lunch and dinner varied little daily, with *frijoles*, *nopales* and tough pieces of pork that smelt of gasoline being the staple diet. If I was lucky, a few jelly cubes were included with one of the meals as a special treat, although I wouldn´t have been surprised if they were laced with some kind of drug to nullify the prison population, reducing the risk of violent rebellion. After my breakfast was taken away each day, it was replaced with a small amount of powdered detergent and a cloth for me to clean the floor and walls of my quarters, after which I was to bathe myself with a foul-smelling flannel and a piece of soap that never created a proper lather no matter how hard I rubbed it. I also had to make my bed each morning by pulling the grubby blanket tightly and tucking it in under the mattress. And every day the same question. Who had made *her* bed? Smoothing the creases out as if eliminating any trace of what had happened. Who had made the bed? Lina? The landlady? Dan? Me?

After my chores were out of the way, I got dressed for the day, although it wouldn´t have made any difference if I´d stayed in the white t-shirt and shorts that I slept in. I wasn´t going anywhere.

I felt like a hamster stuck on a wheel. I had nothing to occupy my mind except my memories and imagination, which thankfully seemed to be the more vivid the longer I stayed in my tiny cell. I regretted, plotted and lamented about my life and what it had become, what it should be, and the hours surprisingly passed by less torturously than I ever imaged they could.

After around a week or so in my new abode, *Robinson Crusoe* appeared with my breakfast. I stared at its faded and creased cover wondering why someone would bring it to me. It was in English, so word must´ve spread about the foreign prisoner that was being held in solitary confinement. I was pleasantly surprised by this apparent random act of generosity, but also a little worried about having my anonymity exposed among the staff and – more worryingly still – possibly other inmates at *Almoloya*.

I read the novel in one afternoon, and then re-read it again the next day. While I lay in bed at night I mutated the story, changing Crusoe´s island for Marcos´ lonely jungle desert, swapping penguins and seals for toucans and howler monkeys, cannibals for Federal soldiers and Friday for myself. If I ever got out of here, I vowed that I´d write the updated version that was spiralling around my twisted mind.

One afternoon, as I was reading *Crusoe* once more between check-ups from the wardens, who´d quickly open the slot to the corridor to see if I was still alive before slamming it shut again, I was jolted out of my literary escape as the door to my cell was thrown wide open. Two short but burly guards gestured for me to stand up and slip on my prison issue plimsolls and soon I was handcuffed and half-walked, half-carried along the corridor I´d seen for the last time just over a fortnight ago. Through gates and doors I was escorted and up the same stairs that had made my right leg cry out in protest. It was easier this time and much less painful and I´d improved physically no doubt, in part down to the passing of time and proper rest, but mostly due to the exercises I´d started to do in order not to waste away far under the Mexican ground. The guards whisked me along another corridor that radiated from the central reception area I´d passed before and then I was pushed through a door and shoved into a chair bolted to the floor. One of the guards strapped me into the austere furniture with a huge leather belt which pinned my arms to my sides. Both of my minders disappeared and I was left alone in the room to try to comprehend what was happening.

In front of me was a table and on the opposite side was another chair. An interview room. Or maybe a torture room. No, why would they fix me up only to tear me apart again. Someone would come in and sit down in front of me and ask me similar questions that the detectives had asked; that Marcos had asked.

The door opened soon enough and through it walked a tall, slim man in an expensive-looking tailored dark suit. He was in his mid to late forties with grey receding hair, wore large thin-framed glasses and carried a stony expression. If anyone could look more out of place in a maximum-security prison, it was this man standing here, this accountant, lawyer or tax inspector. He looked serious, albeit a little nervous, although quickly his thin lips cracked and he forced a cold smile.

"I hope they´re treating you well here," he said in an English heavy with an accent spent from time in the United States. He glanced down at the strap that was holding me in place and then snapped his fingers in the air to summon the guard who was stationed outside and looking in through the small window in the door. He gestured to the sentry to release my bindings.

"*Si, licenciado*," the guard answered servilely. The strap was quickly unfastened and after another gesture my handcuffs were removed by the guard, who after doing so, hesitated briefly, waiting to see if there were further instructions before being waved dismissively outside again. The newcomer sat down opposite me and stared across the table but said nothing.

"Why am I not with the other prisoners?" I asked at length, the English I spoke now sounded completely foreign to me.

I was met with another thin smile. "Please excuse me, but I don´t think it would be a good idea for you to be with the rest of the criminals here. Believe me, you´re better off where you are, on your own." The smile was fixed on his face but his eyes were controlled, hiding the real feelings that were sealed inside. "It´s for your own good," he added.

"My own good? Being stuck in a shoebox for twenty-four hours?" I asked incredulously. I was ready to attack, the pent up anger that had been brewing as my energy and health improved was fighting its way to the surface, bursting up through the ground that had nearly consumed me.

"The others here are in their cells for all but one hour of the day. Do you really want to go to a woodwork class or play basketball with these people? I think, in your condition, you´re in the best place you can be. Anyway, you´re hardly missing much in this …" He looked around the room with a look of disgust that he didn´t bother to disguise. "… facility, believe me."

My Condition? Why do they all say that? I stayed silent and pushed the thought away. I had to admit, despite my predicament, – and my so-called condition – I was definitely much better where I was. The rage subsided and curiosity began to take over. I had no choice other than play along with this.

"I want to make a phone call and see a lawyer," I demanded after an uncomfortable silence in which my interlocutor did nothing else apart from stare at me. His impassive features didn´t move, he´d given up trying to smile.

"It doesn´t quite work like that," he replied. "Here, it´s more of a – how do you say? – a *quid pro quo* basis." He paused again for several seconds. "Anyway, I won´t waste any more of your precious time. I´ll get to the point and be honest with you. We´re going through something of a crisis at the moment here in Mexico, as I´m sure you´re fully aware of." He glared at me, allowing my involvement in the indigenous uprising to wash over my consciousness. "There are certain things that we need to – how do you say? – put into order. So, if you show us a little willingness to help, we may be able to show our gratitude to you in return."

He reached into his jacket pocket and placed something on the table between us. A small burgundy red rectangle, its gold crest shining, reflecting the overhead light. My passport. My heart sank. My throat tightened. Where did he get that? Did I leave it with our generous hosts with my backpack on our way through the jungle? No. I had it with me after that. They´d found the camp, hadn´t they? They´d found La Graciosa. I tried to steady my breathing. It´s OK, maybe it had been abandoned, the EZLN moves around a lot to hide their tracks, don´t they? There was still hope.

"I´m very sorry to take liberties with my position but you must realise that nobody knows you´re here. And nobody cares. Your friends in the jungle certainly don´t. They were simply using you. You´re not one of them. And I doubt very much your Conservative British government would lift a finger to save a Maoist terrorist accused of crimes against the Mexican state. So, I´m afraid, you´re very much on your own." A smile had appeared again on his grey features. "But I can offer you a way out, if you wish."

He reached again into his jacket pocket. What else could he have? I looked down at the table and the second object that had been placed there. My head started to spin, to bulge. I felt dizzy at the sight of the photograph of Dan and Lina sitting and smiling, posing with bottles of Corona in front of them. I wanted to be sick as I continued to stare at the photo.

Black sky. Black earth.

"You know, you don´t have to stay here forever if you don´t want to," the man said softly, almost encouragingly.

My heart was ripped out like the soft centre of the maguey. So that´s why Dan had recommended that I go to San Miguel. He´d been there before. He´d been with *her* before. The same special place I´d shared with her too, the same table, the same drinks. I looked up at the messenger that had delivered this poisoned gift, wondering how much more fucked up my life could get from now. Hadn´t I gone through enough? Hadn´t *we* gone through enough? Why had he produced the photo? Did they have Lina held captive somewhere too? Impossible. It´s just my imagination protecting me from the inevitable truth. The unknown, familiar truth. Softening the final blow that would end my world. A tear escaped, on its way to freedom, and ran down my cheek.

"Please, take your time. Think about what path you want to take and the World is yours."

My visitor stood up, his work had been done and I could tell he was satisfied with the result. He scooped my passport up and tucked it away again inside his jacket pocket. His hand reappeared quickly and he produced a wad of crumpled sheets of dirty white paper. He threw them down on the table and stared at me. The trap was sprung, it crushed my leg, smashing my hope into shards of irreparable desperation.

"If you want your sweetheart to hear these beautiful words from your own lips, then you need to think carefully."

I gazed at my thoughts, my promises, my desires. Something broke deep inside of me. I heard it, felt it.

"You need to decide how much of yourself you're willing to give up to get what you really want."

With those icy, measured words that would replace *Robinson Crusoe* as I lay awake at night, the man turned around and was let out by one of the stocky guards that had been keeping vigil outside.

I was left in my solitude with an unclear choice to make, a vague task to carry out that could secure my freedom and possibly Lina´s. I was left with doubts as to what I had to do, what was to come and why I was now sitting in a prison interview room staring at a photo of my beloved Lina smiling, arm in arm with the man I´d grown to despise more than anything else in the World.

We all have important decisions to make that will lead our life into one direction or another. I thought I'd already made my most vital ones when I left San Miguel de Allende and again when I was blindfolded in my first incarceration in the Highlands in Chiapas.

But sometimes the choices have already been made. They take us towards what has already been written for us in our lives, the future we're destined to live, and whatever path we decide on will always lead us inevitably to the same conclusion; if I choose to fight my reality, I will lose.

As I lay on my thin mattress, I listened to the same first lines of the faint song that floated down the corridor to me each day after lights out. "*No vale nada la vida … La vida no vale nada …*"

Hearing those sad lines serenaded to me time and time again, I vowed to myself that I wouldn't spend the rest of my life rotting away in *Almoloya*. This was not where it would end. I'd do whatever it was I had to do in order to write the next lines in my story. My song. *Our* song. I wouldn't end up here forever. Life isn't worth nothing, as my fellow inmate sang. Life is worth something. *My* life is worth something and it will not finish with a drab full stop in my four by two prison cell. I'd destroyed and created before and now was the time to do it once more. It was time to create a new life, a new world from the bones of the old; time to create a new Sun.

*

I waited for the door to open, I *willed* the door to be opened and for me to be dragged along the corridor outside and then hauled up the stairs and dumped unceremoniously onto the chair in the interview room. The days passed by and I grew increasingly impatient. The calm with which I'd accepted my fate in solitary confinement faded away and I spent my days pacing, prowling and turning around in my cell again and again and again. Waiting once more. Freedom is contagious and I wanted mine. Ours.

Doubts forced their way into my solitude. Accompanying me like my insect companions in the jungle. Why patch me up? Was I just some kind of play thing to them all? A way to satisfy their thirst for manipulation. An experiment. Marcos´ experiment. A diversion from their lives. A novelty, a joke played on someone who wasn´t part of them. Controlling someone from the First World and for once not the other way around. Maybe my suited visitor was right, maybe the Zapatistas had used me. I was on my own. I´m not the prodigal son, I´m not the chosen one. I will not be welcomed back from my voyage of discovery like the rest of them. The jungle had taught me to survive, and I will. It had welcomed me into its arms, and it was the only thing I could really trust.

And now I was a revolutionary. I was trying to change what´s around me. A system. I was lost in a cause but could the real change that would save me ever be done?

Everything mocked me. The sink, the squat toilet, the characters in *Robinson Crusoe*. The book that had been my faithful cellmate, accompanying me throughout the day and stimulating my imagination at night became my chagrin, the eyes of the bearded Crusoe on the cover following me wherever I went, haunting me from every angle. My notes, the story of a burgeoning love written in the depths of the jungle in Chiapas, lay undisturbed. I tried to ignore them, put them out of sight but they unnervingly remained seared into my mind, their generous gift to me having the desired effect on my fragile psyche. But worst of all was the photo that the slim, suited visitor had also left for me in the interview room and which I´d now propped up on the small shelf on the wall above my table. This snapshot of treachery was my motivation. This image of two happy lovers a reminder of what was wrong with me, what had become of my life and what now needed to be done.

*

Eventually, a week after I´d last left my cocoon, the door opened. Like the light that washed inside my cell, relief flooded through me, even though I knew not what awaited me beyond. I didn´t care. I´d do anything to have the opportunity to be out of here and try to find Lina. I slipped on my plimsolls, stuffed the photo inside my shirt and then let the guards take my full, passive weight – much to their displeasure – and after the usual security checks I was soon impatiently sat at the table in the interview room ten metres above my residence below.

I didn´t have to wait long for the vampire to enter the room. This time he made no attempt to placate me with a smile and got straight to the point of his visit.

"There´s a lot at stake. Are you with us?" he asked bluntly, the formality of my answer a foregone conclusion judging by the briskness of his question.

I nodded. He didn´t reply, nor did his expression change as he summoned the guard outside with a raise of the hand. Several seconds later, a television set was wheeled in on a metal trolley to which it was bolted. The guard plugged it into a socket on the wall and the TV came to life, black and white lines of static hissed angrily on the screen. As the guard left the room, my visitor – my saviour – opened the briefcase he´d brought in with him and took out a video cassette, which he fed into the mouth of the player underneath the television. It whirred and whined and the static was replaced by another image and the white noise ceased. He pressed the pause button, preventing me from making out what it was I was to about to be shown.

"In Mexico, there are no untouchables," he said, before smiling crookedly. He hit the play button, gathered up his briefcase and left me alone to watch the video.

The screen flickered back to life as the interview room door clicked shut. On the television the huge crowd that was gathered in the square waved flags and shouted in excitement as their idol made his way through the multitude of supporters, shaking as many hands as he could and waving in all directions. Behind the seated audience the golden dome of the enormous stone monument that dominated the square shone in the bright sunlight. All eyes were on the man in the dark suit as he stepped upon the stage, pumping his fists and raising his arms in defiance. The crowd roared louder, thrilled to see in person the man that would finally change the country after so many years of corrupt government.

He reached the centre of the stage and took his position at the microphones that awaited him, pausing as the cameras panned across the thousands of people that had come to cheer him on. The stony-faced men in dull suits in the front row clapped slowly, among them the gentleman who´d only just left the room in which I sat. Colosio smiled his charismatic smile and began his speech.

"Companions of the party. Compatriots. Here is the PRI with its strength. Here is the PRI with its organizations, with its militancy, with the sensitivity of its women and men. Here is the PRI with its strong political vocation. Here is the PRI ..."

My head was spinning, I wanted to throw up. This man. This man that had been in the background of my life over the last few months, admired, discussed and then forgotten, was now there opposite me, talking to me. Why *this* man? My escape that just a few seconds ago seemed to be so simple, so within my grasp, now seemed like an indomitable mountain to climb.

I watched him revel in his role, pause, smile and hold the crowd – the country – in the palm of his hand. I watched but I didn´t hear what he had to say. My head, my ears, were pumping with the sound of my own rushing blood. I was gripped with a fear of what I would have to do, the consequences of my actions. What *was* it I had to do? Was this a test for me? Should I be looking for clues to confirm what was screamingly obvious? I tried to focus on Colosio´s words and forget the rest but all I could hear were snippets of promises being sucked into the vortex that was dragging me away from reality.

"... old practices are left behind ... the PRI today does not have guaranteed victories ... we do not want concessions outside the votes or votes outside the law!"

Few people in the front row clapped at the powerful prose they were privy to. The line of political dinosaurs was unmoved by the words of the unprivileged newcomer from the north of the country. My recent visitor did applaud, albeit unenthusiastically, keenly aware that his own actions were being broadcast nationwide.

I´d heard Colosio speak before on numerous occasions. With Lina, with Carlos, but this time was different. Through my haze I could still see that this was a carefully aimed shot across the bow of the old ship that was the Partido Revolucionario Institucional, a warning as to what was going to happen in order to bring the corrupt behemoth into line with a society still shaking off the hangover of the unforeseen indigenous uprising in the south-east of the country. I strained hard to listen to each and every word.

"... today we need to transform politics to comply with Mexicans. We propose the reform of power so that there is a new relationship between the citizen and the State. Today, before the PRI in Mexico, before the Mexicans, I express my commitment to reform power, to democratise it and to put an end to any vestige of authoritarianism."

Billboards, posters, leaflets, barroom discussions ... and now here with me in this room. Eyes that have followed me, words that have been spoken, promises repeated. White teeth. Fake smiles.

"Reforming power means a presidential system strictly subject to the constitutional limits of its republican and democratic origin. Reforming power means strengthening and respecting the powers of the Federal Congress. Reforming power means making the system for the administration of justice an independent instance of the highest respectability and certainty among the institutions of the Republic. Reforming power means bringing government to communities through a brand new federalism."

I began to smile to myself. Marcos had done this. Marcos and the EZLN had woken up Mexican society and the government had no choice but to adapt to this new normality. I didn´t know if he was alive or dead but through the man standing there being watched by millions, something new was on the horizon. Subcomandante Marcos had indeed made it to the capital.

"I see a Mexico of indigenous communities, which can no longer wait for the demands of justice, dignity and progress; of indigenous communities that have the great strength of their cohesion, of their culture and that they are willing to believe, to participate, to build new horizons. I see a Mexico of peasants who still do not have the answers they deserve."

I began to relax, to enjoy what I was listening to and just momentarily forgot the macabre reason why I was sat here in this sterile room watching the rousing speech in the first place.

"I see a Mexico of women who still do not have the opportunities that belong to them; women with a great capacity to enrich our economic, political and social life. Women, who demand a fuller, fairer participation in the Mexico of our time."

I thought of the women I´d seen on my journey through Mexico, the women abused by drunken husbands, the women who got up in the middle of the night to look after children and animals, the women with babies slung across their bodies with their hand outstretched begging for money, the women who carried huge bundles of firewood in the misty hills of Chiapas, the women who wore balaclavas and commanded battalions, giving their lives for a brighter tomorrow.

"I see a Mexico that is hungry and thirsty for justice. A Mexico of aggrieved people, of people aggrieved by the distortions imposed on the law by those who should serve it. Of women and men afflicted by abuse of the authorities or by the arrogance of government offices. I see citizens distressed by the lack of security, citizens who deserve better services and governments that comply with them. Citizens who still do not have defeat in the future; they are citizens who have hope and who are willing to join their efforts to achieve progress. I see a Mexico convinced that this is the time for answers; a Mexico that demands solutions."

The camera panned out to capture the immensity of the scene. The crowd, fans flapping cooling down faces, umbrellas raised as people tried to shelter from the harshest of suns. The glare of the dome of the monument to the Revolution reflecting in the windows of the surrounding buildings. The enormous white cross that loitered behind the speaker. The spectacle, the show, the occasion.

"I express my deepest commitment to Chiapas. That is why we must listen to all the voices; we must not allow anyone to monopolize the feelings of the people of Chiapas. I express my solidarity to all those in Chiapas who have not yet told their truth, to all those who have a voice to transmit and to all those who have a word to express."

Chiapas, Chiapas, Chiapas. A place I had never known; a place that I will never leave. I will always wear the balaclava, the red bandana. My blood will always stain the fertile soil. My identity will be theirs and theirs forever mine.

"It is time for the great fight against inequality, it is time to overcome extreme poverty, it is time to guarantee education, health, and decent housing for all … It is time to do justice to our indigenous people, to overcome them being left behind, their shortcomings; to respect their dignity … It is time to celebrate a new pact between the Mexican State and the indigenous communities. It is time for new opportunities for the Mexican countryside … It is time to decisively and firmly confront poverty and improve the living standards of peasants. It is time for Article Twenty-seven of the Constitution to express itself in well-being, in justice, in freedom for the men of the countryside. And it is time to put an end to all traces of latifundism forever. It is time to give certainty to the ejido, communal lands and small property. It is time to promote agrarian reform for our time."

Had the battle been won? Had the EZLN triumphed and had its demands been met? If it had, where were they? Why weren´t the comandantes up there with Colosio hand-in-hand celebrating a moral victory? The shoo-in for the next president was echoing the words of the Zapatistas alright, but they were not there. What the hell was going on? Something was wrong.

"... I am a man of my word, a man of my word who is committed right now to dedicate myself to the change that I have proposed; a change with direction and responsibility."

Never trust a politician, even the ones that want to speak freely. Isn´t that the truth? This man … why *this* man?

"The great demand of Mexico is democracy. The country wants to fully exercise it. Mexico demands, we will respond."

This man. This politician. I know what you are. A Traitor. What you are capable of. What have you done with Marcos? The eyes of the snake. He has the eyes of the snake. Dan´s eyes. Snake eyes. It´s always the snake that comes down from the sky, eliminating life, destroying dynasties. He´ll betray the indians as they have all done before.

"As a Candidate for the Presidency of the Republic, I am also ready. Let's give our best effort in this election. Let's get excited."

And there he finally was in his true guise. Quetzalcoatl, with his brightly-coloured feathers and fangs ready to sink into the flesh of the innocent, contaminating them with his desire for power disguised as knowledge and compassion. And I, Tezcatlipoca, his reflection, his brother. Vengeance personified. I had to beat him down. Merge into one supreme being and destroy what we had created together.

"We must not lower our guard. We go for the victory. Let's win it with Mexico and let's win it FOR Mexico. Que viva el PRI! Que viva Mexico!"

Luis Donald Colosio Murrieta wrapped up his speech and all but a handful of people in the crowd rose in unison, cheering their hero as he waved at them and pumped his fists in the air soaking up the applause and the standing ovation. As he disappeared into the arms of his adoring fans, I noticed that he was closely shadowed by the stern man in the thin-framed glasses that had presented me with a glimpse of freedom.

Voices then barged their way into my head, brought to me by the thin air of the Altiplano. Dan´s, Lina´s, Javi´s, Marcos´, shouting together at me, screaming contradictory messages that I couldn´t understand. Stop it. Stop the noise, please. I gripped the sides of my head in an attempt to squeeze them out of my brain, to get rid of them forever. They vanished, replaced now by another voice suddenly pushing them away into the distance, a quiet voice gently blowing the others to another place, a voice from another age.

The sharks will get him ... you'll see ... the sharks will get him.

*

I stared at the ceiling as I lay on my paper-thin mattress, a tray of regulation prison food untouched beside me. I looked at the grey concrete that pressed down heavily on me and I rose up through the uneven gaps in the wooden slats that made up the roof, caressed by the upper branches of the forest canopy and out into the clear night as I travelled towards the stars. Past the turtle, the rattlesnake, the bat, the scorpion, the space between the stars. I soared into the very heart of the creation.

The choice. So hard at first, was now so easy, so clear. Zapatism would survive. It can never be hijacked, held to ransom. An intuition in each and every one of us that will never be stopped, never beaten down no matter who the protagonists. Something innate in the deepest most natural feelings of everyone. And we will survive; the messengers. We'll be waiting in the darkness, ready to come out of the jungle and down the mountains. Out of the cities, towns, villages. We will not stop. We will be watching.

Freedom is contagious yes; but love – the love that is keeping me alive – can be even more so. High up on the Altiplano, surrounded by thick walls and high fences, I prepared myself for instructions.

Through the large windows of the departure lounge I watched the flashing lights of the planes as they taxied on the warm tarmac outside. I´d be on one soon, flying out of Tijuana, out of a Mexico I´d grown to be part of. Out of a Mexico fighting with its own identity. A Mexico, in the early spring of nineteen ninety-four, that was in emotional and political turmoil.

A plane pushed back away from the terminal building. Another took off in the distance, hauling its weight into the dry night air. I watched until it had passed out of the frame of glass, not caring where it was going. I was alone again. Nobody else was looking out of the dirty windows, seeing what I was seeing. The rest of the passengers waiting for their flights were crowded around the television screens behind where I sat.

A solemn, middle-aged newsreader, a telephone pressed to his ear, listened to the reporter on the other end as the call was simultaneously broadcast to the nation, to the millions in their homes, those that were huddling around sets with neighbours, in *cantinas* or anywhere else they could see the news. To the groups of shocked people watching and listening at my back.

"*... when he left the church, two individuals approached him through the crowd with hand guns, pistols, and managed to shoot him directly in the head and in the stomach. He was immediately taken by ambulance to the central hospital in Tijuana, where he´s undergone an operation to try to save his life. We don´t know, at present, his current condition,*" the crackling voice on the telephone explained.

"*And what do we know about the individuals who carried out this terrible act?*" asked the newsreader.

"*One of the perpetrators was apprehended immediately by the security services at the scene and is being interviewed by the state police as we speak. The other, we understand, is still at large.*"

"*Can you please tell us where you´re transmitting from at the moment, Oswaldo?*"

I wasn't listening to the television. I didn't hear the other eye-witness accounts of what had happened. I didn't see the images of the gun raised to the side of the head of the presidential candidate and the chaotic aftermath. I knew exactly what had happened less than four hours before. I knew the past and the present. But the future was unclear. I knew that the bullet I'd fired had guaranteed my freedom. What I didn't know was that eventually it would kill any chance of a peaceful agreement with the Ejército Zapatista de Liberación Nacional.

The people behind me stood gaping at the scenes of crowded hospital corridors full of a swarming mix of reporters, medical staff and police. Outside on the steps of the building, candle-lit vigils had sprung up as worried followers prayed for a favourable outcome to the unfolding tragedy.

As the death of Luis Donaldo Colosio Murrieta was officially announced to painful cries on the television and those watching here in the departure lounge, I rose from my seat and headed to my gate.

I paused briefly, looking down at the boarding card that I held in my trembling hand. I double checked the gate number and then stared at the name printed there. My name. Daniel Robert Graves. My head hurt; my scar hurt. I pushed my glasses up the bridge of my nose, sat down in front of the gate and waited to board my flight.

A NOTE FROM THE AUTHOR

The book you´ve just finished is a work of fiction but grounded in fact, with the main characters based on real people, either explicitly or implicitly expressed in name, deeds or essence.

Without doubt, the standout character in *Desert of Solitude*, from a historical point of view, is Subcomandante Marcos, the charismatic leader of the Zapatista movement. Known as Galeano since 2014, he declared himself "dead" to the World in October 2023, reclaiming his original identity of Rafael Sebastián Guillén Vicente and stepping back from the movement in order to hand over to a new generation of revolutionaries. Although we have never met, I hope through extensive research and countless hours of listening to his captivating interviews and speeches I´ve been able to replicate the authenticity of his words, his ascorbic wit and the image of the man once described as the new Che Guevara.

Luis Donaldo Colosio Murrieta, whose assassination in March 1994 rocked Mexico, is another real-life person. Heralded as someone who would unite a fractured country, we can only image what life would have been like for Mexicans, and in particular the indigenous population, had this hugely popular figure lived to fulfil his weighty election promises. Would Mexico be a more inclusive country today? Or would his promises remain vacant, his hands tied by the party he represented and his reputation stained by his endorsement of the North Atlantic Free Trade Agreement (NAFTA) and the effect it would have on the poorest of the population?

We will never know.

Comandante Javi, as he appears in the novel, is in truth a fictional character. However, his thoughts and feelings echo the hopelessness and anger that most of the indigenous members of the Ejército Zapatista de Liberación Nacional (EZLN) felt towards the central

Government. In a way, he is an embodiment of many of the commanders that made up – and in some cases still make up – the EZLN, such as: Comandante Alejandro, Comandante Daniel, Comandante David, Comandanta Esther, Comandante Moisés, Comandante Tacho and Comandanta Ramona.

Other characters that we come across have their roots in real-life, but naming them here would serve no purpose other than to use more ink on this page and reveal identities that mean little to anyone else but myself. Suffice to say, with them they have brought their own inspirations, challenges and idiosyncrasies and all have touched my life to such an extent in one way or another that they simply couldn't have been left out of *Desert of Solitude*.

But why write this book in the first place? Why Mexico? Why Marcos? Why the existential fight between Max and Dan, Quetzalcoatl and Tezcatlipoca?

In 1999, five years after the uprising, I found myself in the heart of Chiapas in Palenque and someone threw something hard that struck my head. Who had done that and why was – and still – remains a mystery to me, although it was clear my presence wasn't exactly welcome. Whatever the reason was, it woke me up. I had been making the footsteps that Max and Dan would follow, in both place and manner, paying little attention to the bigger picture of a country still trying to get to grips with the indigenous uprising just a few years earlier and much of the native population in Chiapas suffering at the hands of corrupt and violent governments at both national and regional level.

That small rock or stone that had hit me made me open my eyes to the government road blocks, the bag searches at gunpoint, the graffiti of indigenous corn farmers with their faces covered dominating the sides of wooden buildings, the untrusting eyes I just couldn't gauge as I walked around and gawked at endless markets and temples.

The twelve-day war five hundred years in the making had brought hope to the downtrodden of Mexico and millions more throughout the globe that there could be an alternative system of governance from the bottom up. Subcomandante Marcos' eloquent words were heard around the World and the cause was spread as much in the media as the jungle itself. But as I got to know the area and its inhabitants more deeply, it was clear that the conflict the people living there had suffered was far from over.

Just two years before I'd set foot in Chiapas for the first time, paramilitaries allegedly supported by the national government, burst into a church in the village of Acteal and massacred forty-five people, including eighteen children. Their target: the indigenous human rights organisation Las Abejas, who publicly supported the Zapatista movement. This barbaric act, among many others, is a clear indication of the persecution that the indigenous population faced many years after the uprising on the first of January 1994.

And so, the seed for *Desert of Solitude* was sown without me realising it at the time. I'd dreamt of someday publishing my own *Motorcycle Diaries,* and even kept my own daily journal of my journey from Mexico City to Buenos Aires but what I'd seen and learnt in Chiapas and the awakening to the plight of the indigenous population and the Zapatista movement was stifled, forgotten and replaced with notes about journeys across salt flats and tales of altered perceptions after taking ayahuasca.

But the seed didn't die. It lay dormant somewhere inside, slowly growing every time I stumbled across an article about the Zapatistas or a report commemorating the tenth, twentieth and now the thirtieth anniversary of the uprising. I began to dream of writing a sweeping epic love story set against the backdrop of the conflict. I didn't want to romanticise war, it is an evil that should not exist, but I was captivated by the Zapatistas´ cause. Everything seemed so simple, so right. How could it fail? But in truth, many things in Mexico and Latin America remain unchanged or even worse than they were thirty years before.

I returned to Mexico several more times and the more I learnt about the political and emotional turmoil that the country faced during the mid nineteen-nineties, the more the schema of my novel changed, morphing into a version of my own travels and momentous moments in modern Mexican and World history.

As with the factual background to the majority of the characters in *Desert of Solitude*, most of the events in the novel actually happened as well. NAFTA came into effect on the first of January 1994 as the EZLN began their armed uprising, the stolen dynamite was used to blow key bridges, the remnants of a doomed group of ELZN fighters were holed up in a market during the Battle of Ocosingo, and Donaldo Colosio was indeed murdered while meeting and greeting the public in Tijuana (several conflicting theories exist about those behind the assassination).

Every effort has been made to ensure historical accuracy throughout this book, using official records, archives and the help of renowned historians in Mexico. Any inaccuracies and misrepresentations are purely accidental and not intended to cause any offense or harm in any way, shape or form.

This book is based on history, it´s true. A history that did happen, a history that might have happened, and a history that will, undoubtedly, sadly happen again.

"We live surrounded by mirrors. Mirrors of the past and mirrors of ourselves."

One look around us today will make you realise that Subcomandante Marcos was absolutely right.

THANKS

How can I thank the countless people in Chiapas, wider Mexico and beyond for their sacrifice in fighting an often losing battle so that others can live a better, more just life? How can I do justice to what they strive to achieve in the face of insurmountable odds? How can I put down in words the gratitude that myself and many others feel for these selfless people?

It is highly unlikely that they will ever read what I write here, but I want to thank these people from the bottom of my heart all the same for what they have done, continue to do, and will do in the future.

I can, however, give personal thanks to a few individuals who have contributed directly to the existence of this book.

Firstly, to Natalia, my wife, for being my inspiration, best-friend, life-coach, critic and so much more. Without her, this book would definitely not exist. To Ann Cyphers, historian at the Universidad Nacional Autónoma de México, for her input on San Lorenzo and assisting with the historical accuracy of many of the archaeological sites I have described. I am sorry you never got to see the finished product. May you rest in peace. To Nick Henck, professor, author and expert on Subcomandante Marcos, for his keen eye for detail and advice on corrections. To Toby Charlton-Taylor, for being one of the first people to read the manuscript and giving much-needed feedback. To Carmen Rioja, Editor at Atención San Miguel (de Allende) for allowing me to delve into their newspaper archives. To Juan Gómez, for his help with the beautiful Tzotzil language. And to Robin Furby, without whom there would be no Dan.

REFERENCES

Extracts of speeches by **Luis Donaldo Colosio Murrieta**:

p85-87 – Acceptance speech of the pre-candidacy for the Presidency of the Republic, announced before the National Political Council from the Comité Ejecutivo Nacional (CEN) of the Partido Revolucionario Institucional (PRI). Mexico City. **November 28, 1993**.

P94-97 – Acceptance speech for the official candidacy for the President of the Republic for the Partido Revolucionario Institucional (PRI). Mexico City. **December 08, 1993.**

p233-237 – Speech given at the celebration of the 65th anniversary of the Partido Revolucionario Institucional (PRI) in front of the Monument to the Revolution, Mexico City. **March 06, 1994.**

Extracts from *El Despertador Mexicano* (published **November 1993**) – Official bulletin of the Ejército Zapatista de Liberación Nacional (EZLN):

p102-104 - Contents of envelope left by Lina, including the First declaration of the Lacandon jungle.

P193-196 – Reading of the First declaration of the Lacandon jungle from the balcony of the Palacio Municipal, San Cristobal de las Casas, Chiapas. **January 01, 1994.** Extracts from *El Despertador Mexicano* were also simultaneously broadcast on the radio (including by Radio XEOCH in Ocosingo) and leaflets and posters were widely distributed throughout the region.

Cover design by: Natalia Gómez Álvarez

Steven Richard Harris was born and raised in the United Kingdom but has now spent half his life living in Spain. He gave up teaching at universities in 2020 to concentrate on his writing.

Other novels available by Steven Richard Harris include:
The Butcherbird Series:
The Butcherbird Tree
We Are the Tide.

For more about Steven Richard Harris, go to:
stevenrichardharris.com
twitter.com/srharrisauthor
amazon.com/author/stevenrichardharris
facebook.com/SRHauthor

If you would like to help him reach a wider audience, please leave a review of *Desert of Solitude* on the platform from which you bought this book. If purchased via bookshops, a rating on Goodreads would be highly appreciated.

For any other comments, please contact Steven Richard Harris via the website and social media links given. He will do his best to get back to you as quickly as possible.

Thank you.

www.ingramcontent.com/pod-product-compliance
Lightning Source LLC
LaVergne TN
LVHW092345170726
843489LV00001B/48